AF488860

Dragon's Treasure

Maya Starling

Self published
Zagreb, 2016.

DRAGON'S TREASURE

Copyright © 2016 Maya Starling

Author Maya Starling

Edited by Laura Perry

Cover by Maya Starling

Self published by author

Zagreb, 2016.

Printed by Createspace

ISBN: 9535936603
ISBN-13: 9789535936602

For my family.
Thank you for all your love and support.

For my little munchkin.
I wish you a bright and hopeful future.

CONTENTS

ACKNOWLEDGMENTS

Blurbs, dedications, and acknowledgments are not my forte. Hope I do this one justice, because so many people helped me to get to this point; my first published book.

First, I would like to thank Mareliza Viljoen for pulling me up on my feet, for encouraging me to write. Thank you Gitte Ekhdal for teaching me and helping me to walk steady. Thank you Melissa Julian-Jones for showing me how to strut my stuff. Thank you Laura Perry for keeping me on track, for improving my gait. My fabulous beta readers... I am thankful for your honest constructive feedback. You made the book even better.

Emerald Paslay and Kim Fry, you were a great support, you were my people on the line as I sprinted by, toward the finish. You provided me with much needed water, and towels, and cheers.

And most of all, I need to shower my Wattpad followers with much gratitude as well. You persevered, you supported, read, commented, voted, gave me faith in myself and the self-confidence to do this.

Thank you.

CHAPTER 1

The most heated arguments lead to the dumbest choices, Olivia berated herself as she stumbled through the unfamiliar forest. The boughs creaked above, parting only briefly in the breeze to allow a glimpse of the tiny, brilliant stars. She glanced up at the cloudless sky and gave thanks for the full moon above, its beams fighting through the branches to illuminate her path. She sped up her pace, seeking comfort in the folds of the forest, lost and no longer sure whether she was running away from home or back towards it.

Maybe marrying Sebastian would not have been so unfortunate... Olivia sighed. *What was I thinking? I could be at home, safe and warm.*

"I am so spoiled," she mumbled, shaking her head. She drew in a deep breath of the chill forest air, hoping to ease her trepidation, but the scent of wilderness infused her senses, reminding her just how far away she was from anything familiar, from home. The realization seeped deeper into her heart, quickening its already racing beat.

An owl's screech pierced the night, and a muffled crunch sounded behind her. She halted mid step, and turned to glance over her shoulder. It was no hedgehog bobbing along through the undergrowth, nor a cricket, for she had heard plenty of those chirping in the moonlit shrubs. But now they too grew silent. Another crunch followed—not a branch, but a bone breaking.

Olivia wanted to turn and run but her feet wouldn't comply. The compulsion to know what was out there overpowered her and she began tiptoeing toward the source of the sound. Her heart thumped louder with each step, but soon the sound of growls and the snapping of teeth made her stop. She turned her head to the left and narrowed her eyes towards the moving shadows.

A wolf lifted its head from the cover of darkness and into the moonlight. The beast's muzzle was coated in blood, its eyes filled with voracious hunger. A second wolf raised its head as well, blood dripping down its dark fur as it snarled and snapped towards the first one. The dark wolf bared its fangs in warning, and lunged forward when the other beast would not submit. A fight erupted in a frantic blur of fur. Growls and snarls rent the air and echoed among the trees.

Olivia's voice caught in her throat. She covered her mouth to stem the rising scream. She didn't want to end up ripped apart like the sad, bloody carcass beneath them.

She took small, cautious steps backwards, putting one foot behind the other, never taking her eyes off the wolves. When she had put enough distance between herself and the raging beasts, she turned and took flight.

A few strides later, a protruding root snagged her foot. She toppled to the forest floor. The pebbles and pine needles speared her palms. She barely avoided smashing her chin into the ground. *Oh, no, no, no!* Pushing herself up, she winced as she put weight on her bruised knee, and continued to flee. She chanced a glance back to see if the wolves had noticed her. The shadows of the undergrowth were too dark for her to see into, despite the dappled moonbeams shining on her path.

At least the moon was on her side.

She swerved past the bushes, but its thorn-filled, gnarly fingers grabbed for her, shredding her dress, and clawing at her skin. She sprinted over jutting roots, stones, and mounds of dirt. She shivered. The cold crept up her spine, but a warm wetness seeped into her dress as pain pierced through her right arm. The wooden-taloned limbs grasped for her dark brown hair and tried to hold her back, securing her as an offering on which the forest's children would feast.

Tonight, the first to sate their hunger on her would be the wolves.

Olivia's lungs cramped from the strain, and her breath came out in short pants. Still running, she gripped the fabric at her chest in an attempt to ease the pain.

A howl resounded from behind.

Her wild pursuers plowed through the underbrush. She pushed forward, faster. Her calves burned like fire, as if the forest itself was trying to brand her.

Wide eyed, Olivia searched for a way to escape. Panic rose and her heart threatened to pound its way out of her chest, the thumps reverberating in her ears with each frenzied step. Her legs threatened to buckle beneath her.

The approaching growls and clawed paws striking the forest floor forebode her end. They were toying with her. Enjoying the chase before pouncing on her, while she sought for a place to hide, to no avail.

She knew she was too weak and too slow to outrun the wolves. Hiding from them was pointless. The smell of her fresh blood was like a guidepost pointing in her direction reading, 'Easy catch, this way'.

What have I done? What AM I DOING? Obviously I have no idea! Having Sebastian's children would NOT have been as bad as this! I am going to die here and once the wolves are done with me, not even my mother will be able to recognize my remains.

The wolves' snarls drew nearer. Olivia considered whether or not she should just give up; stop running and let them tear her apart. Fear of pain kept her moving, though. And hope. Hope that maybe, just maybe, *something* would turn her luck around.

A light flickered.

There! Hope!

She cut to the right. A cave entrance opened up not far before her, barely hidden by the surrounding shadows. The run-and-hide instinct prevailed and she turned toward it. The soft light of the fire was her guide. Maybe someone in there could help her?

As she neared the opening, it occurred to Olivia that it might be the dumbest plan she had come up with so far. If no one was there, she would be trapped in a cave, served up to the wolves, all soft, bloody and warm. But it was already too late to turn back.

She dashed into the cave with the wolves on her heels, ready to pounce. As she passed into the thick darkness of the cave she looked over her shoulder. Fangs! And blood matted fur. Reaching the fire, she grabbed a wooden stump. *A chair leg?* The surprise was fleeting as she spun to face the beasts; alone against them.

The wolves slowed to a cautious walk as they left the shadows of the forest and entered the cave. They sniffed the humid air. Growls reverberated throughout the cave and Olivia's body. She swung her makeshift weapon left, then right. Fire, *they should be afraid of fire, correct?* The wolves hesitated, lips pulled back. They snarled, and paced left, then right.

I still might live!

"Shoo!" She waved the fire-stick. "Go away, leave me

alone! I have enough trouble on my hands as it is. I do *not* need you as well." She stabbed the fire-end toward them.

Unease crawled up her spine like a dozen tiny spiders. She shook it off. The wolves lay their ears flat back, hackles raised, tail tucked.

"Yes! Smart wolves! Fire is bad, you want to flee. Go!"

Emboldened by the wolves' timidity, Olivia stepped forward with the fiery weapon stretched far in front of her.

The wolves backed off, paw by paw, soft and silent.

Air shifted behind Olivia. *A draft?* She took another step toward them.

The wolves whimpered, almost laid flat to the ground, belly crawling back.

"Ha!" Olivia let out a victorious cheer when the wolves turned and fled, their claws scraping against the cave's rocky ground.

A smile tugged at her lips. Finally, something good had happened to her today. A fortunate break.

The flame at the end of her wooden stick flickered, danced after the wolves, and a soft breath tickled the back of Olivia's neck. A presence moved and a shadow appeared from above.

With a white knuckled grip on her dying torch, Olivia turned. She looked up, and up, straining her neck. Fire light reflected off a long reptilian snout covered in shiny, smooth scales. Her breath caught in her throat. The creature inhaled slowly. The low sound of air slipping past its open jaws vibrated through Olivia's body as the beast showed off a row of deadly sharp teeth. When it exhaled, smoke billowed around its nostrils.

She waited for the monster to flambé and devour her. When nothing happened, she drew in a deep breath and held it.

"I could have taken them on," she said, voice flat.

A pair of large, amber, slitted eyes stared back at her, and a warm puff of breath fanned her face. Once again she froze, too stunned to breathe.

Then her world turned black before she had a chance to scream.

CHAPTER 2

Olivia lay on the cold, hard floor. She blinked a few times but darkness still surrounded her. Rain murmured in the distance. A chill seeped deep into her bones, contracting her muscles. She shivered. She shook her head to dissolve the fog that clouded her mind but all that did was cause a fierce throbbing in her temples.

She struggled to remember what had happened and where she was. The hazy recollections trickled into her mind: the heated argument with her father, his disappointment at her words and the sadness marring her mother's soft features broke Olivia's heart all over again. The whirlwind of emotions still burdened her heart, just as they had assailed her when she had fled to the safety of her chambers after the quarrel. Thunder burst nearby, echoing the slam of the door in her memory. She had let her temper make her choices. She was just as impulsive as her father; even the kind-hearted nature she had inherited from her mother hadn't helped.

Glimpses of more recent memories trailed through her mind: sneaking out under the cover of night with what provisions she remembered to bring along, dashing for the forest, being drenched by the chill rain. Then when the sun rose and Olivia welcomed the warmth of its rays, the bear had appeared. Her heart quickened again as she recalled the incident when terror and instinct prompted her to race from the makeshift camp. A bear woke her up and determined the way the rest of her day went, and had a feast for his trouble.

Everything else came flooding back as well.

The wolves. The chase, the running. The cave… *THE CAVE!* She sat up and scooted backwards. Flutters of panic swarmed inside her belly, nesting around her heart as her back hit the stone wall. *Was it real? Was there really a d-d-dragon?* She stuttered in her mind, afraid to even think the word.

I am alive, I think. She patted herself over. *Yes, still alive and in one piece.* She exhaled in relief. Rubbing her eyes with the heels of her palms, she winced as the motion irritated the scrapes on her hands. She pushed a shoulder-length lock of dark hair behind her ear. The smell of dampness tainted the air, mixed with a slight acrid undertone.

Overwhelmed with despair, Olivia wished for home, her soft bed and a warm bath. She now missed the safety her parents always provided. Safety and comfort. The current predicament was her own fault, all because of her selfishness, her head stuck high up in the clouds. She could have had it all, save for the one thing she wanted the most, and now she found herself further away from that dream as well.

Olivia rose on trembling legs, leaning on the cave wall for support. She tilted her head to the side and listened, trying to hear where *It* was, if *It* was still there. The darkness suggested she was farther away from the cave entrance than she had been before she fainted, or maybe there were no more moonbeams since it was raining. What disturbed her most was the thought of having been moved by the dragon. *Why would it do that? Maybe it just wasn't hungry and is planning to feast on me later?*

A cold shiver snaked down her spine and she shook the morbid thought out of her mind.

The sound of rain echoing off the walls of the cave reminded her of the sound of waves breaking on a shore. She forced a happy daydream for a moment to keep the panic from overwhelming her. *Oh, what I would give to be at the seaside – the sun warming my face, the scent of the ocean on the breeze, the soothing sounds of the crashing waves surrounding me.*

Another quiver shook her, jerking her back from the sun and the sea to the cave and the rain.

Olivia took a deep breath as if trying to suck courage from the humid air. She squared her shoulders to appear brave, hoping the move would turn her boldness into reality.

Fingers gliding over the rough surface of the cave walls, she felt her way around the grotto, thinking it likely that she would reach a passageway at some point. *Hopefully one that will lead me outside.*

And then what? Bitterness invaded her thoughts as her hands made slow progress. *I will deal with it when the time comes.*

As the shock wore off, pain tore through her body. She dragged her legs as if she were struggling against the oncoming current of a rushing stream. Her burning muscles and stinging palms were almost enough to crush her to the ground. The wound on her knee throbbed as it reopened and warm liquid trickled down her leg. The sleeve of her dress was glued to her arm with dried blood. Her body demanded that she just lie down and let time take care of some of the aches and pains. But she pushed on, desperate to find a way out.

"Oh God, let me perish now so I can finally get some

respite." She groaned and her stomach grumbled a threat in return: *Get me some food or I will eat your spine.*

Warmth.

Olivia felt warmth under her questing palms. The texture now was soft and silky smooth. She had the urge to press her face against it, but these stones had shapes, repeating shapes. She halted her exploration, fear gripping her as she realized what those contours meant.

Muscles glided and rolled beneath the sleek surface. The sound accompanying the movement reminded her of bales of silken cloths brushing against each other.

The surface moved again and hot breath swept across her face. Olivia remembered what this creature was capable of. *Oh my, Oh my… it is going to eat me! It is going to fry me to crispy bits and eat me!* She hyperventilated, the pulsing in her ears deafening, as she stood petrified in place.

The warm breath left her face and the creature took a lungful breath. *This is it… This is the end.*

Facing the beast, she saw a bluish light forming in the back of its throat. It traveled upward, expanding and brightening. All Olivia could do was stand paralyzed, overwhelmed.

Her life didn't play out before her eyes. She just watched, wide-eyed, as death approached. *I hope it does not hurt…*

The dragon spouted fire from its maws. Olivia closed her eyes and screamed. She sucked in air and screamed some more. She let all of her fear vent through her voice as she waited for the scorching flames.

But the fire never reached her.

She stopped her screeching vocal onslaught and opened her eyes, one lid at a time. A soft, warm, golden glow flickered from somewhere beside her but she didn't turn to seek its source. Instead, her eyes focused on the creature in front of her with what looked like a single raised brow on its scaly draconic face.

She didn't know what perturbed her more: the fact that she was facing a dragon again and was still alive, or that it actually raised a brow at her as if it were trying to say, *"Are you done screaming?"*

The soft yellow firelight reflected off its deadly fangs, coal-colored elongated horns and dark blue scales. Its amber slitted eyes peered down at her, filled with curiosity.

The dragon opened and closed its jaws. Olivia stared up, gaping, as the creature, she guessed, struggled to produce actual words instead of fire, apparently preferring not to burn her. Or so she hoped. It took the creature a few moments; all the while Olivia just stood there, scared beyond all reason.

"Stay," it said in a deep and raspy voice, the command seeping deep into Olivia's muscles. The dragon snaked its way through a passage that its body had hidden from her view.

Olivia obeyed, astonished that the dragon had spoken. The only movement she dared was to turn her head and look around. Not much was visible, since the meager light didn't penetrate far enough into the surrounding darkness to reveal details. The cave wasn't large; the dragon took up half of it and he couldn't even stand up straight. It was a male, or so she guessed. It didn't have breasts. *Do female dragons have breasts? It is a reptile, right? Do female reptiles have breasts? No, I do not think so. But, reptiles do not talk either.* Olivia hoped she was right or she would have to face an insulted dragon, a dangerous situation at best.

She glanced down at the source of the light and the heat. It looked like a blob of some gooey substance that was slowly burning out. The ashes and remains beneath it spoke of a past fire, probably the one that had drawn her into the cave.

Olivia cherished the warmth it provided as it enveloped her in a gentle embrace. She didn't even mind the slightly acrid smell, so welcome was the warmth.

Tattling, followed by heavy thuds, came from the direction the dragon had disappeared to. He returned, walking on four strong limbs, holding a wooden chair and some fabric in his mouth. Olivia eyed him, her brows furrowed and head tilted to the side.

He put the chair down near the fire. Then, he approached her as if he were approaching a petrified foal. The two pieces of fabric he spread out slowly, close to her feet.

"You didn't run away," he said as he tilted his huge head to the side, mirroring Olivia.

"You are a dragon," Olivia retorted while she studied him. His head was barely smaller then her whole person, all of her five feet and four inches.

"Point taken." He bowed his head slightly.

"You could eat me." The words slipped out before her brain caught up with the implications. *Shut up, Olivia!*

"I could," he said, sounding amused.

"You could hurt me." Olivia's mouth took a life of its own, and she couldn't stop producing the words, offering him unwelcome ideas. She frowned at herself.

"Probably, but I truly wouldn't." His tone was soft and Olivia found his deep, slightly raw voice quite lulling.

"Torture?" Olivia said and then cringed. It was becoming embarrassing.

The dragon's eyes bulged. "Now why would I do that?" A frown drew his brows down. He glowered and Olivia shrank into herself.

"But-but… You… You are a dragon."

"Thank you for stating the obvious. Twice. Now, be

quiet and don't move. I do *not* wish to harm you." After he issued the command, the dragon turned back to the chair and smashed it to pieces with his clawed hand.

Olivia let out a startled yelp and covered her mouth with her hands. Her eyes widened as she watched the dragon shove the wooden pieces roughly towards the fire. The flames engulfed the wood, warming her even more. The fire now burned steady and its dance held Olivia mesmerized. She yawned, exhausted.

She didn't notice the dragon leave until he came back with a large cooking pot hanging from his fang. He passed her by and disappeared through the other passage. Olivia heard him bang the pot against the stone wall, and grumble under his breath. The sound echoed throughout the cave and a hysterical giggle erupted from her. *This surely cannot be happening, not really... I must be dreaming.* She expected to rouse from sleep any moment; she even pinched herself.

When the world around her didn't dissolve and she didn't wake up from the dream, Olivia studied the fabrics at her feet. She picked them up. One was a simple, cotton, light-blue dress with long sleeves that could be rolled up and tied around the upper arms; the other was a soft, woolen, dark-green cloak. The two pieces of clothing, added to everything else the dragon had done, perplexed her even more.

The most recent bout of adrenalin faded and she yawned again. She hugged the garments to her chest and watched the flames dance. The dragon had told her not to move, so she wouldn't. *A dragon... A real dragon, and I am still alive. The stories I have heard...They were real!*

The beast returned carrying the pot now filled with water. He put it down near the fire, the flames warming it.

"When the water heats, clean yourself up and put those clothes on," he said and returned to where he had been curled up when she had discovered him. He exhaled. Smoke billowed from his nostrils.

Olivia sat near the fire with arms wrapped around her shins. Even though her knee ached, it felt good to bend her legs. She gazed uncertainly at the dragon on the other side of the fire. "Will you let me leave or are you planning to eat me later?"

The dragon snorted. Smoke puffed from his nostrils and the gooey slime splattered around, lighting up part of the cave in candlelight-like fire.

Fortunately, the goo missed Olivia.

"What is it with this persistent idea of me eating you?" he said, words laced with agitation.

Olivia considered him. More often than not, she guessed, people assumed he would harm them simply because he was a dragon.

"I am hungry," she responded and shrugged her tired shoulders. "And because—"

"— I'm a dragon," he said, to which Olivia smiled shyly and nodded her head.

"Am I then to be your sacrifice?" Olivia blurted. She really should think before speaking, but she was tired and the anticipation of what the dragon might do with her made her nervous. She just wanted to know her fate so she could make peace with it.

"My sacrifice? Hmmm… now that is a novel idea." The dragon grumbled. He cleared his throat, probably not used to speaking. Who would speak to a dragon after all? He hesitated, but answered nonetheless, "You've heard one too many stories about dragons, Little One. As for you leaving, you're safer here for now."

"Why do you care?"

"If I let you go now, you'll probably get yourself killed, which would make my… helping you save yourself from those wolves futile."

"All right. Then why did you save me from those wolves?"

"Because you drew them to my cave..." It almost sounded more like a question than an answer. The dragon didn't know which answer to supply; he wasn't expecting so many questions from her just yet, but obviously her fear didn't suppress her curiosity. It intrigued him, *she* intrigued him. He hadn't interacted with a human in such a long time. Her tired, slightly downturned eyes would sparkle with inquisitiveness and then, just as quickly, turn dull and sad. That constant shifting interested him.

The young woman merely raised her eyebrow and gave him a pointed look while she took off her abused leather boots, making herself more comfortable, hopefully assured she wouldn't be eaten.

"Fine," he grumbled. "I wanted to talk, and I had a feeling… an intuition, that you would be the right person to make that possible."

The woman glanced up from studying her sore and blistered feet. She winced and wriggled her toes before asking, "Talk?"

"Yes, to talk, Little One. You know, exchange intelligent words with someone else? I haven't had a decent conversation in decades." He puffed a longing sigh.

"Decades? Why?" His personal inquisitor prodded further. She leaned back on her hands and straightened her legs in front of her, bringing her aching feet closer to the fire. He found the whole scene amusing, but her questions too probing.

"Do you have to ask?" he said, dripping sarcasm. "People usually try to kill me to prove something. From some I steal so again they want to kill me and some are just plain scared – "

"Why do you steal if that makes people hate you and want to kill you?"

"You ask an awful lot of questions. I think that is enough for tonight. My throat hurts, so I do not wish to speak anymore," the dragon said. Her questions disturbed him. He couldn't talk about it. No matter how much he wanted to and wished it was possible, he just couldn't the correct words past his reptilian mouth. Instead, he turned his head and faced the other direction.

Olivia thought the dragon's pouting amusing even though she was still wary of him. After all, he was a massive beast capable of who knew what. For a moment she pondered sneaking away, but fear kept her there. He might hear her, see her sneaking out and he could easily catch her. The dragon could then punish her, hurt or even kill her. But somehow those thoughts didn't feel right anymore. As big and scary as he was, he didn't give off the aura of menace, or danger.

She glanced at him. The dragon was facing the other direction. His whole body rose and fell in a lulling motion to the rhythm of his deep and steady breaths. It appeared he was sleeping but she knew better.

Olivia decided to use the moments of privacy while he was facing the other way. She stood up and peeled the dirty and torn clothes from her body. She kept an eye on the dragon, but he did not disturb her solitude.

She threw most of the filthy, shredded clothing into the flames but saved the cleanest piece to use as a wash cloth. She dipped it into the water and washed herself as thoroughly as possible, scrunching her face at the stench, wishing she had her favorite lavender soap, and a real bath. She was careful of her wounds and cleaned them as best she could.

She glanced a few times at the presumably sleeping

dragon. She wanted to be sure he wasn't looking. His scales gleamed and the shadows of the flames danced across his body. From what she had been able to see, he was magnificent, elegant with smooth scales and strong limbs. She found herself looking forward to seeing him in daylight and witnessing all his glory with his wings spread out and sunshine reflecting off his scales. Or seeing him whirl and soar through the air. Olivia wondered what it would be like to fly. *Maybe he would let me. I should ask… or yet, better not, I do* not *want to get eaten.*

Once she finished cleaning herself, Olivia threw the improvised washcloth aside. With one last look towards the dragon, she dipped her head into the water. She wanted to wash all the dirt from her hair as well.

The dragon heard the splash and turned his head back around. She was not as young as he had thought. Her body was a vision that left him wordless and his eyes transfixed, unable to look away, for he had been long deprived of such a sight. He had always preferred voluptuous women, and now he fantasized about the feel of her curves under his touch and the taste of her fair skin on his lips. *Lips! Ha!* He didn't have those anymore.

He could barely remember the last time he had held a soft female body in his hands, or had one wrapped around his own, but he remembered her name… Lucia. *It has been too long.* The glow of the fire caressing the little human's skin did things to him. He shivered with an urge, a desire awaking deep inside of the forgotten parts of him. He wanted to run his hands over her back down to her buttocks, giving them a gentle squeeze. His eyelids drifted shut as he tried to imagine if she would feel as soft and velvety as she appeared. That was all he could do, just imagine.

The dragon opened his eyes in time to see Olivia lift her

head back up, splashing the water around. She smoothed her hands over her hair to squeeze out the remaining moisture. He let his eyes rove quickly over the front of her body and her full, perky breasts. He didn't dare let his gaze linger, because if he looked any longer, he would be left staring and she would catch him doing so. That would create a whole batch of new problems. He shifted his gaze back around, just as she wiped the water from her eyes.

The first thing Olivia did was look in the dragon's direction. She had had a feeling he was watching her, but he was still facing the other direction. She huddled near the fire a bit longer, letting her body dry. Olivia just stared aimlessly at the flames and listened to the crackling and popping sounds.

After a while, she donned the new dress and wrapped the soft woolen cloak around her shoulders. She pulled the hood up and over her still damp hair. After some squirming and turning, she finally settled on the hard ground while staying near the fire for the warmth it provided. She used her arm as a pillow and let her eyes drift shut.

"Just one more question?" she whispered and her request lingered in the air.

"Fine."

Olivia's lips quirked up at the dragon's irritable response. "What is your name?"

"Kaden."

"Good night, Kaden." Olivia yawned and welcomed the sleep that descended swiftly upon her.

When the dragon heard her breathing even out as she succumbed to slumber, he returned his gaze upon her. She was so innocent, her features soft and peaceful until a shiver wracked her tiny body. *She is cold.* Kaden noticed the fire dwindling. He decided to take a risk, because he was a dragon after all, as the Little One would say.

His tail slithered towards her and he wrapped it around her body, careful not to harm her. He half carried and half dragged her closer to him, and tucked her at his side. The dragon chuckled inwardly, imagining her reaction when she woke up.

He covered her with his wing to keep her warm and whispered, "Good night, Little One."

CHAPTER 3

Nausea tugged Olivia out of the dreamless sleep. Her stomach rumbled as it cramped painfully. She gave her lips some respite by moistening them with her tongue.

Once her eyes fluttered open, she found herself under a dark, silken canopy. *I must be dreaming still.* Her pillow, too, brushed silky against her cheek, but not as soft. The surface she lay on though was hard, uncomfortable.

She snuggled deeper into the warmth and pulled the cloak tighter around her shoulders.

Olivia remembered her encounter with the dragon and didn't feel the need to panic this time. He hadn't hurt her thus far and, hopefully, he wouldn't. She recalled falling asleep on the cold floor of dirt-covered stone. Not long after, the chill had seeped through the woolen cloak, making her shiver and interrupting her slumber. At the time she had been too tired to care but now she remembered being wrapped in a bubble of protective warmth after which peaceful sleep finally descended upon her. Olivia furrowed her brow once she became aware of the change in her sleeping arrangement.

When she reached out with her hand and touched the surface she had been snuggling into, she recognized the source of the warmth as soon as her palm made contact with the reptilian scales.

The silky warmth moved, and Olivia smiled. In all the stories and legends she had heard about dragons, the great beasts were always described differently and given various terrifying attributes, but one thing was always the same: they were all evil, ungodly creatures. Yet Kaden had proved to be anything but; he was caring and gentle. At least, he had been up to now.

Her eyes popped wide open when she couldn't remember thanking the dragon for all he had done for her. She was taught to have manners, to show gratitude. He twitched beneath her palms and Olivia felt the soft, lulling movements against her face stop and the sound of his deep, slow breathing cease.

"Good morning, Kaden," Olivia mumbled against his side, her lips almost brushing his scales. She had decided not to panic or throw any more tantrums; it would be useless. If he wanted to harm her, or eat her, he would have done so by now. He had only taken care of her, and she had no choice but to trust him.

Kaden suppressed a shiver that wanted to show its appreciation at having female lips so close to his… scales. He sighed inwardly. He wondered about the change in her behavior but didn't want to complain about it because he welcomed the female companionship. *Any* companionship. As limited as it was.

"Well, it is almost morning outside. So yes… Good morning."

The sound of his soothing deep baritone reverberating through his body sent a shiver down Olivia's spine.

"Olivia," she said through a yawn.

"Hm?"

"It is my name, Olivia. Well Olivia Violet Moore, most

call me Olivia, my father calls me Violet." She peeked out from under his wing.

"Hmmm... Olivia." His voice still sounded raspy from the lack of use. "Are you still cold? I should start the fire again." The dragon gently extracted himself and tried to stretch but failed due to the size of the cave, which now included a human in addition to his gargantuan bulk.

Olivia rose to her feet as well. She winced when her knee protested against the movement, then stretched her hands above her head. "I am actually quite alright. This cloak is warm... oh... which reminds me—" She yawned, squeezing her eyes shut as her mouth opened, and didn't notice the dragon caressing her body with his gaze, looking her up and down as she stretched.

Olivia turned to face him again and he diverted his stare, hoping she hadn't noticed his silent appraisal. He would've blushed if he could. It had been too long since he had last been this close to a woman, and she had slept in his embrace all night.

"Thank you," Olivia said, tilting her head back so she could look up at him.

"For what?" The dragon's eyes landed on her again. He liked the way the short dark curls danced around her soft face, but he couldn't stand that sad look in her bright blue eyes. The color reminded him of soaring high in clear skies. It was an exhilarating feeling, not an unhappy one.

"Everything, of course."

Kaden quirked his brow up and almost asked for an explanation, but then he understood. "Oh, 'twas nothing."

Olivia was about to argue but her stomach decided to make its presence known yet again. Blushing profusely, she looked down at her own feet, put a hand on her stomach and mumbled quietly, "I apologize."

"Why are you apologizing? You are merely hungry." He

shifted and snaked his head out through the passage that led outside. "It's still raining. I should go and get you something to eat."

"Oh, no. I do not wish to impose any more than I already have. I will find myself some food."

"Nonsense!" The dragon's voice shifted back to that cold and commanding tone he had first used with her. "The rain does not bother me, so you will stay. Keep warm while I go and get us something to eat. When I return, we will talk. Wait here."

He didn't give her a chance to respond as he turned around and snaked his way through the passage leading deeper into the cave. Olivia simply stood there, frozen in place. When he spoke like that, the fear rose in her again and she couldn't bring herself to disobey him.

Kaden returned a few moments later carrying a new chair, different from the one he had produced during the night, along with a mattress and a blanket.

"Where do you find these things?" Olivia said.

"In the back." The dragon set the mattress and the blanket down, facing the exiting passage. The chair he smashed, and again gathered the splinters into a pile of wood.

"There... You should be nice and cozy now." He maneuvered himself slightly to the side and brought his wings around the chair as best as he could in the cramped space, protecting Olivia from his fiery breath as he set the wood ablaze.

Olivia gaped and the dragon smirked, amused by her speechlessness.

"Nice to know you can stay your words." Kaden snorted smoke from his nostrils but managed to stop himself from accidentally spouting fire this time.

After she limped over to the mattress Olivia said, "You

just confuse me." She lowered herself down, careful of her wounds, but thankful for the soft cushioning she sank into. She pulled the blanket around her, for emotional comfort as much as for warmth.

Perplexed, he ignored her comment. "I should be back shortly." It had been a long time since he had had to socialize with someone. As he recalled, he used to be quite the charmer. He would have to remember how to act that way with her.

"Oh, may I make one request?" Olivia said as she looked up at the dragon, eyes pleading.

"Somehow, I knew not to expect anything less from you." Kaden smiled inwardly. "So, what is it, Little One?" His voice returned to that warm, caring rumble.

"Please do not bring back anything alive... or twitching... or barely dead. I just would *not* be able to eat it afterwards." Olivia scrunched up her nose in distaste.

Kaden would have laughed if he could have remembered how. "How did you survive in the woods alone? No, never mind now, we'll talk when I return. So, nothing alive and twitching. I think I can manage that. But it might take me a bit longer. You wait here and stay out of trouble. You are not to go to the back cave, understand?" he said in a no-nonsense tone.

"Yes, sir... dragon... Kaden," Olivia responded, her gaze dropping to her hands where they lay in her lap. She had disobeyed her father and it hadn't really turned out well, and Kaden was a dragon. She knew when to speak her mind and when to bite her tongue... most of the time.

As Kaden padded out of the cave, Olivia raised her head and watched him leave. She sighed in relief. He was just so overwhelming in stature and presence. But with him gone, she also felt a lot less safe, and lonely. The cave seemed so much bigger without him. The stone walls were drab, grey and boring, and the floor beneath her feet was a mix of rocks and dirt, just as dull as the rest of the cave. What was she to do? Just sitting and waiting for Kaden's return would give her too much time to think, and the thoughts that were uppermost in her mind - when she didn't actively squash them — centered around the actions that had led her to the dragon's lair. Olivia just wasn't ready for that. The wound in her heart was still raw and aching while the rising guilt would suck the air out from her lungs, so she pushed it further away, until she was ready to face the consequences of her actions.

Olivia sighed. She stood up, stretching her legs carefully and walked to the cauldron the dragon had brought in the night before so she could drag it out into the rain that was still falling fiercely. Outside the cave, the rising sun hid behind the angry, grey clouds. A fog of lifting clouds obscured the trees and the surrounding foliage, allowing only enough visibility for Olivia to see the few trees looming over the entrance to the cave.

She set the pot down in the downpour, hoping it would fill with rainwater. As she waited, she cupped her hands and held them out to catch some raindrops, using the fresh water to wash her face and moisten her lips. When she realized her dress was getting wet, Olivia drew the cloak tighter around her, but not before having a good look at the dress. Even if it was simple, it was quite fine, a beautiful shade of blue that matched her eyes. All she needed was a girdle to look proper. *But who cared about proper out here?* The cloak, on the other hand, was made of soft green wool and was finely crafted in a way that spoke of obvious wealth. She had a few of her own back home.

She shook the thoughts of home away yet again.

She was disappointed at how long it was taking for the pot to fill with rainwater; she barely had enough for a cup or two. She wondered where Kaden had gathered the water earlier in the night, as he surely hadn't gotten it from the rain dripping in. It would have taken too much time. She carried the small measure of rainwater back inside and placed the pot next to the flames.

While she was waiting for the water to heat up, she folded the blanket at the foot of the mattress as if making her bed. Once done, she searched for something to do. She had never been any good at just sitting around. Unfortunately, there was absolutely nothing she could distract herself with inside the cave.

Hmmm… I could run away now that the dragon is gone. But where would I go? Home is not an option. Olivia didn't want to think about home, but her thoughts kept drifting back there. She especially didn't want to revisit the disappointment clouding her father's eyes; she never imagined that it was his worry about her that kept him up these past few nights instead.

Sitting down on the mattress, she sighed and huddled up with her arms around her knees. *They probably wouldn't want me back anyway.* She was probably too much of an embarrassment now.

"So senseless!"

She chewed on her bottom lip. She couldn't stay in this cave forever, it was so…. So… *A Cave! No soft beds, warm baths, hot meals. Not to mention living with a dragon.* Olivia snorted at the thought and shook her head. *What kind of a life would that be?*

She sighed. Certainly not the kind she had. She missed her parents though, her mother's warm gaze, father's mischief. Running away was a mistake. Sure, it had been thrilling when she first set off, the anger fueling her determination, and… but oh the excitement. Finally she had done something she wanted, not something that was expected of her, she had felt free, now though, she felt miserable and lonely.

She looked around the cave again as it perfectly mirrored her mood, her feelings, growing even more hopeless knowing that for now she was stuck there until she figured out what to do next. At least she was safe with Kaden, or so she hoped. He hadn't eaten her so far, and it seemed less and less likely that he would.

Determined to keep herself occupied, she considered her options for entertainment. Going out in the rain was out of the question. The downpour was too merciless and the last thing she needed was to catch lung fever. And she didn't want to make Kaden angry.

She spotted the back passageway and remembered Kaden's warning, but the only thing she could do was find out what he was hiding at the other end of it.

Argh! Olivia pushed herself back up onto her feet. She was both curious and bored, wanting to keep her mind occupied as well. *How would he know I went there? I will only take a peek.*

"And besides, he would probably mind me snooping around less than getting drenched in the rain."

With that as her reasonable explanation, Olivia stuck her chin out as if daring the invisible forces to prove her wrong as she set on making an improvised torch from the leftover discarded fabric and one of the chair legs.

Determined, she marched towards her destination. Adrenalin surged through her veins and her heart beat faster, warming her up and dulling her hunger.

She found it exciting to do something forbidden, just like when she had run away. Olivia had never done something like that before and it had been thrilling. But it hadn't turned out too well for her. The thought slowed her march as she doubted her decision. *Well, depending on the point of view actually*, Olivia reasoned with herself and continued on her stubborn mission.

With one last glance over her shoulder to make sure Kaden wouldn't suddenly appear and catch her sneaking about, she stepped through to the back cave.

CHAPTER 4

Tall trees looming over the cave's mouth prevented Kaden from taking flight near it. He simply could not spread his wings in the dense forest. And he never had the need to clear the trees, liking his leisurely walk. His scales scraped against the bark, chipping bits off, leaving a breadcrumb-like trail behind him as he strode toward the clearing where he usually took off. The soft earth sank under his weight, creating dragon-foot-shaped puddles that quickly filled with rainwater in his wake.

He didn't like flying in the rain. He preferred the bright sun and clear skies to the gloom of the rain. But he would just have to endure it now. At least he had some company waiting for him to come back.

Once he entered the clearing, a green pasture cradled in the arms of the forest, Kaden lifted his head and looked up at the dreary clouds as raindrops splashed against his craggy features. The wetness of the rain never bothered him, for he could barely feel the tiny impacts of its drops. The weather mirrored his mood, the hopelessness and loneliness of his heart. This time, though, he looked forward to the sunshine that would disperse the dark mantle clouding his mind.

Olivia…

The dragon sighed. What he desired could never come to pass, he knew that, but he would enjoy the companionship while he could. *It has been too long.*

He spread his silky smooth wings and beat them downward hard.

Once.

The air strained against the webbed membrane.

Twice.

His wings drew taut under the pressure of the draft and he rose up on his hind legs.

Three times, and his feet lifted off the ground.

The raindrops scattered and merged in a frantic dance around him. The low hum of wings slicing through the air was the sweetest melody to his ears. He loved flying, and the freedom that came with it. If only the sun wasn't hidden behind the clouds so he could soak up its warm rays. The dragon would have to wait for the weather to clear up for that; maybe he could even show off to Olivia, seduce her with his aerial performance. He quickly shook the thought out of his mind. *Don't forget yourself; you're a dragon now.*

When Kaden reached the desired height, he stopped working so hard, only beating his wings languidly to keep himself afloat, generating intermittent gusts of wind that kept the rain at bay. He craned his graceful neck and perused the undulating sea of green below. His tongue darted out now and then, licking the dancing droplets right out of the air.

He scanned the surrounding woods for any sign of food. A doe darted through the bushes seeking shelter from the rain while a pair of squirrels circled up a tree and into a den in the hollow of the trunk, branches swaying in the wind.

Plenty of food moved through the forest, all alive and twitching as Olivia would say. But he couldn't skin, clean and prepare it for her and he knew she wouldn't be up to the task either. So he took to flying wider circles in search of a more convenient food source.

The dragon sniffed the air, but even with his heightened senses the rain thwarted his attempts to pick up a scent.

After circling about for some time, he headed in the direction where the rain fell more gently and beyond that, where it had never fallen, where the sun's rays kept the dark clouds at bay.

As he soared through the air, beating his wings fast and hard, he reached a region where there was no more rain and the air grew warmer. The darkness above him gave way to the bluest of skies, and a pair of eyes just as blue but dulled with sadness gazed out at him from the depths of his thoughts. Determination surged through him and he resolved to make those eyes sparkle with the brightness of the summer sun. Maybe she would stay longer then.

Beneath him, farmlands and homesteads rushed past. His senses were on overdrive, as he was overwhelmed by the desire to find food fast so he could go back to Olivia as soon as possible.

He worried about leaving her alone for this long. What if those wolves returned? He somehow doubted that would happen – he had given the wild canines a taste of his fury and he knew they didn't want a second course – but something worse might come by, and without him there to protect her—

The scent of roasted meat tickled his flaring nostrils. His mouth watered and he sniffed the air again, trying to pinpoint its source.

His eyes narrowed while his pupils dilated. He sighed.

This will be a mess. The dragon's gaze was transfixed on his prey in the distance below: a pig with two chickens on each side of the same spit, roasting over an open fire. The problem, however, were the people surrounding it, dancing, laughing, mingling. A celebration of sorts was in progress, and when he got closer he figured out what kind.

It was a wedding. Just his luck to have to intrude.

He had to collect his meal as painlessly as possible, without too much mess or too many casualties.

There goes my reputation... or my bad reputation. I shouldn't care anymore. I should be proud. Me. The big, bad, evil dragon. Kaden cheered himself on, only to slow down as his shoulders slumped under the weight of the sarcasm in his words. He was going to have to forge on, though, if he wanted to fulfill his promise to Olivia. The need to keep her around longer, to talk, to sit quietly… just to be with him, to fill that loneliness even for a short while, fed his resolve.

The dragon narrowed his eyes and flicked his tongue over his protruding fangs. He sped up, then tucked his wings closer to his body as he speared the air at an even more incredible speed. The wind whooshed past him in a deafening song.

As he neared his target, Kaden roared to frighten the people away. When his shadow slid across the ground beneath their feet and his mighty growl reverberated from above, dozens of wide eyes snapped up in disbelief. A blur of movement erupted as the throng of people shrieked and ran for safety, trampling each other in their haste. They had no idea he intended them no harm. He had always tried to avoid hurting people. But it wasn't as if he could've just flown over, landed among them and asked them politely for their roast. That strategy hadn't worked before when he had been crazy enough to try it. This was the only way he could keep the confrontation and injuries to a minimum.

When he got low enough, Kaden spread his wings and beat them backwards, slowing his progress. He inhaled deeply. He needed to take careful aim when spouting the fire from his mouth; he only meant to scare the people away from his path towards the roast.

A few arrows and stones flew close to his head. He switched his attention towards his assailants, roared and spouted fire in their direction, but not hard enough to reach them.

They took off running.

Kaden descended and swooped in toward the pole with the still-roasting meat. His front claws wrapped around the iron rod as he snatched his prize. With a firm grip on it, he beat his wings hard again, dust and ashes rising as he flew higher and higher. The outcries of panic and disbelief faded as the distance between the dragon and the human crowd stretched on.

He took one last look at the gathering.

People were creeping out of their hiding places, hugging each other or searching for their loved ones. He hated upsetting them like that, but he didn't know of any other way he could have done it. Some were pointing up in his direction but Kaden's attention was drawn to an unmoving boy who gazed up at his retreating form. The boy's eyes widened and then determination poured over his features. The young lad jumped on his horse, dug his heels into the animal's flanks and urged it in the direction of a nearby town.

A feeling of foreboding welled up inside Kaden, like a myriad tiny needle pricks running down his spine.

The dragon faced forward again and focused his thoughts on returning home.

The mountain which he claimed his own, even though no one knew of his claim, grew bigger as he approached it, and the rain pelted on him once more while he squinted to spot the cave, wondering whether Olivia was still there.

A familiar tug in his mind, the unwanted intruder on his life, urged him to look below. He noticed a trading caravan crawling along on the wide path that wound through the sparse part of the forest.

A groan rumbled up from his throat. *Not now!* Fury surged through him and he gripped the pole even tighter, almost snapping it apart.

His heart pumped faster, raging against his ribcage as a plume of smoke, of pure fury, puffed out of his nostrils. With his eyes narrowed, brows pulled down in a scowl, Kaden clamped his jaws tight, suppressing a mighty roar as he fought the inevitable. He couldn't resist it; the urge to take what was not his was overwhelming.

Might as well get it done and over with.

With a heavy heart, Kaden swooped down once more, quiet as the wind, drawing no attention from the folk below. No one was in his way. Before the caravan leaders had any idea what was happening, he grabbed the first thing he could snatch with his hind claws and swiftly flew away.

The merchants stumbled at the sudden outburst of wind. Once they regained their senses they stared at the dragon's retreating form in bewilderment and probably thanked God for their good luck in surviving what they would describe to anyone who might listen as a mighty dragon attack.

CHAPTER 5

In a small town called Atrav, a boy dressed in his Sunday best galloped on his horse towards the inn called The Woodman's Nymph. His chest heaved with labored breaths and his dark brown hair, wet with sweat, was plastered against his forehead. But it was his brown eyes, open wide and filled with fear and panic, that dominated his features. He had just seen a dragon and lived to tell the tale. The cruel beast had ruined his sister's wedding feast!

The boy jumped off his horse when he reached the inn. He burst through the doors, almost tripping over his own two feet. His eyes flitted over the patrons until he found the ones he was looking for – the ones robed in sapphire blue. Quick footed, the boy strode toward the corner where the knights sat.

"Sir?" he asked for attention while he bowed his head. Hiding his hands behind his back, he wrung his fingers nervously.

The knight raised his eyebrows, his cold blue eyes glaring at the boy as he pushed his shoulder length blonde hair behind his ear. The woman sitting on his lap turned to look at the newcomer as well while she ran her fingers through the knight's soft curls.

The other men at the table also shifted their attention from their casual conversation to the boy, appraising him for any signs of a threat.

"Sir?" the golden-haired knight questioned back, hiding disapproval behind amusement.

The boy's eyes widened even more when he realized his mistake. "I'm sorry Sir – ermm... I mean Your Highness." He bowed again, deeper this time.

"Speak quickly boy, I am currently otherwise occupied." The prince's gaze slid back to the woman and he eyed her as if she were the most delectable meal he had tasted in ages, though actually he had sated himself with her the night before. A flirty smile played on his pink lips at the memory. The woman giggled.

"I've seen a dragon," the boy said with breathless eagerness and the prince's head snapped toward him. "I mean... there was a dragon sighting. Actually, the dragon attacked us," the boy rattled off, unable to hold back his excitement and awe.

The prince, along with his companions, sobered up at the words and viewed the boy with narrowed eyes. The other patrons in the inn quieted at the boy's words, anticipating a good story.

"You better not be jesting with me," the prince said in a cold, hard voice.

"I ain't... I... it happened just a while ago. I–I rode here as quickly as possible. There are other people who saw it. 'Twas my sister's wedding. It came out of the sky spouting fire." The boy's voice rose as he spoke and his eyes grew big again. "It roared in rage! We was all so afraid. We tried fighting it off. It stole a roast and almost killed my sister's wedding guests with its fire. Real dragon fire! A real dragon! We saw it flying away towards the north."

On the prince's request the boy recounted the incident,

reporting everything he had witnessed down to the finest detail.

"What you have told us…" The prince rose to his feet and towered over the young lad, rubbing his chin while considering the import and possible truth of this news. His knights leapt to their feet as well.

The woman who had been sitting on his lap almost slid off to the floor. She steadied herself and spoke quickly. "I know the boy. You're Kalmin, am I right?"

The boy nodded.

"I believe he speaks the truth. It is his sister's wedding day today, and he doesn't have a jesting bone in his body. He's too serious for his age."

The prince studied the boy's face, searching for any sign of treachery. When he found none and saw only panic, awe, excitement and some fear, he nodded.

"Very well. I guess others will come soon to share the tale. You have made the right choice by informing me promptly. Reed, Colin – " the prince turned towards his men " – fetch our belongings and saddle our horses. Lance, go get Charlie. And Cathal… you get the others. It looks like I will finally get my chance. The dragon and its head will be mine; I have spent too much time searching for the beast. But our day is getting closer, I can feel it now." His hands balled into fists at his sides, knuckles turning white.

"Yes, Your Highness." The men bowed and scurried to do as they were told.

"And you boy…"

Kalmin lifted his eyes to his prince and waited for whatever was to come.

"Here… for your trouble."

The boy caught a gold coin that soared through the air towards him.

"Thank you, Your Highness! You are very kind. I hope

you get that evil dragon! And I hope to be as great a knight as you are someday." Kalmin's eyes sparkled with pride that he had done something to please his prince.

The prince snorted. "Not like me, but maybe like one of my knights," he said and winked at the boy. "Now, away with you."

The boy scampered off and the prince turned towards the dark-haired woman who had kept his bed warm the last couple of nights.

"I am sorry, my dear puppet." He lifted his hand and caressed her face with the back of his hand. "But my princely duties await. I swore I would have a dragon's head decorating my halls and it seems my quest might come to an end soon." A wry smile curled his lips.

"Will you come back for me?" The woman's eyes filled with hope as she looked up at her prince. Her hands rested on his chest.

Stupid whore, the prince thought. These small town girls were just too easy for him to seduce and bed; they all hoped to ensnare his heart and become his queen one day. They were useful for one thing, though, and he used them well for it. He only needed to turn his piercing blue eyes on them, run a hand through his soft golden hair as he looked at them with desire twinkling in his eyes, and he had them in his grasp.

"I do not wish to give you false hope, my dear puppet. It might take us some time to finish with the dragon and return to the palace, but if I still remember you by the end of it all, I will send for you." *And use you as my personal mistress*, he snickered inwardly. "If I were to judge by the last couple of nights, I will most surely remember you," he finished with a wink.

The woman giggled at his words, oblivious to the insult threaded through them.

"And of course, if you find someone else while I am dealing with the dragon and tending to my royal duties, I will not hold a grudge." Voice serious and features softened, the prince provided a self-sacrificing and honorable look.

"There'll never be anyone like you, Your Highness," the woman said wistfully. She rose onto the tips of her toes and planted a soft kiss on his lips. "For good luck."

The prince nodded and swiveled on his heel. The innkeeper approached him, gifting him some food and drinks for their journey. He was going to make good profit when the word spread that the prince himself had stayed in one of his rooms.

As the prince marched to meet up with his men, many people wished him farewell while bowing their heads in respect.

He soon spotted the crowd that were his knights.

All nine of them, the finest he could gather and their little traveling whore, Charlie. He liked that woman, for she was as fiery as her hair. She had tried to run away once, but he had taught her a lesson, and he had loved teaching her.

"Your Highness." They lowered their heads in greeting.

Cassiel, the dark-skinned knight, relieved the prince of the sacks of food, while Reed, the closest thing the prince had to a best friend and his second-in-command, held up Magnus' full plate armor, helping him don it. Next came his weapon, a two-handed greatsword which he sheathed safely into the scabbard strapped to his back. Fully armed, he mounted his horse and the others quickly followed suit.

The young woman who traveled with them, Charlotte, sat sulking on her horse as usual. She hated being on the road for days, sometimes even weeks, and it was much easier for her when they stayed in a town. She had some respite from the men then.

When Prince Magnus was comfortably perched on his black stallion, ready to leave the small town, a man approached the group and cleared his throat.

"The Inventor!" The prince gave the man an honest, appreciative smile. "Did you manage to make a duplicate? We have to leave now so I cannot wait." He turned his horse to face the scrawny, ingenious man who would bring great things to this small town, now on the brink of a steam revolution. And then, the revolution would spread across his whole kingdom of Illirya. The town of Atrav was, in the Inventor's words, perfect for such an endeavor; it was surrounded by rich forests with easy access to the coal mines.

"Yes, Your Highness!" the Inventor said, beaming up at his prince. "I was just looking for you at the inn and they told me you had left already. So… here I am." The small, wiry man pushed his spectacles up his nose. From his shoulder bag he pulled out an object wrapped in a cylindrical leather pouch and handed it to the prince. "I've tested it and it should work fine, just like I showed you. Use it sparingly."

The prince grasped the pouch carefully, almost reverently, and secured it inside one of his saddle bags. He was going to play with it later.

"Thank you. You will be paid as we agreed." With a tilt of his head, the prince signaled to his knights that he was ready to go.

"Just let me know how it works!" The inventor's eyes sparkled with expectation.

"I will."

Prince Magnus turned to his knights while running a hand through his golden hair. A wicked smile danced on his lips.

"Knights," he said as they prepared to ride off. "We

finally get to kill a dragon."

CHAPTER 6

Olivia crept through the forbidden passage, wary of unsuspected dangers. The tunnel widened, and loomed higher and higher as she approached its end. When she reached it, she took her first step into a second, much larger cave, marveling at its vastness.

Awe and wonder spread across Olivia's face, her mouth agape, eyes wide open, as she scanned the contents of the chamber. Soon, amusement joined them.

The fire from her torch reflected off the shiny surfaces of the cave's contents and provided Olivia with more illumination. She never expected this. Of course, she had had the same prejudices as everyone else, expecting to find hoards of gold, jewelry and crowns within the dragon's lair. And here, there were indeed some of those treasures, accompanied by beautiful mirrors adorned with precious gems.

The items which brought her amusement and wonder however, were the chairs, tables, chests, and cabinets. She even spied a bench, a pile of fabrics she presumed were clothes, a stack of blankets, several big wicker baskets, half of a wagon, a plow and many other man-made objects, carefully sorted. And books! A whole crate of them. She would no longer be bored.

As she walked around, scanning the contents of the treasure cache, a simple yet elegant leather girdle drew her attention and she couldn't resist putting it on just to try it out. The belt fit her perfectly. She approached one of the mirrors to see how it looked on her. She twisted left and right, appraising the combination of the tooled leather with her gown while ignoring the presence of the dark circles under her eyes and the slight tremble of her hands. Out of the corner of her eye she spotted something rather peculiar. *Is that really what I think it is?* She took a few steps closer. *It is!* She couldn't help but laugh out loud.

Her laughter echoed throughout the cave as she kept her eyes glued to a brick chimney that looked like it had been torn whole off of a house's roof. Once her mirth subsided, she almost started back up again as she spotted a dead tree with its dry roots sticking out in all directions.

She couldn't believe what she was seeing. There were all manner of items, both valuable and worthless, but the cave was so crowded she couldn't get to most of them. It would take time and some skillful climbing to explore it all. She had so many questions she wanted to ask Kaden, but that would mean telling him she had gone where he had forbidden her to go.

The fire on her torch sputtered, threatening to go out. That, and fear that Kaden might have returned while she was snooping around, pushed her to go back where she was supposed to be.

When Olivia returned to her makeshift bed, her knee was throbbing, her stomach growling, and her mind was a whirlwind, trying to figure out how and why Kaden had collected and stored all those things. It seemed he had quite a penchant for human possessions. There was no other explanation for it. It was obvious he had no use for those items, and they were just too random, some of them completely worthless as treasure or ransom. *Oh, a compulsive thief and a hoarder.* The thought made Olivia giggle.

After she had rested her aching body a bit, the water finally reached the boiling point. Olivia then carefully hefted and dragged the cauldron away from the fire, letting it cool down a bit so she could gently wash out her wounds. The rest of water she could drink later.

As she sat back on the mattress, legs straight in front of her while resting her back against the cave's rock walls, she thought about the dragon again, how contradictory he was, one moment gentle and caring, the next cold and commanding. He probably thought he was scaring her, but she saw different in his eyes, even though his voice was hard to disobey. Thinking about his low, rumbling voice made her realize how strange it was to watch a dragon talk.

To know he did talk after all.

His lips didn't move like a human's would. They did move though, in correlation with the pronunciation of the words, but it seemed like the words and sounds were formed in his throat rather than in his mouth, the way a human would speak.

Then there were his amber eyes. She had never seen eyes of that color, probably because she had never met a dragon before. Even though he didn't have human facial features, he was easy to read. He probably wasn't used to hiding his emotions and true reactions; most people probably fled from him, if they ever got close enough to see his features at all.

From what she had managed to see of him, he looked quite magnificent. His scales were silky smooth, their color a shimmering midnight blue. His underside, as she had seen today, was a deep gold and his horns were slender and dark grey, almost black. She hated to admit it but she was quite taken with his appearance, as if he were an elegant gentleman and not a fire-breathing monster.

But the thing she liked the best was the emotion he stirred inside her. He made her feel safe and protected even though she had been terrified of him at first. It was just what she needed after what she had gone through the last couple of days. Olivia was beginning to trust him, but remained prudent. He was still a dragon, after all.

Her eyes traveled towards the entrance of the cave. She could hear the rain dwindling. It seemed like the sun was winning the battle of supremacy over the sky, managing to shine a little more light through the clouds.

She pulled her knees up to her chest and rested her cheek on them while still keeping an eye out for Kaden's return.

She sighed.

It must have been an hour or more since he had left. She hoped nothing bad had happened to him, while, at the same time, she felt silly for worrying about his safety. He was probably quite capable of taking care of himself.

Olivia yawned.

She lay back, deciding on a nap while she waited for Kaden to return. It beat sitting around and doing nothing. Just as she was about to drift off, a shadow appeared at the entrance.

The dragon had returned.

As Kaden made his way in with the roast, Olivia quickly got to her feet and moved towards him.

"You are back!" she said, a happy smile blooming on her face.

"Of course I am." Kaden threw her a confused look as he walked by her to put the roasted pig and chickens near the fire to warm up again.

"And you brought food! Real food," Olivia said as she

devoured the food with her eyes. She could almost feel drool dripping down her chin, she was so hungry.

Her feet moved of their own accord, carrying her towards those tasty-looking chickens.

"Stop!" Kaden said.

Olivia froze in place. His voice spoke of trouble. Trouble she was in. *Does he know?*

The dragon moved closer to her and lowered his head so he could gaze into her eyes.

"You went snooping where I told you not to," he accused, but kept his voice level. He couldn't decide whether to be angry with her.

"No I did not!" Olivia put her hands on her hips and raised her chin. Inwardly, she was surprised she had managed to keep her voice strong and steady.

She had never been good at lying.

This time Kaden actually chuckled out loud and the deep sound rumbled through the cave. He inhaled slowly and saw a flash of fear flit across her face.

"I can smell the lies on you." His voice turned serious again as he stared at her, squinting through his left eye.

"Dragons can do that?" Olivia gaped. Had she angered him?

"No," Kaden responded mischievously. "It would have been easier to believe you if you weren't wearing the evidence of your disobedience." He looked at the belt around her waist and raised his brows.

"Oh," was her clever reply. She pasted on her most innocent smile. "I... ummm..." Olivia clasped her hands behind her back, wrung her fingers and looked down at her own feet. "I might have?"

He shook his head in mock disapproval. "And what did I tell you?"

"Not to go there." A regretful sigh slipped past Olivia's

lips as she looked up at him from under her dark eyelashes.

Seeing her like that, remorseful and vulnerable, melted Kaden's irritation. How could he be angry with someone that innocent? They would have to talk about it, but when he heard that stomach of hers growling again, he let it go, for now.

With a heavy sigh, he took a step away from her. "Eat now. I know you're starving."

Olivia blinked a couple of times, surprised there was no chiding, no lecturing. No breathing fire. She watched Kaden leave the cave. Just as she was about to panic at being left alone in punishment for her transgression, he returned carrying a crate.

Her eyebrows rose high, head tilted to the side as she studied him and the crate. Then, remembering what she had wanted to do in the first place, Olivia hurried to the roasted chicken and tore off a juicy drumstick, warm from the fire.

As she took the first bite, she moaned in delight. Olivia chewed with slow enjoyment, relishing the experience. When she swallowed her first real food in days, she noticed the lack of sound and movement around her. Looking up, her eyes landed on Kaden as he studied her lips with an indescribable intensity.

Olivia cleared her throat to wake him from his reverie because it made her uncomfortable. *Did watching her eat make him want to eat her after all? That couldn't be it. He's been nothing but nice to me so far. He would never harm me, would he? What is that dragon thinking? Was he staring at my… lips?*

When Kaden snapped out of it, his eyes made contact with hers. He couldn't believe she had caught him staring, but it was worth it, seeing a deep blush adorn Olivia's cheeks as they looked at each other.

Kaden's tail twitched. Olivia bit her lip.

She was the one to break the spell that wove itself around them. "What – " She choked on the word and had to clear her throat as she looked away from his piercing gaze, "What is in the crate?"

Kaden looked down at it, glad for the change of subject.

"Let's find out." He cracked the crate open with his front claws and peered inside. Before he could answer her, he started laughing. He hadn't laughed in a long time, and between gulps of air, snorts, and puffs of smoke, he responded,

"Pants. A bunch of men's pants!"

Olivia froze for a moment in bewilderment, but soon she joined his laughter, and their united mirth echoed through the cave.

CHAPTER 7

"My goodness! I just ate a whole chicken!" Olivia said as she nibbled the meat off the last bone and threw it into the fire. "I feel like such a pig."

Kaden groaned as if the thought pained him. "Oh, please don't say that. I just finished eating a pig. That would mean eating you. It is a most disturbing thought."

Before they had started eating, they had settled around the fire. Olivia had put the blanket underneath her so she wouldn't be sitting on the cold ground and Kaden had curled up in his usual spot, facing the flames. He was big enough to be close to the blaze even from his place at the far end of the cave. The rain outside had slowed but hadn't stopped yet; the gentle drizzle created a soft, calming music.

The two cave-dwellers fell into a comfortable silence while they both enjoyed their meals, throwing surreptitious glances at each other when they thought, or hoped, the other wouldn't notice. Only once during the meal did Kaden dare to disturb the gentle hush. Compelled, he shared with Olivia the details of his quest for their dinner. She was a little upset with him for stealing but admitted relief that he hadn't harmed anyone. Finally, she had the presence of mind to express her gratitude to him for the meal, and he responded with good manners.

That was yet another odd little fact about the dragon that she found so surprising. All the stories she had heard over the years about the dragons of old made them sound mostly bloodthirsty and vicious, but here she was, safe and relaxed, having lunch with a supposedly dangerous beast. She was also surprised how at ease she felt and how comfortable it was to just sit near the fire and eat while the conversation between them trickled intermittently.

Every minute she spent in Kaden's company, Olivia felt more refreshed and alive. Even though the cave was cold, damp and depressing, having the dragon for company improved her disposition. She never would have imagined finding herself in this situation, but here she was, and she found herself enjoying the experience.

"Have you ever..." Olivia trailed off, too afraid to finish the sentence, and stared into the fire instead.

Kaden had been expecting this question, waiting for it. "Eaten a human?" he finished for her, his voice soft.

Olivia nodded as she sat cross-legged across the fire from him. Even though she was afraid of what his answer might be, she found the courage to look up into his amber eyes.

"Never," he answered; no lies marred his words. "Although there were a few times I wish I had."

His quiet chuckle filled the cave and Olivia tilted her head to the side in puppy-like curiosity. The sadness that had so long dimmed the sparkle in her eyes gave way to inquisitiveness, which he found most endearing.

Again, he knew what she was asking just by looking at her.

"I have encountered many evil people through the years." He decided to be honest with her. "But the most I could bring myself to do was kill them."

Olivia instinctively leaned her body backwards, away from him as she stuttered out, "K- Kill them?" She hadn't expected him to admit to taking lives.

Her fright made Kaden angry and sad at the same time.

"It's better for some people to be dead!" He sputtered irritably as he raised his head higher, his eyes ablaze with long-suppressed anger. "Would you have me leave those murderers and rapists alive? They don't deserve it! And sometimes, I just didn't have a choice. It was either them or me and even though I hate my life sometimes... I still want to live." Kaden breathed out slowly, trying to calm down because he saw her eyes widen with panic and her body tremble in reaction to his outburst. His tone was softer when he spoke again. "Not every situation is black or white." His regretful sigh formed a cloud of smoke around him and the burnt smell of it wafted throughout the cave. "Sometimes, I just didn't have a choice."

Olivia's breath caught in her throat at his sudden outburst. The fear coursing through her body froze her in place but his last words and the sorrow behind them broke through her trepidation. It filled her eyes with unshed tears and when she finally blinked, one tear escaped its cradle.

His eyes softened when he saw that one droplet slide down the soft skin of her pale cheek and he lowered his head in an apologetic manner.

"I am... ummm... I apologize. I did not mean to..." Olivia said as she lowered her head and wiped her face.

"No... Don't. I should be the one to apologize. I am sorry for my outburst. I wasn't trying to take it out on you. I was just angry with my life and concerned that you would still be afraid of me. I mean, I understand you're upset but I've done everything I can think of to keep you from fearing me, have I not?" The dragon's voice filled with hope.

Olivia lifted her head to meet his gaze, and she read honesty there. Her shoulders relaxed down from the knot she had been holding them in. "Yes, you have," she sighed. "I... I believe you would not hurt me." Untangling her feet, she pulled her knees up to her chest and wrapped her hands around them. "Thank you, for understanding my point of view."

"I've had years to learn, but as you just witnessed, my anger sometimes gets the better of me." He sighed in relief, lowering his head to the ground, finding himself eye to eye with Olivia.

"Why are you here?" Kaden asked, voicing the question that had been on his mind since she had first stumbled into his cave.

A half-smile appeared on Olivia's face and an embarrassed flush colored her cheeks. "Oh. The reason just feels so stupid now. Silly even." In hindsight, she couldn't believe what she had done.

But then again... all of her actions had led her to him.

To the dragon. She stared at him in awe.

"Well, I'd still like to know the reason which led you to me," he said, almost as if he had read her mind. What surprised her, though, was his wink.

She laughed.

A dragon just winked at her. She shook her head in disbelief before answering.

"Well. It might not sound serious to you, but I am embarrassed to admit it now. I thought my whole world was crumbling around me." Olivia's voice quivered and she swallowed down the emotions that threatened to clog her throat.

"I live... I mean, I *lived*... not too far away," she said. *Lived* sounded so wrong. She could hardly believe she was here, talking to a dragon – a real, fire-breathing, silk-scaled dragon – and that her parents and her old life were so far away; they had been everything to her, still were. How could she have done that to them? And leave an actually good life behind her... maybe she could have made her father change his mind. "The estate is probably about two days away, east of the mountains, near the city of Remor."

She choked back a sob. Breaking it down to its geography was not helping. "I digress... I am an only child, and my parents are quite wealthy and we have a big estate. As stupid as it is, estates are still handed down from a father to a son or a daughter... *if* she were married. But – I am not married yet." Olivia frowned and picked at her dress.

"My parents had me quite late, just when they started thinking they would never be able to conceive a child. So, you understand, they are not young. And, lately they had started pressuring me to wed so I could inherit everything. I never... I never thought they would force me to marry. I thought my father would let me take over the estate either way. At least that was the mindset I grew up with." Olivia shrugged as she paused to take a breath. She looked at Kaden, pulling her lower lip between her teeth, but she let it slip out when she realized his attention was riveted on her. It was disconcerting, and she felt she had to continue, caught in the intensity of his amber gaze. She saw her own reflection in one large black pupil, her pale face surrounded by the darkness and fire, and the truth came tumbling from her in a nervous rush.

"I did not realize how important it was to them that I marry. It was one of the few things my father is old-fashioned about. Now, though, I understand what he wanted to achieve with that marriage. He wanted me to have someone who would take care of me as he took care of my mother. But I am different. I am quite capable and independent. And I would not be alone. We have plenty of people working for us... I am rambling again." She shook her head, and the image of her childhood home materialized in her mind's eye, the small, romantic stone castle her father had built for her mother, the flowers in the courtyard, the host to all the games she had played as a child... A tear pricked her eye. Olivia found herself swallowing and felt her formal, proper demeanor threatening to crumble beneath the weight of her guilt and the deep ache in her heart.

Kaden tilted his head to the side, studying Olivia's expression. His Little One was quite feisty.

His? He frowned at himself and pushed the thought to the recesses of his mind. He should also stop calling her Little One if he kept having these thoughts about her. She would leave him soon enough anyway. Why would she stay? It's no life for a person... She belonged out there, in the civilized world, not in his dreary cave and miserable life. But his inner most desire was for her to stay and slay his loneliness.

"My father arranged for me to... but I was not aware of it at the time... to wed Lord Mykke. I had never given him any thought, not in that way. Sebastian, Lord Mykke, I mean, used to visit us, and then his visits became more... frequent. He showered me with attention and I did not mind since we developed a wonderful friendship. I never saw him as a possible lover or a husband, but I found more of an older brother in him. What I *did not* know was that my father had chosen him as my future husband and that was his way of trying to make me fall in love with Sebastian. I know not why I did not. I should have done, I suppose. He really was nice and sweet but... I just do not harbor those feelings for him." Olivia shook her head and took a deep, steady breath. She didn't notice the spark in the dragon's eyes, or the tension that had crept into his limbs. At the mention of Sebastian and the arranged marriage, the tip of his tail snaked unconsciously to and fro across the cave floor with feline irritation.

Olivia blinked and continued. "On the day my father told me I was betrothed to Sebastian – Lord Mykke – I broke down. But Father would not take no for an answer. He did not even give me the choice. And that was one of the constants in my life, my choices. We had a… we had a big argument, words were exchanged, my mother cried…" Olivia shook her head, "I cried, and yelled at them like the spoiled child I probably am, and I fled to the sanctuary of my room." She sighed, dropping her gaze to her hands, fingers intertwined in a tight grip, holding at bay the guilt threatening to overwhelm her. She couldn't believe she had done that to her parents. They had been so good to her and she had been so impetuous.

"When night fell, I was still furious and hurt, so I snuck out at the witching hour. I took an old travelling bag with some spare clothes. I raided the kitchen for some food and then left without looking back."

Her eyes welled up as she explained to him about her failed attempt at running away and almost getting killed in the process. Sobs shook her body when she couldn't hold back the tears anymore. She hadn't cried since she had run away and had kept everything bottled up. Now, it all came pouring out, guilt and fear, as she curled up on the cold cave floor, holding herself because she had no one else to hold her.

Sadness and compassion fought with the jealousy coursing through Kaden. To choose was a great luxury for him. He didn't *choose* to be a dragon. He didn't *choose* to steal. He didn't *choose* to be isolated and alone. He didn't *choose* to be hated or feared but it was his poor choices and the actions of his past that had led him to where he was today. Part of him was indignant and bitter, thinking about the freedom of choice that others took for granted, and in that moment he almost agreed with her – this girl was spoiled and should be more grateful for what she had. The rest of him was filled with admiration for her honesty, her courage, and the warmth in her heart. He had lived so long alone, hated and vilified, that he had almost forgotten what a good-hearted person was, and almost lost faith that there were any left in the world who might take pity on him.

The sound of Olivia's sobs penetrated the duel raging in his heart and shook him from his self-pity. He would choose, if he could, to pull her into his arms and comfort her as she cried.

Her sadness and tears won over his self-absorption. *Oh, woe is Kaden,* he sneered at himself.

The dragon moved to the side and carefully approached Olivia. He was afraid to envelop her in his arms because he was so much larger than her and his claws were as sharp as razors.

Olivia, though, was oblivious to Kaden's turmoil and approach until something nudged her gently. She lifted her head and looked through her bloodshot, bleary eyes and came face to face with the dragon. He was so close, with his head almost touching hers; without a moment's thought she threw her hands around his snout.

She clung as tightly as she possibly could... And he let her. She hung on for dear life as her mind drifted back to the night three days before.

"No! I will never consent to be wedded with Sebastian. I thought you would… I thought the estate would be mine. You have raised me so, taught me all about running the business, the accounts—" Her father raised his hand to cut her off.

"It will be yours," Olivia's father said, and the words stopped her furious pacing in front of his desk. She looked up as he continued, *"But the estate is too big and the business too complex for you to do everything on your own. Think of your future family. You need a man at your side to help you and protect you. Lord Mykke is the perfect choice."* Lord Connal leaned back in his armchair and crossed his arms over his broad chest.

Olivia shook her head. *"He is like a brother to me and I... I want to wed for love, just as you and Mother did. And not for the convenience that union would bring."* Her eyes darted back and forth from her mother's guilty features to her father's, stern and unrelenting.

Lady Caroline spoke softly, *"Livvie, my sweet, you know well that your father and I are not young anymore."* She placed a hand on her husband's shoulder and squeezed gently. *"It is the right time for you to take over, but not on your own. Lord Mykke's time to wed has come as well... passed even—"*

"Of course it has!" Olivia threw her hands in the air, exasperated. The light of the fire in the hearth mirrored the blazing anger in her eyes. *"He is almost ten seasons my senior."*

"Do not interrupt your mother. That is disrespectful." Connal narrowed his eyes at Olivia, the hues of blue clashing. This was serious – he was close to losing his temper, something Olivia had rarely seen and had always taken pains to avoid. Tonight was not one of those times.

"No. Your forcing me to marry someone I do not love is disrespectful." Olivia glared back at her father, just as fiercely and with unwavering determination.

"Your love for him might grow," her mother cajoled, pressing her hands together. *"A good friendship is a foundation for a strong relationship. You do not have any other suitors. You do not even try."*

Olivia's eyes widened and she flung her arms out, waving. *"Because I am busy helping with the estate..."*

"We have offered to hold a ball in your name. We were even ready

to send you to Remor, or Asil, but you always gave us a reason for not going, and we have respected that," Lady Caroline said, and Olivia knew it for the truth. She had always dreamed that love would happen spontaneously, just like in the fairy tales, not by hosting a ball and parading herself around for possible suitors. She wanted someone to steal her heart and sweep her off her feet when she least expected it, not because they were supposed to.

"You are not a child anymore." Her father placed his hands on the table. "You need to face your responsibilities."

"My…" Olivia stopped herself, and sighed. "That is what I am trying to do. I… I do not know where this is coming from. I thought you were proud of me. I thought I was doing well enough on my own! Why do I need to wed just to carry on doing the same thing that I am doing now?" She shook her head, her brow furrowing deeply as she looked from one parent to the other, feeling utterly trapped. "Who are you? I do not even recognize my own father anymore."

"That is enough." Connal stood up, the chair scraping against the wooden floor as he pushed it back. "The arrangement has been made and Lord Mykke has accepted."

"H-h-he…" Olivia stuttered and took a few steps back. He did what? The betrayal by her closest friend heated her cheeks as if she had just been slapped. "He did?" Her defenses and defiance crumbled, washed away by a tidal wave, the hard-suppressed tears now wetting her cheeks. She brushed them away, angry, but in vain. "You have all made arrangements about my future, about my life… without me? All of my life you both taught me different. You always said… You always said I was clever enough to make my own decisions." She dropped her gaze and shook her head. "This is just too much." She swiveled around, not looking back at her parents, and fled out of her father's study, up the stairs and into her own room.

A slam echoed through the whole mansion. The wooden door offered a cool welcoming comfort as Olivia leaned her forehead against it. Her body was on fire, hands shaking, chest heaving. She pressed her cheek to the mahogany. Sounds of heavy footsteps approached on *the other side, followed by a click as Olivia locked her door.*

"Olivia Violet Moore!" Her father rattled the handle of the door, trying to force them open. "Open this door! We raised you better than that."

"You raised me to expect better for myself, to value myself more," she said in a determined voice, pushing hard against the oak, although the lock was strong enough to hold out on its own without her slight weight against it.

"Connal, hush!" Olivia heard her mother speak, her voice shaky. "You both need to calm down. She is just as impulsive as you are… stubborn as well. You both need to cool your tempers."

"We have spoiled her too much, she—"

Olivia could only imagine her mother's glare as her father stopped talking.

"We will discuss this further tomorrow," Lady Caroline said.

I won't be here tomorrow, *Olivia thought. She didn't say it out loud.*

"There is nothing to—"

"Connal!"

After a moment of silence, heavy footsteps stomped away.

"My dear Livvie," Lady Caroline crooned, her sniffles tempting Olivia to reach for the key. Her mother was a gentle, caring soul and it hurt Olivia whenever her mother cried. The hardest thing she had ever done was to leave the door locked and refuse to give over her future into her parent's hands just to stop those tears.

After regaining her composure, Lady Caroline carried on, "Your father and I love you very much. We only worry about your future. Please calm down, get some rest and then… think about it, about our side of things. Be reasonable about our request. Just… Just clear your mind of the anger first." Her voice seemed to be coming from somewhere below the keyhole. Mother and daughter huddled on either side of the great wooden barrier, so close, but with an impassable gulf between them. Even yesterday, Olivia would not have believed this could happen. She sat, listening to her mother's voice, turning the key over and over in her hands. The small metal teeth dug into her palm, leaving bruised indentations in her skin, but she still did not unlock the door.

When Olivia didn't answer, her mother sighed and said softly, "Good night, my sweet."

Olivia took a deep breath, clutching the dragon's snout tightly. She couldn't bear to think about it anymore. She had not done it lightly, but... how had it come to this? And were those words the last she would ever hear her mother say? Olivia could no longer contain herself. She gripped Kaden and sobbed.

CHAPTER 8

Kaden controlled his breathing, with Olivia so near to his fire. Closing his eyes, he tried to absorb her sorrow, to ease away her pain. After a while, her sobs slowly subsided and her grip loosened. With a last sniff, Olivia unwrapped her arms from around him so she could brush off her tears and dry her face with the sleeve of the dress. Kaden pulled away and worked out the cramp in his lower jaw.

"So, about those pants," he said, feeling oddly proud when he heard her chuckle softly.

"Next time, please bring something more useful. Like some tea leaves," Olivia said after she had dried her face and tilted her head back to give him a small smile. "Thank you," she mumbled, a soft pink adorning her cheeks in embarrassment.

"Tea," he nodded in confirmation. "I'll try to remember."

"Where did you get those pants anyway?" Olivia asked, eyebrows raised. "I do not remember ordering any pants," she teased.

Kaden gently nudged her before schooling his expression again. "Well, since we're being honest —" He pondered for a moment what to say, and then settled for the truth. "—I stole them."

"You stole them?" Olivia gaped in surprise, eyes widening. "Why would you do that? People already have a very bad opinion of dragons. And why pants?"

"It's a —" He fought his way through the barrier in his mind, wishing with all his heart to tell her the truth. Trying with his whole might, he just couldn't, the words wouldn't come so instead he said, "— an addiction. But I'm working on it! I promise."

Olivia rewarded him with a soft smile, even chuckled because the dragon reminded her of a child caught doing something he was not supposed to.

She glanced toward the back passageway, unable to keep her mind off it for any length of time. "So all the things in the back cave are the items you stole?"

"Yes. And speaking of that part of the cave, what possessed you to go there when I told you not to?" Kaden said while fighting off a grin as he looked at her sternly, but the amused glint in his eyes gave him away.

"Oh, yes. I forgot about that," Olivia quirked her lips into a sheepish smile. "Honestly?" She looked away for a moment, remembering the loneliness, the grief but chose to ignore it now, she had just cried it out. Looking at him again, with the same smile, she said. "I was bored and curious." She shrugged.

"Liv, Liv, Liv… What am I to do with you?" The dragon shook his head as he moved and settled back down in his spot, amusement evident in his rumbling voice, but it didn't escape his notice the her eyes spoke differently; haunted and unhappy.

An involuntary shiver ran through Olivia when he called her *Liv* and his smooth, velvety baritone caressed her soul like a warm summer breeze. Her heart fluttered with nervous delight, so she lowered her head and regarded him from under her lashes. The way he made her feel, she could easily forget he was a dragon.

"Keep me?" Olivia blurted, surprising herself, and she was quick to add, "I mean, I can be quite a handful, and am easily trained." She finished off with a cheeky wink of her own. She liked the dragon's playful side. She could be playful as well.

Kaden's sudden laughter reverberated throughout the cave. He snorted little fireballs, shifting his head so as not to burn Olivia as she joined him with her giggling. Images of Olivia as some sort of a pet flashed through his mind before they morphed into different images; visions that caused his laughter to abate and other feelings to bloom inside him.

Damnation, it has been so long.

It was his fondness for female companionship that had gotten him in his current condition in the first place, that condemned him to this wretched state. If only he could have saved her… if only Lucia's sister hadn't…. no, he would not dwell on his past mistakes. Nothing he could do about it now, not even speak out loud about the events of that fateful night, and of what he used to be.

He shook the thoughts away, but he couldn't help, though, and be mesmerized by the sparkle in Olivia's sky blue eyes. Her hand brushed way the unruly curls behind her ear, giving him a glimpse of her milky white neck, the line of her collarbone flirting with him, peeking shyly from beneath the fabric of the dress. As she drew her other hand away from hiding her giggles, luscious pink lips still pulled back in a smile, he even found the overbite of her pearly white teeth fascinating.

Her lips moved, creating words, but his ears never registered the sound. When Olivia tilted her head to the side and cocked an eyebrow, Kaden shook out the lustful fog clouding his mind, once again chiding himself for wasting time on such thoughts.

"I apologize; my mind drifted."

"I noticed. Is everything well?"

Kaden nodded and then continued their little banter, engaging Olivia in a harmless conversation, wanting to learn about her as much as possible, to live a human life once again, even if only through her words.

Olivia told him about her childhood, her gestures just as vivid and elaborate as her words. She spoke with flourish of the first time she went fishing with her father, even jumping up to her feet, demonstrating how their lines intertwined, and then they tangled as well, falling into the water, getting completely drenched. And the time she snuck into the stables to steal a kiss from the stable master's son, her first kiss, and how awkward it was for both, but they remained good friends. Kaden found himself jealous of the boy who got a taste of her lips.

Also, she told him about the first time she tried trimming the bushes with her mother, and in the end, they molded them into various amusing creatures. Once, she even traveled to the sea, when he father took her on her first trading trip, learning about negotiations and business intricacies, and how, surprisingly, she enjoyed learning that as well. Oh, and the sea, she made it sound so magnificent, even dipping her bare feet into its freezing fold; it was winter. But no one was around to see her. And of course, she spoke proudly of her horse, Starlite; sometimes, when she was younger, Olivia would sneak out and sleep in the barn with the mare. The horse was a gift from her parents for her 16th birthday.

As she spoke about her parents more and more, the sunshine in her eyes drifted away behind gloomy clouds. Her gestures subdued, she sat down again, and spoke of the little things, like her favorite color; purple, favorite foods and such.

In the end Kaden decided that she harbored quite an adventurous spirit for someone who had led such a sheltered life. Her mind was of an uncommon mould, and she was so eager to learn and fill the bottomless bucket of her voracious curiosity. If he hadn't known any better, he never would have guessed her status, with only the little things, like the way she held herself and the manner of her speech, giving her away. Maybe the times have changed since his last interactions with young women of higher social standing. Which was a good thing; women had so much to give to the world, so smart, nurturing, so… resourceful, and dangerous as he had learned.

In spite of her disagreement with her parents – a dispute so severe she ended up running away from them – she spoke of them only in glowing terms. It was obvious she was proud to be their daughter, though that fact might be moot at this point, since her chances of returning home were rapidly dwindling away to nothing.

The sadness in her eyes tore at Kaden's heart so much that, in spite of his burning desire to know everything about her, he forced himself to change the subject to his own past, at least the parts of it that he was able to talk about. With an enthusiasm born out of his desire to distract Olivia from her sorrow, he described the exciting details of his travels, the many places he had seen, his encounters with people – which usually didn't end well – and the wide variety of human possessions he had stolen.

"One time," Kaden chuckled, "as I was out enjoying a beautiful summer day I flew over a small, rickety house and the mule grazing in the field caught my attention. I wondered what it would be like if I just picked up the animal and took it back to my cave. I didn't have to wonder long, since, without giving it much thought, I landed in the field and approached the mule."

Olivia shook her head in disbelief, a smile whispering on her lips.

"Of course the animal spooked and then, out of the stack of hay to the side, an old woman stumbled to her feet. The most tenacious woman… or better yet, old hag I had ever met. She charged right at me with her cane, pounding away like I was just some small lizard she wanted to squash."

Olivia laughed at the images Kaden's words evoked in her mind.

"I deserved it though, and in the end, we came to an understanding and parted ways peacefully." Kaden sighed. "That was also the last time I spoke to a human… almost fifty seasons ago."

"Have you ever just approached someone and talked to them? Tell them you mean them no harm?" Olivia said as she tilted her head to the side, watching the dragon from across the fire, the dancing flames wrapping her in comforting warmth.

Rain murmured outside the cave, and inside the fire crackled and popped.

Kaden paused. "For the longest part of my life, I was just bitter and angry, not caring about companionship, so I didn't even try. I lived far away then. The only contact I had with people was either when I… you know… borrowed things from them for an undetermined period of time, or when those foolish enough dared to come and attack me. My life was always complicated, even after I moved somewhere new and tried being more friendly. In the end, I accepted my loneliness, found this cave and avoided everyone altogether."

"But what about—"

"Have I told you about the horse?"

Olivia opened her mouth to argue, but she saw the pleading look in his big amber eyes and closed it again. He told her about the time he had successfully stolen a horse. He hadn't eaten it, but made sure to bring the animal alive to his cave and stashed it in his treasure chamber. The horse kept him company for two days because it was hard for him to let go of things once he had taken them. On the third day, he had gone out to give the horse a chance to escape on its own. The horse had seized the opportunity and had snuck out, bolting away once it had reached the woods.

He still missed the horse and the company it had provided but now he had Olivia.

She laughed through most of his stories. They were funny, but the bittersweet edge to them was not lost on her. She hoped he would see she was laughing *with* him, not *at* him. She knew being lonely could make a person – even a scaled, saurian person - overly sensitive. Even so, she couldn't remember the last time she had laughed so hard or so much. Olivia listened to his stories about the chimney, the unfortunate apple tree, the wagon and some other silly items he had stolen.

Finally, after one hilarious image too many, she waved her hand, creased up and barely able to get the words out. "Alright, alright... enough... I give up! No more, my stomach hurts from all the laughter," Olivia exclaimed, clutching at her aching sides.

Kaden had been enjoying their last few hours together and didn't want the day to end. The conversation flew easily; the bantering felt natural, as if they had known each other for years. He also admired Olivia's wit and her inquisitiveness. He loved the way her laughter bounced off the walls and he was attracted to the mischievous glint in her eyes when she had something impish or funny to say. He couldn't manage to look away from her face even for a moment. Her joy spread like a salve through him and he was happier than he had been in a very, very long time.

He had almost forgotten what it felt like to be with someone who wanted to be with him.

A soft groan brought his focus back on Olivia's words. She was now standing up and stretching her arms above her head, her soft figure in the form-fitting gown silhouetted in the firelight. Kaden closed his eyes and breathed out the suppressed desire. *Don't think of it. It could never happen. You're a dragon now.*

"I wish I could get out and breathe in some fresh air." His eyes opened at the sound of Olivia's wistful voice.

"I have an idea." Kaden rose to his hands and feet as well. "Follow me," he said as he led the way towards the cave's mouth.

"But it's still raining," Olivia grumbled but followed the dragon anyway. As they drew closer to the cave's opening she inhaled the fresh air, filling her lungs as a gentle but chill breeze caressed her skin. Even though it still rained upon them, in the distance the clouds parted and they could see the sun low on the horizon, its golden rays holding the forest in a glowing, warm embrace.

"Come." Kaden's voice jerked Olivia from her thoughts and from soaking in her surroundings. She noticed he had lifted one of his wings up, offering her a shelter from the rain. Hesitating for just a moment, Olivia took a few steps forward until she was safely pressed against his side, under the protection of the silky membrane.

"Keep your hand on me and follow where I go," Kaden said and Olivia liked the assuredness behind it. It was comforting.

Olivia did as Kaden requested and allowed him to lead her to a small clearing not too far from the cave. A small gasp of wonder burst from her lips as she beheld the sight of the valley spread out before her, painted in the gorgeous colors of the setting sun. The sky was a light shade of blue but the fluffy clouds drifting below were ablaze with the colors of dancing flames. Never had she ever seen the kingdom in such a way before, and she drew the cloak tightly around her shoulders before she leaned her full weight against the bulk of Kaden's body. She drew warmth from him and the dragon curled his wing in nearer to his body, pulling her even closer to him.

Neither of them said a word as they enjoyed the view of the sun slowly slipping below the horizon and the sound of birds singing them a marvelous symphony. Immersed in the beauty of the moment, neither of them sensed the shadow of foreboding creeping up behind them under the cover of darkness.

CHAPTER 9

After the sun had set and the rain receded, Kaden and Olivia took a leisurely walk back to the cave. The fresh air and the freedom of an open space were exactly what she needed.

Filling her lungs with clean, damp air, she breathed in the scents of the forest accentuated by rain; pine trees, wet bark, fallen needles and resin overpowered almost everything else. And even though she was wrapped up in the cloak, Olivia still shivered but welcomed the cool breeze that murmured through the trees. This cold was so different from the cold of the cave.

Calming. Refreshing.

Since darkness ruled the sky and the moon was slimmer than it had been a few nights ago, Olivia clung to Kaden with one hand so she could keep her footing steady. The inky blue sky was streaked with the last remnants of the rain clouds, and even the stars were not as visible as on the night she had ran away from the wolves. *Has it only been the night before? Or more?* She shook her head at the loss of time, everything blended and distorted, as if in a dream. She looked up at the clouds still lingering above them. They drifted away from the misty surface of the moon as the breeze drove them onwards. Owls hooted, crickets called out to their mates as an occasional smaller nightly critter shuffled by, scavenging around. A howl or two echoed in the distance, but Olivia didn't fear them as much with Kaden by her side.

They walked in a comfortable silence, each lost in their own thoughts.

As they neared the cave, Olivia asked for a few moments of privacy. It took Kaden a moment before he realized what she meant. It was a good thing dragons couldn't blush. After he made sure it was safe and no dangerous animals lurked nearby, Kaden retreated to the cave and got the fire going again. Although he tried not to listen, he couldn't help but focus on every small sound. He was almost sure that she was going to come back – but, like the horse, Olivia was a living thing and not a possession. She had a strong mind and a will of her own. When he heard her approach, her footsteps light, quick and eager, a bubbling of hope and excitement, which he had not felt in centuries, rose in his chest.

Once Olivia joined Kaden, he took her to his treasure chamber so she could retrieve whatever she thought she might need for a more comfortable stay in the front cave. He was not used to guests, and had never expected any, but luckily over the years he had stolen an impressively eclectic variety of items. It wasn't as if he could actually use any of them, and by now, most of their previous owners would be long dead. It was a melancholy thought, but Olivia's bright face in the torchlight, shining with curiosity as she rummaged through chests and boxes and loose piles of bric-a-brac, banished Kaden's loneliness. She brought a warmth into the cold recesses of his inglorious past, bringing everything to life again, giving a purpose to these forgotten, dead objects in his reluctant collection.

She didn't take much. Just a padded chair, some extra blankets, a book, a piece of cloth she could use as a towel, a handful of candles, a brass lamp to set them in, and an old bone comb she found in one of the chests. She loved the design on it, a swirling pattern of carved ivy and roses, and she wondered how old it was and what history it had witnessed.

After they had settled in for the night, Olivia didn't tuck herself under the blankets on the mattress but again, and of her own choosing, snuggled up close to the dragon. *For the warmth*, was her explanation, *and safety*, she assured herself.

The events of the day had exhausted both of them, and before long, they were sound asleep.

ဆ

As the dawn crept over the horizon the next morning, gently coaxing the world into wakefulness, Olivia stirred.

Kaden had been awake for some time but hadn't dared move in case it would rouse her. Her eyes fluttered open and she found herself facing Kaden's smooth scales. She yawned while pressing her forehead into him and inhaled the scent she had started to associate with her dragon, the faint odor of smoke mixed with the fragrance of the forest.

My dragon.

Hesitantly, Olivia reached her hand up and softly pressed her palm to Kaden's scales. Even though she had touched them before and enjoyed their silky smoothness, this time it was somehow more intimate. Her fingers traced around one of the scales. Kaden shivered beneath her touch and it made her smile. Olivia continued gliding her fingers over his scaly draconic skin, marveling at its glistening blue color, its sleekness, and she fought back the urge to rub her face against it.

She failed.

Pressing her palm flat against the dragon's now slightly taut muscle, Olivia leaned her forehead against his flank. As she closed her eyes, her nose brushed his scales, making slow circular patterns.

Kaden sucked in a breath through clenched teeth and held it. He hadn't felt anything this intimate and affectionate in a very long time. When he looked far enough back through the recesses of his memories, he came to the startling realization that he had actually never experienced anything like it, such a simple, gentle touch. Not even with Lucia.

He shivered again when Olivia pressed her cheek against him while she ran her hand over his scales, caressing him as far as she could reach. His scales might have been strong but they were also sensitive to every little caress of Olivia's wandering fingers and every brush of her warm breath.

When her fingers found an especially sensitive spot on his lower ribs, Kaden brought his head around and gently nudged her. "That tickles." He affected squirming and held back a chuckle.

"Does it now?" Olivia teased while she ran her fingers over his ticklish spot one more time and giggled.

"Oh, hush you... you little imp." Kaden nudged her gently again.

Olivia detached herself from the dragon. "Good morning, Kaden," she said as she sat back on her heels. She covered her mouth as a deep yawn escaped her. Contentment whispered across her lips, eyes bright with wakefulness. She sighed in relief as she stood up, working out a cramp or two. Her muscles ached less, and her knee was only a bit sore.

"Morning, Liv." Kaden pushed up to his hands and feet,

claws scraping against the rock- and dirt-covered floor. As he turned his head toward Olivia, he was almost blinded by her bright smile. It lit up the cave like thousands of fireflies. Her cheeks were flushed; she was probably still shy about her daring exploit.

When Olivia raised her intertwined fingers above her head, wanting to stretch, Kaden turned away so she wouldn't catch him staring at her again. Even though they flirted a bit, he assumed she felt at ease with him because he was a dragon and not a human. Kaden doubted she would relinquish the proper etiquette and behavior if he were a man.

Using his tail he moved the leftover roasted chicken closer to the fire.

"Hungry?" He glanced over his shoulder and saw Olivia drying her face next to the pot that still had some water in it.

"Mmhmm," Olivia responded as she picked up the comb and settled closer to the fire. "Must be a beautiful day outside, after the yesterday's rain."

"We'll go out after you've eaten." He was rewarded with a grateful smile.

True to his word, after Olivia had finished eating, Kaden grabbed a big water sack and some ropes he had found in the back and led her outside. The sun was still low on the horizon and the fog was slowly dispersing, creating the illusion that they were walking among the clouds.

While Kaden led her to the clearing where they had watched the sun set, Olivia surveyed her surroundings. She could now see the trees she had caught whiffs of last night. They were spaced wide enough so that Kaden could walk between them with his wings tucked in by his sides.

Since she had been a good study Olivia now recognized the pine, blue spruce, fir and birch trees. Beneath them hid dwarf honeysuckle bushes and an occasional milkweed.

The forest floor, which was still muddy from the rain, was littered with pine needles and patches of grass in the spots where the sun reached it. Dotted here and there in bright patches of color were flowers in bloom including saffron, primrose, snowdrop and woodland cyclamen, scattered around in a wonderful harmonic mess of lilacs, yellows, whites and purples. The colorful carpet reminded Olivia of her mother. She sighed, pushing away the sadness and worry.

Movement in her peripheral vision caught her attention and she saw a squirrel winding its way up a tree. Olivia thought she also spotted a rabbit darting away to its hiding place. From what she knew, she was sure there were some roes living in the forest and probably some badgers as well. The forest was teaming with life, in addition to the wolves and bears she had already witnessed. She welcomed the distractions.

The caress of the spring breeze against her face tugged at her lips and brought her feet to a stop. Sunbeams reached out to her smiling face, warming her cheeks. She closed her eyes, faced the sun's rays, and listened to the birds sweetly chirping away.

Kaden heard Olivia's steps falter so he stopped as well and turned to watch her. To study her. The content, peaceful smile brightened her soft features. Her hands were hanging loosely by her sides and her face was turned upwards, soaking up the sunshine. He wished for that peacefulness and that innocence. He had taken the simplest things for granted back then.

The things he now missed the most.

Observing her like that, he breathed in deeply as he tried to look at his surroundings and feel them as she perceived them. She made it easy for him to truly relax and enjoy the moment, to search for that peace deep within him.

The dragon found it when he settled his gaze back on her. He watched her open her eyes and beam at him as she started walking again. There they both were, the girl who longed for the freedom of the dragon, and the dragon who longed to be a man.

When they arrived at the clearing, the fog had dissipated. With not a cloud in sight, and the air crisp and clear, the view stretched endlessly onward. Olivia gazed at the forest below, an undulating sea of green that gave way to a lush valley. Her blue eyes widened in delight and a smile danced on her lips. She drew in a deep breath of fresh mountain air mixed with the scent of dew and conifer trees carried by a soft breeze.

Olivia asked to rest for a while, because she couldn't get enough of the view as the rising sun chased away the chill of the morning, its rays catching the sparkle of dewdrops on the grass. Afterward, she suggested they head off to get some fresh water from a nearby stream.

Kaden lay down facing the view, and Olivia nestled in the crook between his neck and his shoulder. She pulled her knees up but leaned fully into Kaden, her head against him. The same easy conversation flowed as the day before, the chatting and flirty banter. Both were comfortable with this dynamic, aware of the odd kind of chemistry and not denying it. Olivia, for her part, had no idea what it was about Kaden that had drawn her in – she didn't feel as if she were talking to an animal or to a savage, fire-breathing monster like the ones in the stories she had heard.

She had loved horses as a young girl and had spent hours grooming her favorite mare, Starlite, and talking to her and pretending she could talk back, but this was so different. If she closed her eyes, Kaden was to her mind just as human as Sebastian. Except, she was sure, Kaden would not have agreed to anything without asking her first. She knew nothing more could develop from their bond, however. When she opened her eyes again, Kaden was not a man, he was a dragon. She sighed.

Olivia slipped her feet out of her boots and wriggled her toes, loving the feel of the grass tickling them while the breeze gave her feet some respite from being all cooped up most of the time.

Kaden watched with amusement as she tried to pluck out the stalks of grass with her toes. Olivia was intent on this activity, and her concentration on the grass – and away from him – gave him the courage to ask about something that had been on his mind.

"Why did you run towards the mountains? You said you heard the stories and warnings but you still came here." When they had been talking yesterday, she had told him about the rumors going around about a dragon living up in the foothills, guarding the forest. "Didn't you believe those stories?"

"Oh, I thought those were just fabricated stories, intended to keep the children from wandering the forest alone. And, at the time it made sense to run towards the woods and the mountains and not towards the city where they would most likely follow me. I was also not quite rational at that moment." She shrugged her shoulders, brushing against the dragon's scales. "Actually, I have a question of my own that I have been wanting to ask since yesterday," Olivia said. Encouraged by Kaden's nod she continued, "How many dragons are there?"

"I don't know. I've never met another dragon."

Olivia's head left his side as she leaned away so she could face him. She gaped for a few moments, blinking those big blue eyes at him. "You have never encountered another dragon? How is that possible?" She quirked her head to the side.

"I... You see..." Kaden wished he could tell her the truth, the truth he couldn't even think about. "I really don't know if there are any out there besides me. I have heard rumors but I'm not sure if those were about me or some other dragon. The world is a really big place. If there are only a few of us, and if they are hiding away like me, I'm not really surprised I have never met them."

"What about your parents? Your mother? Did you really come from an egg?" Olivia fired off the questions.

"Take a breath, Liv," Kaden chuckled, "One question at the time. It has been such a long time, over a century, almost two… I think. So I don't remember much." The lie rolled of his tongue easily, and he was thankful Olivia wasn't looking into his eyes but had settled back down against him. "Since I can remember my draconic existence, it has always been just me. And I think the presumption about the egg is correct." At least those words were truth. He hated the lies. It felt as if he were marring their... friendship. But he had no other choice; he couldn't speak what had really happened to him. The words lodged in his throat, twisting and morphing into the lies that came out. At least the way he had phrased it was less of a lie.

"That is sad." Olivia sighed. "I miss my parents." She was absentmindedly caressing Kaden's neck, right next to where her head was pressed against his gleaming scales.

"You do know you could go back?" Kaden said despite his desire for her to stay. He wanted to encourage her to think that she should stay here, with him, forever, but that would be selfish. He had been that way too many times in the past.

"No!" Olivia stiffened against him. "I could *not* do that. I have embarrassed them and disappointed so much. You should have seen the look on my father's face. I am afraid they would not want me back."

"You don't truly believe that." Kaden frowned at her, and even though she couldn't see his face, Olivia could imagine it quite clearly.

"I... I ... I am scared," she conceded.

"I think those are silly thoughts. After all you have told me about them, I believe they're worried sick and scared for you and surely want you back."

"You are probably right. They really are the kindest people I have ever met." Olivia sighed. "But I am not ready."

"You will have to go back sooner or later. Why keep them in agony any longer?"

"It is not that I am not ready to face them." Olivia scooted away from Kaden so she could face him as she sat back on her heels.

Kaden lifted his head and stared at those blue irises filled with emotions he hadn't seen since ... He forced the thoughts of his past away and gave Olivia a slight nod to continue.

"I am not ready to leave you yet." After she got the words past her lips, Olivia stared into the dragon's amber eyes for a few moments, finding surprise and gratitude in them. The intensity of his gaze startled her and she looked down at her hands in her lap, playing with her fingers.

Kaden nudged her. It seemed he liked doing that, and he rested his head near her lap.

"Thank you."

Olivia knew he was thanking her for not leaving him yet, alone again. It meant more to him than anything at that moment.

"Come on." The dragon shot up all of a sudden and waited for Olivia to do the same.

"Yes?" Olivia rose to her feet as well and looked up at

her dragon. She liked calling him that, even if only in her head.

What she saw then left her speechless. Kaden rose to his feet, his hands leaving the ground as he spread his wings wide. Olivia had to shade her eyes from the sun as she looked up at him in wonder. The sunlight glistened off his scales, bringing out their color, the midnight blue accentuating his golden underside. His wings were spread out as far as he could extend them, and he gave them a few soft beats. The dragon's movements drew Olivia's attention to his muscles, rippling beneath the silky surface, especially where the shoulders of his arms met the shoulders of his wings. He was beautiful, he was elegant, he was –

"Magnificent," Olivia spoke out loud. "You are a magnificent dragon, Kaden." She was still looking up at him, eyes wide with awe and amazement.

Kaden's gleeful chuckle echoed through the forest. The birds in the nearby branches shot out of the trees, flapping away in fright.

"I'm honored you like what you see," he said, followed by a cocky wink, "but wait till you see this."

The dragon beat his wings. Once, twice, gaining momentum as he always did so he could gather the wind beneath his wings to help him take off into the air.

Olivia shielded her eyes from the dust which had risen and she struggled to hold a steady footing against the gusts of wind. On the third and last beat of his wings, he lifted off the ground. The torrent of air blasted Olivia back. She stumbled, and losing her balance she fell on her backside with a squeak of surprise.

She was glad Kaden had missed that. *This is so embarrassing.* Olivia scrambled back to her feet and then watched the dragon circle above her. He soared up high and then swooped down with great speed, spreading his wings so he could glide gracefully over her head. She just couldn't help the silly smile that seemed to be stuck on her face. She didn't even dare blink; she wanted to see it all. She spun around, following his movement, wondering what it would be like high up there, off the ground, where she would no longer be part of the world below, leaving her worries behind as she reached for the heavens above.

When Kaden twirled one last time and neared Olivia again, slowing his flight, she took a couple of steps back and braced herself against another blast of air.

The dragon beat his wings back and hovered over the ground a few moments before touching down. A silent return, as he tucked his wings against his sides again. Olivia expected the earth to tremble beneath her feet as the dragon landed, but it didn't. How could something so… bigger than life itself be so quiet and graceful, his flight like a downy feather swirling through the air, gentle, carried by the breeze and then ever so softly gliding back to the earth. A tender caress of the sharp claws against the lush green grass.

As the dragon padded towards a still mesmerized Olivia, he scooped up the rope he had brought with them, into his mouth. Reaching Olivia, he placed the rope at her feet and lowered himself before her.

Olivia's brow furrowed. "What am I to do with *that?*"

"You will need it because I want to take you flying. I've seen the look in your eyes." He continued before Olivia could argue, "You're going to wrap that rope around your waist and tie it really tight, and the rest will go around my neck. It's a safety precaution. I don't want you to fall off once we're up. I think you could get settled comfortably near my wings, a bit behind. The ridges of the scales should be a bit further apart there, so you can sit in between two.

You can also hold onto them for support and balance. You will have to keep your knees tucked in tightly. You have ridden a horse before, so you should know how to hold on with your thighs."

"Alright," Olivia said, not a hint of hesitation in her voice.

"Alright? You aren't going to argue?"

"No," Olivia's grin grew even wider, "I do *not* want to miss this opportunity. This is amazing!" Kaden chuckled at her response, shaking his head in disbelief as he helped set her up.

⁊∽

"Now, you have to hold on tight, especially when we're gaining height. I will not take us very high because it's cold up there and the air is thin. It would be harder for you to breathe. We'll glide above the tree line. If at any point you feel uncomfortable or think you might slip, give the rope a hard tug." Instructions finished, Kaden helped Olivia up so she could get settled.

"Yes, sir," she mocked and giggled.

"Olivia..." Kaden said, a stern edge to his voice and a serious glint in his eyes as he looked back at her.

Olivia shivered. Now she knew why. His commanding tone was hard to disobey, yet she liked it.

"Hold on tight."

Without another warning, a whoosh sliced the air, followed by a blast of wind against Olivia's face as the dragon's wing swung down.

Chin tucked to her chest, she kept her eyes shut tight, knuckles turning white, wrapped around his spine ridge. They lurched higher and higher until her whole body jerked back. Olivia squeaked and leaned forward, the wind deafening in her ears, whipping her curls back.

"Open your eyes, Liv," Kaden said as he glanced at his rider over his shoulder.

She did as she was told. A gasp slipped past her lips. "Dear Heavens above!" she said.

Pride swelled within Kaden, lifting away the years of darkness that had consumed him as joy filled him for making her that happy. It was a wonderful feeling, after so long alone in the dark, to indulge someone else's desires.

Olivia's eyes had never been wider and she was sure her jaw was going to hurt for days because of how much she was smiling. She also didn't care how many bugs she was going to swallow along the way. Her heart pounded against her ribcage as fear, exhilarating fear, coursed through her veins mixed with a rush she had never felt before. She couldn't put it into words; it was so much more exciting and liberating than the first time she went galloping on her own. So liberating. The world far beneath her feet.

Trees rushed by under them in a blur of greens, but as she squinted ahead, she was once again amazed by the view.

Looking at the treetops, Olivia thought that she could just reach down and brush her hands through the leaves, caressing the forest itself. All the green below them and the blue vastness above them made her realize just how big the world was, how tiny her role in it.

So this is what it feels like to fly. Right then, a new addiction bloomed inside her. She had to experience it again. Kaden would surely agree to such request.

Olivia wrapped the little bit of loose rope she had around her hand until it was taut as she sat upright, gazing all around them. She closed her eyes for a few moments and cherished the wind whipping at her face, the chill leaving a trail of gentle nips on her flushed cheeks. But she didn't mind any of it. She feasted on it; it fed her mind and her soul, refreshing her spirit.

Opening her eyes, Olivia laughed out loud and a happy whoop escaped her lips.

Kaden veered to the left, circling around then flying back to their little clearing. As they glided above forest, the dragon spread his wings wide. He looked back at Olivia when her happy laughter reached his ears.

The healing balm of her being, her joy and innocence spread over his wounded soul.

I'm smitten.

He shook his head and minded their path again. Never before had he thought he would experience love, especially for it to bloom so fast, almost painfully so. Was it only his loneliness being quenched or were his feelings genuine? As soon as the question flitted through his mind, he knew the answer. Nobody could blame him after meeting Olivia. The adoration that grew within him in such a short time, like a spell of a masterful seductress woven around him, surprised him, but he had heard the stories of men succumbing to women's charms as fast as in the fairytales. *It doesn't bode well for me. She will leave and I will be left alone again. And probably heartbroken too...*

A gentle caress of Olivia's hand against his scales brought him out of his reverie. He didn't care about a broken heart anymore. He would cherish her companionship for as long as he could. It would be worth it.

Olivia was worth it.

That last thought filled the dragon with contentment and happiness as they soared on the arms of the wind.

CHAPTER 10

Only a day's ride away from the dragon's cave, Prince Magnus and his knights rode into a small trading town.

Heads turned as they entered the small town. Some people recognized the royal crest and whispered words spread. They never expected to see their prince here. Awe lingered on their faces as Prince Magnus and his contingent of knights rode by.

Magnus held his head high, face grim, eyes narrowed. Pride coursed through him at the reverence of these peasants. They had probably never witnessed such an intimidating and magnificent sight. He led the way as his weathered knights followed; most of their faces just as grim, riding straight, chins tipped up, as their armors and sharp weapons spoke of proficient use… nothing fancy, nothing expensive, but practical and well used. Except for Magnus's gold engraved breastplate.

Magnus had chosen his men wisely. He made sure he had some of the best fighters, with two sworn knights at his side, and the rest, besides being good with a weapon, had skills in other fields as well.

Reed was his right man hand, his brother in arms, his best friend. They were so much alike that they would feed off each other's anger and temper. If it were not for Cassiel's cool-headedness and calming presence, they would have probably encountered plenty of problems during their journey. Reed wielded his long sword as if he were born with it, the weapon as much a part of his body as his arms or legs. His mother had been the prince's wetnurse, so the two had grown up together, fought together and whored together. A scar cutting alongside Reed's jaw was left as a reminder to the man that without Magnus, Reed would have been just another lowly servant, emptying chamber pots or cleaning out the horse dung from the stables. They had been fourteen seasons old when Magnus put Reed in his place with the sharp edge of a knife, and the knight had stayed there.

The prince's second sworn knight was Cassiel, a dark-skinned warrior and the only true, honorable knight among them. As unique in his fighting style as in his appearance, Cassiel fought with a short sword in one hand and a battle axe in the other. Cassiel had sworn his oaths to Magnus' father and, honor-bound to serve his king, had been given to the prince to use his talents in Magnus' service. He did not take oaths lightly, and in Magnus' presence was always silent and stern, the rational one. But there was a softness in Cassiel's eyes that Magnus didn't approve of. They needed to man him up, the prince thought. He wanted to take the knight aside with a woman and make a real man out of him, teach him that women were there for his pleasure.

Theo, the red-haired scout, and Damien, the quiet hunter, kept to themselves and had developed a close friendship, always going off on their own, scouting they said, and hunting. Magnus had his suspicions, but when it came to tracking and acquiring food on their long travels, while stuck in the wild, the two were the most efficient and valuable men to have at his side. As long as his concerns were left unconfirmed and the men followed his lead, he would ignore his doubts.

The prince chose young Donovan for his resourcefulness and quick thinking amidst the battle when his brothers in arms needed to be patched up. The boy looked up to him. He was the youngest of the group, with no family of his own, and was hoping for a brother in Magnus, even though Magnus never gave him anything in return. It seemed the more he ignored the boy, the more Donovan sought out Magnus' approval. He had a natural healing touch; some might even say magic flowed through his fingers. Magnus didn't care, as long as the boy did his job.

The twins, Cathal and Galor, who really looked nothing alike but were as close as two peas in a pod, depended on Magnus and their position as royal knights. Their wives and children were well taken care of on account of their job. Magnus also found Galor quite useful when food needed to be cooked over the fire.

Lance and Colin, he knew the least well of all of them. They were hired men but still loyal to the crown and Magnus respected them for the veneration they had towards him.

Of course, they also had Charlotte, whom they called Charlie, a prostitute he had paid to travel with them, and her story was a different one.

After receiving a nod from Magnus, Reed rode forward to the main market square and asked about dragon sightings. He returned with three men following him on foot. One of them stepped out, wringing a hat in his hands.

"Your Highness, these men claim to have seen a dragon yesterday," Reed said, sitting atop his horse as he maneuvered the animal behind the three men, while Cassiel and Galor flanked their prince.

Magnus eyed the men warily as he patted his horse's neck. "Your name?"

"Rhett, Your Highness," the man said, keeping his head lowered.

"Tell me what you know," Magnus demanded. "And look me in the eye as you answer."

The man looked up as instructed. "Yester we was traveling with our caravan to here for some trading on the market. Took the same road you has. Then, out of nowhere, actually... from the south - " The man called Rhett glanced at his men who nodded in agreement, "- yes, south. It swooped down like this," he made a swooping motion with his hands "and attacked us somewhat fierce. The beast tried to take our whole wagon! Including horses! It almost burned us alive. But not us... Oh no! We... we fought back with our swords, sticks and stones. We was not going to let it take from us. We was fiercer. So, the dragon fled defeated but managed to take away with him one of the crates with our most precious wares," the man finished off with a self-satisfied nod.

Magnus was no fool. He knew the man was lying, at least about the fight. The three of them were clean and completely unharmed. If they had fought a dragon, at least one of them would have been wounded or burned, and they were neither. The man also hadn't mentioned any bystanders being injured. Magnus presumed the other parts of the story to be true, though; the direction and the day matched.

"Where did it fly off to?" inquired the Prince.

"To the mountains, Your Highness." Rhett waved his hand to the west.

"Have you ever seen the dragon around here before?"

"No, Your Highness. We're new to this route. It's been

quiet. But there is stories going 'round 'bout dragon attacks surrounding the mountain area, some years back I guess… or were they only sightings?" Rhett scratched his balding head. "Should talk to the locals about those."

"My prince?" Reed spoke, requesting Magnus' attention.

"Yes, Reed?" Magnus quirked an eyebrow.

"If I may suggest we rest here for the night and ask around about those attacks. It has been a long day of riding."

Magnus agreed so they settled in for the evening. They would probably head towards the mountains in the morning, following yet another trail the dragon had left. And if the rumors were true, he was one step closer to having the monster's head, first on a pike and then on his walls.

CHAPTER 11

"I can't wait 'til he kills that dragon," Charlotte exclaimed as she burst through the door into a room of the inn where they were staying, long flaming curls bouncing on her shoulders. She paused a moment in thought, tapping the cleft of her chin with her finger. She closed the wooden door, locked it and continued as she walked towards the bed, "Or better yet, if the dragon kills him."

"Charlie!" two male voices hissed from the direction of the bed. They both jumped up blushing.

"Don't say that!" Theo said as he settled back on the bed. "Someone might hear you. And you shouldn't have burst in like that. What if someone followed you in?"

"Well, you should've locked the doors. You two've become careless. Lucky for you twas just me this time," Charlie said as she plopped herself on the bed next to Theo, leaning back against the headboard. Damien lay crosswise to them with his head on Theo's lap and his feet hanging off the side of the bed. Charlie put her feet up on Damien's stomach.

"Umph! Thanks for the warning, Charlie." Damien turned his head to glare at her. The look was short-lived however, because Theo brought his hand back down on

Damien's head and started running his fingers through Theo's short, dark curls again.

"You're welcome!" Charlotte retorted with a giggle.

"Bitch!" murmured Damien, which caused her to shrug her shoulders. She had heard it all before and she knew he was actually angry with himself and Theo for leaving the door unlocked.

"He's grumpy today," the red-haired woman pointed out as she rested her head on Theo's shoulder. Seeing the two of them like that, one would guess they were siblings. Both had red hair and similar soft features, but Charlotte had mischievous green eyes while Theo's were light brown, and his nose and cheeks were peppered in light freckles. Damien, on the other hand, was the complete opposite of the two with sharp, high cheekbones, short black curls, and dark blue eyes that stood out against his tanned skin.

He had his eyes closed as Theo's fingers massaged his scalp, relaxing him. His pulse slowed to a steady beat.

"Anyway, you two are still my favorites," Charlie said through a yawn, and then grinned.

"I wonder why..." Damien rolled his eyes behind his closed eyelids. "Must be our amazing personality and great skills in bed." A small smile slipped onto his lips.

Charlotte giggled. "Yeah, great skills in bed, if only you were to share. So selfish!" She poked him in the ribs with her bare toes.

"No. Sorry. I don't share my man." Damien opened his eyes, winked at her and beamed at Theo.

"Such a waste!" Charlie pouted.

"You know your womanly wiles and those pouty lips won't work on us, Charlie."

"Well, you can't blame a girl for tryin'." Charlie grinned back but the smile left her face when she remembered why she had come to their room in the first place. "Reed said he's gonna look me up tonight," she sighed wearily. "I can't handle him yet; he was too rough the last time."

Theo brought his hand around her shoulders and pulled her in closer. "We'll cover for you, you know that. So don't worry about it tonight. But..."

"I know. I won't be able to avoid him much longer. At least Magnus's been keeping himself busy with other women this last week. I shouldn't complain; this whole deal could've been much worse. You all could've been all over me. What was I thinking?" She groaned.

"You weren't. It was your stomach and your empty purse that did the thinking for you." Damien rubbed her calves which were resting on his stomach.

"I know. Hopefully it'll be over soon, one way or the other. Then," she sighed, "I just need to bear the trip back and I'm done."

"Why not ask him to leave you behind when we go back?" Theo said.

"You think he will? After the last trick I pulled?" Charlie extracted herself from Theo's embrace, crossed her hands over her chest and looked up at the ceiling.

"Yeah, that was really a stupid attempt at running away," Damien said, angry at her for trying and at himself for not helping. No one should go through what she had gone through, what she was still going through.

"'Twas worth it... seeing his fuming face when he caught me. He was so embarrassed that I managed to get that far with his own horse. I thought his vein would burst and he would die right there." She smiled wistfully, imagining the prince's demise, seeing him falling at her feet, reaching out for help or mercy, and she would just kick him over and leave him to rot. "Now, that would've been a wonderful sight."

"But was it worth it? The beating and... other things?"

Theo turned his angry eyes at her. He had been the one who had helped patch her up afterwards.

Both men heard her sigh and could see her lip quivering as she fought back the tears.

"I'm sorry... I shouldn't have..."

Theo gently wiped away a tear that ran down her cheek and brushed a red curl behind her ear. He hated seeing her like that. He was starting to really care about her, as if she were his own blood. "We... we should have helped you. We still can."

"No!" Charlie's eyes widened in alarm as she shook her head vehemently. "Don't you dare even think of it. He'd kill ya if he found out. He's the prince! Our future king. If you betrayed him like that, if he found out... no, no, no," she shook her head and then narrowed her eyes at Theo. "It's not worth it... *I'm* not worth it. I made the deal with him and I'll stick to it. I've handled men like him before..." She winced at the memories of what had happened when she fought back. "I've learned my lesson."

"But—"

"No. Please don't, Theo. If you try something like that, I won't cooperate. As long as there's a possibility of you two gettin' hurt on my behalf... just no." Her voice softened, wavered. "I wouldn't be able to handle the guilt. It'll be easier to handle him, and Reed, for a few months longer, and then I'll have enough gold to stop selling myself around."

Theo closed his eyes, but nodded his assent.

"Anyway," Charlotte cleared her throat, "since we're talking about working for the Prince Cur, I've wondered for a while now, why're the two of you even working for him?"

Damien turned his head and looked up at them, "At first I wanted the money, he offered a lot, and then I wanted him," he said as he smiled at Theo. "I got him, so now I want money for us. So we can settle down somewhere."

Theo leaned forward so he could place a loving kiss on Damien's lips, who met him halfway. They would've deepened it if not for Charlotte's squeal of delight.

"You want to settle down!! That's so adorable!" she squealed again loudly, clapping her hands out of happiness.

Banging on their door cut her merriment short. They froze, anticipating.

"Charlie! Is that you in there?!" They heard Reed's slurring voice boom from the other side of the door.

"Shite!" "Oh no!" "Fuck!" The trio exclaimed at the same time as they sprang into action.

Theo and Charlie moaned loudly while he was unbuttoning her shirt. She yanked her skirt down, leaving her only in her chemise. Damien, at the same time, attacked her neck, leaving a few love bites.

"Charlie! I can hear you, you whore! I recognize those moans! Those moans belong to me tonight." Reed's deep voice boomed again. "Open the fucking door!" The door shook with the force of his banging.

"Quickly!" Theo murmured and then let out a loud moan as he ruffled her hair.

Charlie bit down on her lip hard, almost drawing blood, so it would appear kiss swollen. Her cheeks were already flushed with adrenaline. She slid off the bed and went to open the door. Looking back, she saw that both men were already undressing themselves.

"Wha's got your breeches in a kink, Reed?" Charlotte said in a breathless voice when she opened the door and leaned on the doorframe, twisting a lock of red hair around her finger.

"You!" Reed growled as he leaned closer and his

alcohol-laced breath fumed her face. Instead of gagging, she managed to plaster a wide smile on her face, proud that she still had all her teeth, strong and white.

Theo appeared naked behind her, hugging her close to him by wrapping his hands around her waist.

"I haven't finished yet, and Damien still hasn't had his turn." He planted a kiss on her neck and nibbled while Charlie faked a giggle. "We got to her first tonight. You know the deal, Reed."

Reed shuffled on his feet, diverting his gaze from the sight of a naked, lustful man before him. As he was about to respond, Damien walked by nude in the background, barely containing his laughter at Reed's distress.

"Ummm, yeah, yeah... sure. Plenty of other whores around." He looked everywhere but at them before his bloodshot eyes settled back on Charlie's face. "But you're still my favorite." Reed ran his big thick finger down her cheek. "Next time I'll be faster," he said before turning around and stumbling away as Theo closed and locked the door behind him.

The room was filled with three sighs of relief.

"That was too close." Theo broke the tense silence.

"Yah. Thank you, both." Charlie turned and couldn't stop her eyes from roaming, admiring their naked bodies. "What a...waaaeeeaaste," she said through a yawn.

Damien and Theo chuckled.

"Come on, little red. Let's get dressed and sleep. It's going to be another long day tomorrow," Damien suggested and the other two agreed without hesitation. They pushed their beds together after getting dressed for the night. Charlie put on one of their shirts, and they all snuggled up together.

"Good night, my-oh-so-edible-but-unattainable-saviors."

Theo and Damien chuckled before drifting off to sleep.

98

CHAPTER 12

Olivia had never had so much fun in her life. She compared it to the feeling of getting her first horse, the first gallop, catching her first fish, seeing the sea for the first time, stealing her first kiss from the stable master's son… all the cherished firsts, but none of them measured up to flying with a dragon. She had been ecstatic, and she still was, the leftover tingles still coursing through her body to the very tips of her fingers. And Kaden had promised to fly her again!

My dragon.

Olivia smiled, sitting on the soft, moss-covered bank of a gently meandering stream. Kaden had taken the slightly longer route to reach the place where the water flowed at a slower pace. Now, Olivia soaked her weary feet in the cool stream. Water cascaded over lichen-covered rocks, gathering in small pools before overflowing and continuing its downward path. She leaned forward and, cupping her hands, she drank. She studied her reflection in the mirroring pools, her flushed cheeks, bright eyes, surrounded by a dark halo of unruly curls. She glowed, and Olivia smiled at her reflection as the water murmured by, gently lapping at the rocks as the birds sang in the trees behind them.

"Enjoying yourself?" Kaden's deep voice rumbled in amusement as he lay down next to Olivia. He circled his claw in the water, creating little whirlpools.

Olivia beamed. "Very much so! It is so lovely out here." She glanced around the little natural cove at the surrounding trees, the forest's ever watchful guardians, and the colorful flowers dancing across the clearing. The air demanded to be breathed deeply into her lungs, refreshing her very soul. The sun, now high up above, held her in a warm embrace with its shining rays. She looked back at the water, swirling her feet, imitating Kaden's patterns.

"I am glad." Kaden nudged her with his head, earning himself a tinkling laugh from Olivia as she splashed him with her feet.

Kaden returned the favor. Olivia reciprocated, and soon she found herself almost completely drenched from head to toe, claiming that their little water-war was unfair since the dragon could just shake the droplets off while her clothing would take time to dry.

"I want to come back tomorrow. To wash myself properly. It has been *days*," Olivia said as she lay back on the grass, the sun drying her dress, a forearm covering her eyes.

"We can return tomorrow. I will show you later which roots and leaves you can use instead of soap."

Olivia turned left, shielding her face with her hand. Kaden's large amber eyes peered down at her as he nestled along her side. For a moment, she marveled his size; she guessed him to be five or six horse lengths long.

She raised her eyebrows at the dragon.

Kaden rolled his eyes in return. "I know herbs and roots and plants... I know a lot about a lot of things. I have been around for a very long time. I learned."

Olivia nodded, accepting this fact, then went back to soaking up the sun.

℃

Once Olivia's dress was dry, they decided to catch some fish. Kaden would make an improvised pool around a fish or two with his tail and Olivia would wade in, laughing and squealing while trying to catch the slippery fish with her hands, and then throwing them back on the grass. She didn't mind getting her dress wet again.

Kaden was relieved she didn't have a problem with cleaning and then eating the fish. With his help, they caught quite a few, cleaned them and prepared to take them back to the cave along with the water they had come for.

As they strolled back to the cave, the sun sank low and was swallowed by the horizon, painting the sky in numerous shades of orange, pink and violet, all turning into a slowly darkening blue. The air in the forest was tinged with an orange hue, giving it an unearthly glow, and the spring breeze had ceased. The forest had reached its most peaceful moment of the day. The trees stilled their swaying dance, and only the chirping of the birds and the sound of their shuffling steps could be heard.

"Kaden?"

"Yes?" The dragon glanced at the little fascinating human walking beside him.

"It is easy to forget you are a dragon," Olivia said as she looked up at him.

"What do you mean?"

"The way you talk and act, if I did not know any better or if I were not able to see you, I would bet my life you were a human." She bumped him with her shoulder, which of course had no effect on him.

Kaden chuckled at Olivia, but inwardly he panicked, his heart pounding, and at the same time he hoped she would discover his secret, that she would figure it out.

The words slipped past his lips, "Well, if you consider that I have been living around humans for over a hundred years, even if I only had occasional contact with them, does it really surprise you? I have seen them interact quite a bit." It wasn't a lie, but it wasn't a complete truth as well. He managed to twist the words into a somewhat honest answer. As close as he could.

"I guess it makes sense. So, why the mountains and the cave then? Why stay in one place when you could travel wherever, whenever?"

"Oh, I've done my fair share of traveling, but after a while, the novelty of it fades. The sights might be refreshing, but the people are the same. I have had enough of people and just want some peace. What better place than somewhere secluded? I like it here. I had to scare a few wanderers away, but once the word spread that it was dangerous up here, they mostly left me alone."

"Mostly?"

"Yeah, mostly. There's always someone stupid enough to think they have the skills to kill *a monster haunting the mountain* and boast about it."

"What happened to them?"

"There you go again, asking all those questions." Kaden bumped Olivia lightly. She stumbled as her foot caught on a protruding root but he flung his tail around her to keep her from falling down.

She laughed. "What was that for?"

"I'm sorry. With you, I seem to forget I'm a dragon." He winked but didn't let go of her; instead he picked her up and put her on his back. "I bet your feet hurt."

"Actually, it is my knee that is throbbing," Olivia

admitted shyly when she settled on his back, relaxing into the lulling movement, almost as if riding a horse, albeit a gigantic one.

"Why didn't you say something?" Looking back at her, Kaden could see her wince. "It must've hurt when we were flying too."

"Yes, but it was worth it." A silly grin adorned her face.

Kaden just shook his head and walked on again. They enjoyed the peaceful quiet, and neither had the urge to speak. Olivia absentmindedly caressed Kaden with her left hand as she held on with her other, looking around and about.

"Stop!" Olivia's voice echoed around them as she pushed up from her sitting position, both palms flat on the dragon's neck.

If he could have bristled, Kaden would have. Instead, he inhaled sharply, smoke forming around his snout, ready to blow up whatever danger might happen upon Olivia. A roar itched to come forth from his mouth.

Olivia felt Kaden's muscles tense beneath her thighs. When she noticed the smoke rising from his nostrils, a slight tremble crawled up her spine.

"Kaden?" She lowered herself back down, even lower, pressing her body flush against him as best as she could. "It is alright. I apologize for ummm… scaring you. I just got excited," she murmured against his neck and felt his heartbeat pulse through him strong and fast. She caressed the dragon while waiting for him to calm down.

"I…ummm… I am alright. I am safe with you." As she said that, Kaden's muscles uncoiled.

The dragon swallowed back his fire and let out a long calming exhale. When he heard her speak those words, it helped him rein in his temper and emotions.

"I wasn't frightened," he spoke once he gained his

composure, "just…just disturbed by your distress. If you haven't noticed, you have come to mean a lot to me and I tend to be overly protective of what is mine." The dragon closed his eyes, letting her scent fill his lungs and the touch of her body soothe him.

"I apol—"

"You have nothing to apologize for. I was the one who overreacted," Kaden said as he walked on again, his rhythmic movements causing Olivia to sway on his back.

"Kaden, please stop. The reason I got excited is over there and I need it." Olivia pointed to a stand of plants on their right. "It's burdock, great for cooking the fish. Just some clay and we are almost set."

Kaden stopped as she requested and then stomped over to the plants. "That is what got you so excited?" He eyed the large leaves - he knew of burdock's medicinal uses but had never realized that it could be used for cooking.

"Yes." Olivia smiled, abashed, when Kaden looked back at her, now amused.

"Alright." Kaden lowered himself so Olivia could pick a couple big burdock leaves which she then tucked under her belt. "Great. Thank you."

The dragon rose up and continued on their way back. Olivia's thoughts swirled in confusion around her head.

He cares. A lot… He called me his… Did he not? She knew that she should be outraged at the idea, but it wasn't about being a possession or a pet. *Why did that set my heart racing? He is not human. Nothing could come of it. Why do I let this continue?* She paused, feeling the movements of the firm muscles beneath her. His scales glistened, dazzling her with their shimmering colors. She hadn't noticed how beautiful they were until now. *Why am I…*

She had to take a mental pause, unwilling to admit her feelings even to herself. They were all wrong, weren't they?

Everything was so confusing and so confused. Yet there was no point in denying it. *Why am I letting myself fall in love with a dragon? It should not be this way, it could not, and so fast...* Yet her soul called out to his, as if finding its other part. *He needs me, probably more than I need him.* She had been so disappointed to realize that money and prestige were all she was valued for as a marriage partner, even to a man she had thought of as a close friend, now it felt so good to be needed. *Needed for the person I am and not what I could provide or own. The way he treats me,* Olivia sighed, *no one has ever treated me like that. Not with that kind of attention and affection... Have I even heard him right? Well, if he needs me, I will be there for him. I need to be needed.*

Olivia absently stroked the burdock leaves tucked in her belt and allowed herself to rant on in her head. She kept telling herself that getting close to him, getting attached wasn't good, but yet again she wanted it and never made any promises to herself to stop. Without noticing, her hand dropped from the leaves to the scales beneath her, and she let the dry, silky smoothness of the scales soothe her as she stroked them.

"So, what's the recipe?" Kaden could almost hear Olivia thinking, her thighs clenching around him, her hand ceasing the tender caresses. The air had gradually filled with tension, so he decided to try and tame it.

"Hmm?" Olivia jerked out of her reverie with a guilty start, as if he had caught her doing something illicit. "Oh, right. Yes. You take the trout, season it with salt and thyme, wrap it up in a burdock leaf, and then enfold it all with clay or I guess mud could work, too? Then you set it close to the fire and wait for it to cook. It is also good to bury it in the ground next to the fire and cover it with hot coals." Her mouth watered at the thought of proper food.

"Alright. I will find you clay. I think I remember where I

can get some. I know this forest like a squirrel knows its tree," Kaden said.

"Did you call me yours?" Olivia blurted before her brain caught up with her mouth.

"Yes," Kaden said without hesitation. He really didn't want to lie to her or keep anything from her, so he decided to speak as much truth as he possibly could. He waited for the indignation, the vehement denial, the stream of objections.

"Good." Butterflies erupted in the pit of Olivia's belly. It was an odd feeling but she liked it.

Kaden's butterflies, though, were already flying around but with her acceptance of his declaration, they took off in a beautiful, yet frantic dance.

Olivia's mind picked up on other little details which he hoped she wouldn't ask about.

"So... who else is yours?" she asked in a soft voice.

"Huh?"

"You said you get protective of those you consider yours, or something like that."

I really hate my life sometimes, Kaden thought. Olivia had just asked another question which he could not answer. *Think, Kaden, think...*

"The horse," he said, voice serious and unwavering.

"The horse?" Olivia echoed in disbelief.

"Yes, the horse. It was so hard to let him go. But you know the old saying: *You have to set free the ones you love, and if they come back they're yours; if they don't, they never were.* But he never came back." Kaden sighed.

Laughter echoed through the forest and Kaden was happy to once again be the one to make Olivia laugh. She even snorted, much to her embarrassment.

When her mirth subsided, Kaden knew she would ask more questions; he knew she would want the real answer.

He knew vague or false answers would disappoint her, so he intercepted her predictable train of thought. "Do you want to know why?"

"Why what?" Olivia held onto Kaden with both hands, leaning forward, as they made the slight ascent towards the cave.

"Why I care..."

If there had been any more laughter waiting to bubble forth from her, it died down with those words and the butterflies took off again.

"Why do you?"

"You see, he was a wonderful horse. He had these soulful, doe-like brown eyes..." Olivia's laughter and a slap to his back made him pause for a moment. "It was like he could see right to your soul. And his coat... I could never forget it, oh so soft..." He teased on as Olivia shook with laughter, clutching at her belly and almost sliding off.

"Stop. I will be really worried if you honestly think that way about a horse," Olivia said as she tried to rein in the merriment.

"It's your eyes..." Kaden said in a soft voice as he slowed his gait. "When you really smile, your eyes remind me of soaring high on a sunshiny day, flying among the clouds. And that smile... it can light up the darkest of souls." He paused, letting his words sink in. "There's also this innocence about you; it gives me hope. Your touch is soft and gentle like your heart. And your inquisitive mind is quite fascinating."

Olivia had stopped laughing, words dying on her lips. Her heart beat like a master drummer playing the crescendo on his drums and her cheeks heated up as a blush crept up her face.

"Oh... funny too, especially when you speak before you think. It is amusing to see you surprise yourself and then your face when you silently chide yourself as well," he chuckled.

The silence stretched as Kaden waited for Olivia to respond, to blurt something. He stopped and turned around so he could look at her. It was unusual for her to be so quiet. He saw her holding a hand over her mouth in disbelief as tears rolled down her cheeks.

No one had ever described her like that before. She sounded beautiful.

Kaden kept his eyes locked on hers. "You know, you make me wish you were a dragon, or better yet, pray I were a human. Our love would have been—"

"— I know." Olivia nodded in agreement and rewarded him with one of those dazzling smiles that he came to love.

They reached the cave as the last rays of the setting sun said goodbye to the day. Olivia ate the fish and Kaden promised he would find the clay for her tomorrow, so she could prepare it like she wanted to. By then, he would have done anything she asked of him.

Afterward, Kaden pulled the mattress closer to his spot so Olivia could sleep on it, instead of the floor, and still be cuddled up against him.

"Good night, Kaden." Olivia nuzzled her face against his silky smooth scales before she settled down for sleep.

"Good night, Liv." The dragon brought his wing down and around her, protecting her from the chill of the night and from the rest of the world.

Excitement still ran through Olivia's veins. Memories of flying flashed behind her closed eyelids and her heart fluttered each time she remembered Kaden's confession.

"I like you too," she said, "very much. It doesn't matter to me whether you are dragon or a human. I still want you in my life."

"Thank you. I do too." Kaden sighed. "Now sleep,

because tomorrow is a brand new day."

CHAPTER 13

"Liv…"

Silence.

"Olivia…" Kaden coaxed in a soft and low voice. He had been trying to wake Olivia but was afraid to speak louder in case he scared her.

"Come on, Olivia. It's time to wake up." He nudged her gently before nuzzling at her side with his snout.

"But I do not want to," Olivia whined, still tired.

Kaden's chuckle rumbled through the cave and the now familiar shiver trailed its warm fingers down Olivia's spine. Waking up though, she didn't want to. Being curled up next to her dragon was just too comfortable and cozy, lying on the soft mattress while being snuggled up to and surrounded by everything Kaden.

His scent. His warmth.

Protection, safety and love.

She didn't want to move anywhere, except maybe closer to her dragon, which she promptly did.

"Come on, love. It is a beautiful day and I will take you flying again." The endearment slipped past Kaden's lips as he cajoled Olivia to get up. Her lips, curling into a smile, brushed against his draconic scales. She obviously approved.

"Yes, you will. Just like you will give me a bit more time here... with you." Olivia yawned. She placed her palm against his side and caressed him, cherishing the feel of his scales under her questing hand.

Kaden closed his eyes, relishing her touch. If he could have purred he would have at that moment. Instead, a rumbling sound came forth from his throat, a sound of enjoyment which had Olivia smiling even wider.

"My dragon," she murmured, voice filled with tender affection, before placing a gentle kiss on one of his scales where her face had been pressed.

"Do you want me to stop?" Olivia asked mischievously, still not opening her eyes as she relished the feel of Kaden's heartbeat quickening under her ministrations, the blood pulsing and running through his veins.

"No," Kaden answered through a rumbling moan. He was utterly mesmerized and completely under her spell.

Eyes fluttering open, Olivia looked up at her dragon and an impish smile curled her lips.

"Well, it seems we have a problem then, my dear dragon. You want me to get up and at the same time you do not want me to stop. Which will it be?" She raised her eyebrow.

Kaden gazed down at her and almost got lost in the sky of her eyes as she continued with her gentle ministrations. The wicked yet innocent smile playing on her lips kept him floating, rather than flying, high.

"I was wrong, you're not an imp. You're a little minx. You're doing this on purpose." He tried to give her a disapproving look but his eyes gave him away. They were happy.

"But we really shou—" He was interrupted by one of his own deep moans when Olivia scratched him gently.

"Olivia..." was all he could say while she marveled at the new power she had over him. He was big enough to crush her with a single swipe, but here he was, tamed and helpless as she petted him. *If he were a man...* She shut that thought down swiftly, filled with embarrassment and surprised at the thrill of longing that washed over her. He was *not* a man. He was a dragon.

"Hush, Kaden, just enjoy it for a bit," Olivia said as she pressed her face against the silken scales and continued to scratch him softly. After a few more peaceful moments, Olivia pushed herself away from him.

"But I don't want to." Kaden threw back one of her own excuses, making Olivia laugh.

"Who is whining now?" She sat up and leaned her back against Kaden while, at the same time, he unwrapped his wing from around her and tucked it back. Her legs were stretched out in front of her, so Kaden just twisted his neck and lowered his big head, settling his snout over her lap.

Olivia brought her hand down on his head and traced his features. The feel of the scales on his head was so very different to those on the rest of his body. They were much harder, sturdier and a bit rougher.

She feathered her fingers from the top of his head, between his eyes and over the ridge of his nose to his jaws. She traced his mouth, his protruding fangs to the side of his head and his cheek. There, she spread her fingers wide, gliding them upward gently over his closed eyelid, making a mental map of his draconic features.

Her fingers stopped their wandering at a scar that cut through his eyebrow and continued above. It was vertical and as long as her hand from the bottom of her palm to the tips of her fingers. She leaned over and pressed a soft kiss to it, her lips lingering a moment longer.

Kaden huffed out a sigh of contentment.

"Where did you get that scar?" Olivia's fingers traced the edges of it.

"It's still there? That is an old one, probably the only one showing. There is a good story that goes with it." He opened his eyes and looked into the distance, reminiscing.

"Those might have been the only people who didn't fear me or who wanted to kill me, at that time, after everything that happened. I haven't thought about them in a long while. Almost forgot."

His amber, slitted eyes turned to her, but his head was so large that only one had a view of Olivia. "I was travelling at night, flying over a fairly deserted region of land with a few homesteads scattered around when I spotted a fire. One of the homes was ablaze, so I went to see if everyone was alright. A family was out. They were all crying and calling out a name as they held the mother back. It seemed that someone was stuck inside the burning house. Without giving it a thought I just charged in. The house was already falling apart but I managed to hear, above the noise of the crackling fire, a crying and coughing child. When I spotted her, I took her into my hands. Fire doesn't harm me because it's a part of me." He puffed out a cloud of smoke as proof, making Olivia roll her eyes at him.

"Anyways, as we were on our way out, there was a loud crack and a main beam broke in half. All I managed to do was hide the child beneath me, enveloping her with my wings as I waited for the roof to collapse on top of us. It landed on my head, where the scar is now and we were buried under the debris. I lost consciousness then. I usually heal very fast, but the wound was seared before it had the time to heal, thus the scar."

"What happened to the little girl?" Olivia said, eyes wide

and voice tinged with worry.

"She survived. They found us among the ashes in the morning. My body protected her from the impact and fire, and I presume the cocoon of my wings saved her from choking. To say they were shocked by what I did would be a great understatement. But once they saw their little girl alive and clinging to me, the fear and shock wore off quickly."

"I... I... I really do not know what to say..." Olivia stuttered. "...except that you are greatly underappreciated."

Kaden just shrugged it off and Olivia smacked him on the forehead.

"What was that for?" Kaden frowned at her, confused.

"Do *not* do that!" It was Olivia's turn to frown back at him.

"Do what?"

"Do *not* bring yourself down... do not shrug it off like that. What you did... there are not even many *people* who would do that." Her voice rose but settled back down. "That was very heroic of you," she said with a defiant tilt of her chin, and her stern gaze dared him to say otherwise.

Kaden loved the fiery side of her, standing firm for what she believed. He didn't want to contest her, so he simply lowered his head in submission even though he considered himself far from heroic.

Olivia nodded in approval. Kaden reluctantly lifted his head from her lap so she could get up. They went about their morning routine.

"So, I'll go and try to get the clay you wanted, and then I'll fly you over to a valley where you can pick some thyme. You can make yourself a real feast tonight." One part of his plan he left out. He needed to find himself a decent meal, without having Olivia witness that side of him - hunting and eating raw meat, because the few fish they caught could never sate his hunger.

Olivia followed him out of the cave. "Just be careful and return hastily, before I get bored."

"Oh yes, who knows what mischief you might be up to this time. Roam the back cave all you want, just don't go too far away from the cave all together. Promise?" Kaden faced her as he said that.

Olivia tilted her head back almost all the way, so she could look up at him. "I promise," she responded sweetly. "I will behave," she added with a wink.

Kaden shook his head. "Just... just be safe and I'll see you in a bit." He turned and walked away.

Olivia lingered outside, breathing in the fresh morning air and enjoying the scents of blooming spring. A light breeze courted the branches, and the leaves celebrated the union in a murmuring dance. Olivia's curls brushed her cheek. She tucked them behind her ears, and with a smile on her face, she returned to the cave. She spent most of her time exploring the back cave and decorating the front one, making it resemble a real room. It made her feel useful and gave the cave a bit more of a homey feel. She managed to keep herself busy that way.

After Kaden returned with a full belly and the promised clay, he and Olivia went flying for a while and searched for the thyme.

The experience of flying with Kaden again was just as exhilarating for Olivia as it had been day before. The sense of freedom elated her and extreme happiness filled her being.

Kaden kept glancing back at Olivia. He just couldn't help himself; seeing her happy like that made their situation feel less... ominous. Also, he couldn't shake the feeling of foreboding which had stuck with him from the day when he had gotten food for Olivia the first time, when he had intruded on the wedding. It hung around him like a haunting ghost, never visible but always there. He had been ignoring the feeling and enjoying the emotions his little human had awoken in him, but now, the ill-omened vibe was stronger. He was hoping it would go away and that nothing bad would happen to Olivia. As long as she was safe and happy, safe above all else, he could deal with anything.

They spent a good part of the day at the valley where Olivia picked some thyme. They talked more, never seeming to run out of topics to discuss. They also had a few playful moments, where Olivia chased Kaden around, trying to reach his ticklish spot. She found it hilarious to listen to a dragon's squealing laughter. The day was innocent and full of memorable moments: laugher, joy, cuddling and caressing. Kaden was getting addicted to her displays of affection, she was obviously a very tactile person. Olivia even managed to take a nap and this time Kaden didn't have any problems waking her up.

As they flew back, soaring playfully above the treetops, the same feeling of danger tingled down Kaden's spine like a crawling swarm of spiders. He glanced over his shoulder at Olivia with every second beat of his wings, making sure she was safe.

The tension and unease spread from Kaden to Olivia. She sobered, the smile slipping off her face as she leaned forward.

"Is everything alright?" she said above the sound of whooshing air.

"It's just—" Kaden looked back over his shoulder but something that he saw from the corner of his eyes, down below among the trees, drew his attention. A flash of red mingled with the green. He shook his head. "Just another bird," he said as faced forward again. *I think.* But he didn't voice his worries out loud. His tail twitched. Olivia bounced and then squealed in alarm, which soon turned into laughter as she held on tighter.

The dragon exhaled in relief.

ॐ

"Please Kaden, I really need some privacy. What could happen? You will be nearby and if I need you I will call out. I really need to wash, completely. I stink!" Olivia argued, wanting Kaden to leave her alone by the stream so she could bathe herself, all of her.

"You do *not* stink! You smell wonderful! And... I don't know but I have a bad feeling following me around today, Liv," the dragon said, reluctant to leave Olivia all alone and away from his protection, even though she did speak the truth; if anything happened to her, or even threatened her, he would be there in a heartbeat, trees or no trees in his way.

Olivia took a step closer, and Kaden lowered his head toward her. She put a hand on his snout, between his nostrils, stroking him gently. "Please? I promise I will not venture anywhere. I will stay right here, go into the stream, wash the dress, let it dry as I wash myself and when I am done I will call for you. Honestly, what is the worst that could happen?" she said, her slightly downturned eyes working to her advantage; she batted her lashes pleadingly.

Kaden couldn't resist that look on her face. She wanted this and it would make her really happy, but still the sinister feeling had him doubting. He hoped he wouldn't regret leaving her alone, even for such a short time. Nevertheless, he knew and understood her needs and reasoning, so he exhaled a sigh of defeat and stepped away from Olivia.

"Alright, but if anything... I mean anything threatens

you or makes you feel uncomfortable, even if it's a frog giving you weird looks, you call me right away."

Olivia jumped and squealed in delight.

"Thank you, thank you, thank you! I will be quick, and I promise to behave this time. Even if a mosquito lands on me I will scream for my heroic dragon to come and save me from the blood-sucking monster."

Kaden couldn't help but chuckle at her enthusiasm. "You can be such a child."

"I know! I am still a big child at heart." Olivia shrugged her shoulders. "But you like me the way I am."

He shook his head in disbelief. "Yes, I do. I better go now. I'll be at our clearing, waiting *impatiently*."

"Do not worry. I will miss you, too." Olivia winked.

Kaden's eyes smiled at that. He leaned his head forward again and nuzzled her side gently as Olivia gave him a quick hug. With great reluctance, he forced himself to step away and checked the surroundings for any signs of threat. With a last nod towards Olivia, he turned around and walked away.

When Olivia thought Kaden was far enough away, she looked around again and strained her hearing for unfamiliar sounds. Hearing none and seeing nothing out of place, she timidly started taking off her clothes. She had never been naked outdoors before. Now, she would not only be naked in the forest, she would also be swimming with no clothes on. Even though nobody was around she felt shy, so she quickly made her way to the stream with her dress in one hand and some leaves and roots, which she was going to use instead of soap, in the other.

As the water reached her knees, she sucked in a deep breath and held it. *Cold, cold, cold, so cold,* she chanted as she took slow steps further, deeper. *Oh dear God and heavens above this is cold.* Her breath sped up, hitching, while goose bumps spread over her body, prickling her skin like a myriad tiny needles as the water reached her waist. Taking another deep breath, she plunged in, letting the water glide over her head. When she came back up for air, she panted rapidly, teeth chattering, swimming around in a way that was more like crawling over the rocks, so she could acclimate to the freezing water faster.

She washed the dress swiftly and spread it on a rock to dry under the sun. Before going back, she "soaped" herself as best possible, scrubbing the dirt off and washing her hair thoroughly. She plodded back into the deeper end to rinse off and repeated the process twice more; only then did she feel like a proper human again.

Once out of the chill water, she turned the dress over, letting the other side dry as well. Shyness thrown away, she stood on the bank of the stream, the warm rays of the sun caressing her body dry. Closing her eyes, she enjoyed the sunshine, the breeze, the scent of the spring and the now familiar sounds of the forest. An elk called for its mate, and she smiled. She could never get enough of it. This was where her heart belonged.

Her mind drifting away, she didn't notice when silence descended upon the forest. Opening her eyes, she picked up the dress and as she pulled it over her head, she heard a deep male voice behind her, "Do not cover that fair body, my Princess. It is a shame to hide it, and keeping it from my view should be outlawed."

CHAPTER 14

At the birth of dawn, even before the roosters croaked out their morning song, Magnus and his men, including Charlie, were up and preparing for departure.

As usual, Charlie sat alone at a table and Lance came over with breakfast for both of them, joining her. She accepted, giving him a coy smile then looking away. He flushed hot crimson in response and ate his food without saying a word. Charlie grinned to herself, making sure to gaze at him under her lashes until he noticed, then glanced skittishly away. She lived in hope that one day his feelings would give him the courage to stand up to Reed, if not to Magnus, but so far he remained cowed by the older knight and no help at all when it came to the prince. She was secretly glad about that, if she was honest with herself – she really didn't want to bring Magnus' wrath down on anyone else's head. Or their back.

She swallowed her food, barely tasting it as her grin faded. She would bear those scars for a long time. Lance caught her expression and tentatively moved his hand across the table to cover hers. She stiffened but did not draw it away until he stroked her fingers with his thumb. He didn't argue, but stood up with a sad tilt of his head, withdrawing from her and leaving her to finish eating alone. Lance must *know* she didn't have the same kind of feelings for him as he did for her, she thought, watching him go, and sighed. She pushed the food away, catching sight of Reed fetching the prince's breakfast.

They would be moving on again soon, and she couldn't wait to be out of the woods and back somewhere dry and warm, with a proper roof over her head. *I can't wait for him to kill that dragon*, she thought. *Then we can all go home.*

ꕥ

After breaking his fast, Magnus and his men geared up and mounted their horses. The prince gazed at the mountains, squinting, eager for a glimpse of the dragon rumored to haunt those slopes. He hoped the stories were true and the monster lingered somewhere in the forest. He would not go back until he fulfilled this self-imposed quest. It would make him look puny in his father's eyes if he failed and returned empty-handed, and this was the closest he had gotten to the dragon since his journey started two months ago.

He glanced back at his men. The horse shifted underneath him, sharing his master's anxiousness. No words were uttered as he gave a nod to his following, tugged the reins and started for the mountains.

The aura of anticipation, the apprehension of the unknown, and excitement settled over them. They could only grit their teeth and ride on. A few hours later, they reached the foothills, just as the sun blazed down on them, and they were grateful for the shade of the trees that forest provided.

"We'll stop here to rest," Magnus said after trekking for four hours. "Theo… Damien. Scout ahead for any signs of the dragon and bring back some meat."

"Yes, Your Highness," Theo said, nudging Damien with a covert grin. "We'll be very thorough."

Only Charlie caught the flicker in Damien's eyes as he shared in the smile, and she rolled her eyes. They would take a while, being very... meticulous. *"What – a – waste"* she mouthed as Theo turned back to wink at her, and the two bounded off into the trees.

Dismounting her horse, Charlie ignored Reed's attempts to gain her attention, but still, the unease prickling in the back of her neck and creeping down her spine made her aware of him and conscious of the fact that he would not give up until he had her all to himself. She closed her eyes as she heard heavy feet stomping closer to her.

"Reed, come here," Magnus said, and Charlie's shoulders sagged in relief. As soon as her horse was untacked and brushed down, she joined Cassiel. The dark knight always looked out for her best interests when they spent time together, and he never used her services, a true gentleman... a true knight, like the ones in the fairy tales. A rare find these days, she decided. Still, he had always puzzled her. She understood why most of the knights had ended up in the prince's service, but not this one. His armor was of a very fine quality, so she guessed that unlike Theo and Damien, he wasn't in it for the money. He certainly didn't share the prince's particular interests, like Reed. The others... the others hadn't really had a choice, as they had been chosen to serve, like her. You didn't say no to Prince Magnus, and you certainly didn't say no to his father, the king. Not if you wanted your house to remain standing and your family to remain free.

One day, she would ask Cassiel about his oaths. With a determined nod, she watched the dark knight inspect his horse and check his belongings. With him, everything always had its proper place.

At the sudden sensation of a grope of her behind, Charlie swiveled around and found herself face to face with Colin. Him, she didn't like. He wasn't as… aggressive with his demands as Magnus and Reed, yet he wasn't as mindful about her as Lance, not to mention Cassiel. He ran a tongue over his teeth behind his closed lips and his beard moved as if living a life of its own. It sure could chafe and bruise that way.

"What do you want, Colin?"

"Oh, you know what I want."

Charlie swatted his hand away when he reached for her. "Not now."

"As I remember, you don't have a say in that." Colin cocked his head to the side and a wicked smile dance on his lips, showing off the gap where his front tooth used to be. He looked her up and down with those poo brown eyes.

"Well, Reed claimed me next, so you can take it up with him." Charlie placed her hands akimbo to hide their trembling and glared at him. Her heart pounded but she kept her breathing under control, taking in deep measured breaths when all her lungs wanted to do was pant to the rhythm of her rising panic. She gulped it down when he took a step closer.

"Seems he's busy with the prince. I bet—"

"Colin…" Cassiel joined Charlie's side and she took a step back, hiding behind her savior. "It would be prudent of you to heed Lady Charlotte's words. This is neither the time nor the place. The Prince is high strung as it is and he would not approve of you being… distracted at this moment. At least wait till nightfall."

Colin narrowed his eyes at Cassiel. "But then Reed will—"

Cassiel raised his hands. "You deal with him on your

own as you see fit."

Colin opened his mouth to argue again but Cassiel intercepted, "It really is my *personal* suggestion you do not do this now, Colin. Stand. Down." The command behind the calmly uttered words didn't go unnoticed by Charlie or Colin as the man swiveled and stomped away.

Charlie exhaled a breath of relief. "Thank you, Cass."

The knight turned and offered her a small smile. "It is the least I can do." He spread his hand to the side. "Would you help me gather some wood?"

Charlie nodded vehemently. "I would love that." She was willing to take up any chore Cassiel offered as long as it kept her away from those seeking her services.

&

Horses left grazing, and a small fire blazing, Reed still stayed away from Charlie, tending to his prince's whims. The rest spread out the small makeshift camp, relaxing and resting, or talking in hushed voices.

Two wolves burst through the bushes to one side.

Snarling and growling.

A black wolf pup hid behind the pair in the shrubberies. It had been playfully running away from the two wolves and would have stumbled upon the humans if its wolf parents hadn't overtaken it and jumped out in its defense. One of those wolves turned back now to growl at the pup, compelling it to run away to safety.

Shackles raised, ears perked forward, the two wolves bared their fangs at the humans, wanting nothing more than to protect their young and give it a chance to run away.

But Magnus had other ideas.

"Reed, how about some soft wolf pelts. They would

make a nice addition to my lovely collection, don't you think?" The prince took a few steps back and closer to his sword, hand wrapping around the hilt.

"Yes, Magnus, they surely would." Reed unsheathed his own weapon and stalked forward.

The wolves snarled and snapped towards him, eyes darting about at the rest of the people, wary of danger.

Charlie stepped back, hiding behind a tree while others took defensive positions in front of Magnus, with Lance standing nearer to Charlie. Lance's position didn't escape the prince's notice and he narrowed his eyes at the knight.

"Oh look, the puppies want to play!" Reed taunted, swirling the sword in front of him, slicing through the air in big, heavy sweeps.

"Just make it quick! We don't have the time for your games," Magnus snapped at Reed.

"Yes, my prince," the knight conceded and lunged at the first wolf.

The wolf dodged. The tip of the sword brushed past its ears and it stepped back before pouncing forward. The other wolf attacked Reed too, jaws snapping at the knight's armored feet.

Reed stumbled back as the first wolf leaped onto him and he knocked it away with an iron fist. His low and steady stance, with muscles bunching under the weight of his armor, helped him keep his footing.

Full plate armor kept the wolves' teeth and claws at bay while Reed expertly swung the sword, years of experience guiding his hand. He made short work of the creatures.

Just as one of the animals retreated, limping and bleeding, trying to get back to its pup, Reed stalked towards it, torture and menace glinting in his black eyes. The wolf didn't have much life left in it but Reed decided to make the pain last a little longer.

An arrow flew past him and pierced the wolf's head, killing it instantly. Reed swiveled around and glared at Theo, who had already nocked a new arrow to his bow.

Damien stood by his lover's side, chest heaving from sprinting back after hearing the sounds of battle. They hated this part the most because they shared a love for animals, trying to preserve the natural balance, and hunting only what they needed to eat. At least this way they could lessen the animals' suffering.

Reed roared, eyes narrowed and blazing with fury as he stomped toward Theo. Damien dropped the rabbits he was holding and drew his bow as well, the arrow aimed at Reed's unprotected head. They could kill him before he even reached them.

"Reed, stand down!" Magnus' voice boomed through the forest.

Reed reluctantly obeyed, still glaring at the two, his lip curling into a silent snarl while his hand tightened into a white-knuckled grip on the hilt of his sword. He glanced at Charlie, then back at the two, anger fuming in his eyes.

"You need to stop drinking so much and rein in that temper of yours. Take it out on someone else, not on our group." Magnus stalked forward and stopped right in front of Reed, eye to eye, cold blue against raging black.

"I apologize, Your Highness." Reed lowered his head and turned to clean up the mess and his sword. He managed to angle his path so he smacked Theo's shoulder as he walked by.

"Damien, the wolves are yours," Magnus ordered as he kicked over a dead animal and walked back to sit down and rest.

&

The prince and his knights continued their way up the

mountain not long after they had rested and eaten. Magnus hoped for a dragon sighting today so they could get a general idea of the territory it covered. That would make it so much easier than searching the whole forest for the beast. That could take days, and yet, no promises they would find him at all.

As they hiked up a slope, leading the horses by the reins and silence keeping them company, a shadow flew overhead. It moved too fast to be just another cloud. All their heads snapped up, catching a glimpse of a creature rushing above the tree line, followed by a gust of wind.

"Theo, Damien," the prince said.

The pair dropped their bridles and dismounted. Damien charged toward a tree. He jumped and pushed up, and then wrapped his hand around a branch. Legs locked around the limb, he swung down and extended his arms toward Theo. Forearm gripped forearm as Damien pulled Theo up. The rest of the branches were within easy reach as they both climbed up, swiftly reaching the top. Through the branches and leaves they caught sight of a huge animal flying away.

"Shite! It's real!" Theo looked over at Damien. "I thought it was all talk."

Damien shook his head. "I know," he whispered, never taking his eyes off the dragon, "and we're going after it. Hopefully we won't find it, but knowing Magnus, he won't give up until we do. I hope we survive it. Do you see the size of that monster?!"

Dragon out of sight, they descended the tree, unhurried.

"Let's just keep our heads cool, and if the push comes to shove, we can always turn tail and flee. After seeing that thing, I judge it wouldn't be a cowardly move but a smart one." Theo suggested.

"I agree." Damien nodded.

"So, what did you see?" Magnus asked as soon as he

spotted them.

"A dragon! We really saw a dragon." Theo's eyes were still wide with wonder. He jumped down, followed by Damien. "It went that way."

"Finally!" Magnus said. "Quickly! Move! I don't want to lose the trail!"

Theo and Damien led the way on foot, Magnus tagging along as the rest followed on horses, leading the extra mounts as well. The three cut a straight path, while the group on horseback, zigged and zagged, making their way through the more open areas of wood, but constantly staying in contact.

"How big was it?" Magnus panted, the heavy armor bearing down on him, determination driving him onward on foot. He wouldn't miss a moment of the chase. So thrilling.

"It was… huge. Unlike anything I've ever seen," Theo said as he led the way. "Hard to estimate real size, it was already too far away, but if I were to guess, about five or six horse lengths long, from its head to the tip of its scaly tail."

"Wonderful!" A sinister, gleeful smile crept onto Magnus's face. "No time to waste. We need to find it." After two hours of hiking in the direction the dragon had gone, no new signs of the monster appeared, nor did it fly over again.

"Damnation!" Magnus said once they reached a stream. "Where is it!?" He kicked a rock, a clang of metal on stone, and it splashed into the water.

"We have no way of knowing how far it went, or even if it remained in the forest," Theo spoke up, earning a glare from Magnus.

The prince stomped toward him and fisted Theo's shirt in his gloved hand. "I don't care! Give me the dragon today, or give me your life."

Damien reached for his bow, but a hand on his shoulder stopped him. As he glanced back, Cassiel shook his head no, and squeezed his grip in reassurance. The group had caught up. Damien nodded, trusting Cassiel's judgment.

Theo gulped. He hadn't expected Magnus to lash out that way. Verbally, yes, but not physically. Lately, the prince's behavior had gotten more erratic, unpredictable, and anxious. Not that he hadn't acted out before, usually when drunk, or contented, or wanting a woman, or… Theo's wide-eyed stare moved beyond Magnus' shoulder, seeking help. Reed smirked at him, but movement to the side caught his attention. Cassiel approached.

"Your Highness." The soothing voice of the dark knight did nothing to calm the prince. Maybe reason would. "Not all is lost. There is still a way."

The prince slackened his grip on Theo as his head snapped toward Cassiel. He nodded for his knight to continue.

"Dragons probably need to drink as much as humans. If it lives in this mountain, it could be somewhere close to the stream, or at least we might find some tracks where it comes to quench its thirst. Theo and Damien should be able to discern those."

Magnus narrowed his eyes at Cassiel, but nodded. He shoved Theo away before continuing their trek upstream. Reed followed, after taking the reins to Magnus's horse.

As Charlie rode by, Theo gave her a small reassuring smile and to Cassiel he mouthed, *Thank you.*

Just as Damien reached for Theo, Magnus bellowed, "Theo, Damien. Up front!"

Theo let his hand brush Damien's, and they jogged together to catch up with Magnus, and their horses, all of them continuing the trek on foot.

"I think we might be coming up to a clearing," Theo said. Four more hours had passed, and Magnus grew more agitated, taking the lead alongside his scout and hunter.

The prince raised his hand and everyone stopped. He turned to face them. "If the dragon's not there, we'll stop to rest… maybe set up an early camp. The dragon might show up or fly over again." Fists balled at his sides at the thought of waiting longer, he continued, "We're close. I can feel it. I want you all well rested before we face the beast."

"Yes, Your Highness," voices chorused.

As they neared the clearing, Magnus spotted something, no, someone standing next to the stream. He turned to his men, putting a finger to his lips, motioning forward, signaling caution. Reed took his left side while Cassiel flanked his right. As they sneaked closer, Magnus grinned at the sight and pointed his finger down to his companions. They were to wait.

He cleared the tree line and took a few steps forward, admiring the female form in front of him. An angelic appearance, her body soft and luscious. Warm rays of the sun caressed her skin. Magnus halted so he could enjoy the view for a few moments. The sight of her naked body made his burn instantly. This was how he would imagine the famous water nymphs from the stories he had heard. He wanted her, not in any way possible but in every way possible. What he wanted, he had always gotten. And now, he had finally found her. She had the body to keep him entertained at night, and her innocent glow, alongside her understated beauty, would make her an appropriately attractive companion. At first sight, she had the potential of being a princess, and when he heard her talk, he would know for sure if she had the necessary upbringing. He would work his charm on her then, and she would be putty in his hands in no time. He was sure of it.

The spell her body wove around him broke as she pulled on a dress. He licked his lips, and plastered on one of his best smirks before he spoke in a low, seductive voice, "Do not cover that fair body, my Princess. It is a shame to hide it, and keeping it from my view should be outlawed."

The girl squeaked and whirled around, hand pressed against her chest, soothing the thundering heartbeat.

Magnus liked the face that went with the body. She wasn't the prettiest thing he had ever seen, but blood rushed to his groin at the glint of fear in her eyes. *That's my girl, fear me and let me mould you.*

He moved forward and she took an instinctive step back. He narrowed his eyes at her retreat for a split second before schooling his expression back to that seductive smirk.

ဆ

What Olivia saw was quite a sight. Full plate armor, polished to a blinding shine but the deep grooves and scrapes spoke of formidable use. *Is that real gold?* She squinted as she studied the crest, a golden crown with a pair of golden swords crossed behind it, tips up. *Wait, is that the royal crest?* Her eyes widened, travelling up, back to his face. He had blond hair, a bit longer than most men wore, reaching his shoulders, with curls falling over his eyes which were bright blue, a shade lighter than her own. A day-old stubble accentuated a wide jaw, and the seductive smirk morphed to a wolfish grin which showed off his white, perfectly straight teeth.

He looked like a real knight in shining armor.

As if he had just stepped out of the pages of a fairy tale.

Olivia had to admit he was quite handsome, but she saw something in those eyes, something sinister hiding in the depths.

"So Princess, cannot keep your eyes off of me?"

Magnus' men stayed back, hidden by the trees, but listening in with great interest. They had never heard him call a woman Princess. They were always Puppets to him, whose strings he pulled with ease, manipulating to his pleasure. Hearing Magnus calling someone a Princess did not bode well. They knew the girl would be off limits to everyone but Magnus himself.

Magnus reciprocated Olivia's appraisal as his eyes took her in, toe to head, remembering what she had looked like naked.

Olivia blushed, gaze dropping, and she shuffled on her feet as she wrapped her arms around her middle.

"You have nothing to hide from me. I have already seen it all." The declaration made Olivia look back up. "And believe me when I say that I like what I saw."

Olivia's eyes widened. The prince bit his lip, suppressing the blooming desire.

"Can you speak, Princess?" Magnus took another step forward, slowly, as if approaching a frightened animal. He spotted a green cloak near her feet; it looked well-made and not cheap. *So she probably isn't just some poor girl... Good. Can't have a peasant at my side.* She would be perfect. His father would hate it. But, he would no longer submit to the King. It was time to take over, to make his own choices, starting with his Queen. He would choose his own, not some convenient noble or a foreigner of his father's choosing.

"P... Please stop," Olivia said, stepping back again. Irritation crossed his features at her outburst. Women usually fell at his feet willingly, promptly.

"Whatever you say, Princess. I mean you no harm."

Magnus raised his hands in surrender.

"And... And, please do not call me that. I am not a princess." Olivia quickly scanned the forest and the sky for any sign of Kaden. The whole predicament screamed... wrong.

Very wrong.

When Magnus saw her eyes wander around not so subtly, he put his hands behind his back, giving his men a signal to be cautious of possible ambush. He couldn't be sure if there was anyone out here with her or how many of them there might be. Although, once they found out he was a prince, they'd bend to his will.

"Oh, you will be a Princess soon enough." He winked at her. He really liked the timid demeanor; she could be easily tamed to his satisfaction. "But in the meantime, what should I call you?" He subtly shuffled his feet a bit closer to her.

Her name was on the tip of her tongue but she wouldn't grace him with that knowledge. Instead, she said, "O- O- Ophelia."

Movement behind Magnus caught her attention and a faint sound of unsheathing weapons drifted to her ears, carried by the soft breeze. She leaned to the side and craned her neck, trying to see behind him.

Magnus sighed. He was irritated because she was distracted by the sound of his clumsy knights drawing their swords. There was no point in his men hiding anymore; it would only make her suspicious. He decided to bring them into the game, a game he planned on winning.

"Knights!" He called back, not taking his eyes off his Ophelia's face. At first, he saw surprise when she heard him call for his men. He chose that word deliberately. He wanted her to know they were noble men. Money and status might lure her in.

He didn't get the response he was looking for because the surprise on her face was quickly replaced with fear and panic. Glancing back over his shoulder, he understood how she could find the sight frightening.

Nine men stepped out, leading horses with them, while one of them led two. They wore various sorts of armor, from leather, like the two archers in the back wore, to full plate armors like his and Reed's. They also had an assortment of weapons with them. Charlie was still in the background, where she should be if Magnus were asked. He just hoped she would keep her mouth shut or else there would be trouble for her. As a precaution, he shot her a warning look. She understood and nodded. He turned back to face Ophelia and noticed that she had taken another step back. She was inching closer to water.

Olivia scanned the men behind the one who was obviously in charge. A nobleman of sorts, maybe even of royal blood. He did wear the royal crest. Too young to be the king, old enough to be a prince, but a prince wouldn't be out there trekking through the forest, he would be back at the castle, tending to his duties and taking care of his people. She could only imagine the scope of those responsibilities compared to her own at the family estate. So, if not the prince himself, what would the king's knights be doing in this forest?

She was afraid, for herself and for Kaden. A wave of apprehension swept over her. What if they were among those who braved facing the dragon? She hoped not. If she were to choose, she would have them be passersby and with her lack of interest they would continue on. *When has it ever gone the easy way?*

She spared their armor and weapons only a passing glance and focused more on their faces. The one leading two horses was as big as the leader but much darker, more menacing. The dark-skinned one had a soft expression on his face, as if he would rather not be there witnessing whatever was about to happen. She also noticed the ones in leather armor with their bows strung, because they too looked uncomfortable but wary as they kept scanning the sky with their sharp looking eyes. *Do they know about Kaden?*

The last person who drew her attention was far in the back, on a horse, a beautiful red-haired woman keeping her head low. But as curiosity won, the redhead looked up and their gazes met. Olivia saw sadness in her eyes, and compassion.

She trembled. She understood now the fear of a small animal entrapped, unable to break free, filled with dread and uncertainty. *Who are these people? Who is the man in front of me that instills such loyalty and fear into those who follow him?* Her thoughts brought her eyes back onto him.

Kaden was so much *more* than this man, than all of them together. He was her champion and if it weren't for him, she might have given the blond man standing in front of her a moment's glance, but she somehow knew he didn't even deserve that. Instincts on high alert, unease prickling her skin, she wanted to scream out Kaden's name but it only got stuck in her throat.

"My sweet Ophelia," Magnus crooned.

Olivia was glad she hadn't told him her real name. It would sound foul coming from his lips because – Olivia took a breath, and blinked. Because she was Kaden's. And he was hers. She needed to protect her dragon. She pushed her shoulders back and tilted her chin up.

"My name is Magnus and these are my men. We are on a quest of utmost importance for the crown, and my honest and humble opinion is that you are in grave danger here. You should let me protect you and keep you safe, at least until we get rid of the monster roaming the mountains."

"A monster?" Olivia said, tasting her own panic.

"Yes, a monster, my dear Princess."

"I... umm... I have not seen any monsters here... and... umm my, you see, my brothers should be back soon so I will go to safety with them just in case." The words tumbled past Olivia's lips. Lies were not her forte, but desperation forced her to try. She wanted to divert their attention away from herself.

Liar! Magnus thought. *How dare she deny me!* The seductive sparkle in his eyes darkened and shifted into one of anger, resentment. A wry smile curled his lips. *I do like a challenge.*

"But I insist, my dear Princess. I could not live with myself if anything were to happen to a divine creature like you." Magnus took another step closer to her. They were thirty feet apart, with water only a couple of steps behind Olivia.

The air filled with tension, thickened. Magnus' men waited for her answer, witnessing for the first time someone turning their prince down, wondering if she was even aware he was a prince. Would it really make a difference?

Olivia's hands trembled as she pushed a still-damp curl behind her ear. The gazes, the question, their presence weighed down on her, coiling around her neck, tightening, as if she were dealing herself her own sentence.

Casting a wary glance around, Olivia said, "Maybe I should just call for my brothers."

"No need, Princess. I can send my men to look for them. We would not want to attract the monster's attention, would we? Did I forget to mention it was a dragon?"

When Magnus mentioned the dragon, recognition lit

Olivia's eyes. It didn't escape his notice.

"Oh my," he said. "You do know about the dragon."

Olivia froze, her body locked up.

"Where is it?" Magnus clenched his fists, blue eyes ablaze with cold fire.

"My brother..." Olivia said and then screamed, "KADEN!"

The dragon's name echoed throughout the forest, bouncing on the wind.

The knights raised their swords and drew closer to Magnus. Charlie stayed hidden in the trees near Theo and Damien, who took up the rear of Magnus's guard.

"STOP!" Magnus's voice boomed. While everyone stood frozen, he listened.

When he didn't hear anyone approaching, he took a step closer towards Olivia.

"Please stop!" Olivia panted, panic mingling with her breath, eyes watering with tears. "KADEN!" She called for her dragon again. She took another step back and slipped on moss-covered rocks. Grasping a stone, she scrambled to her feet and threatened Magnus, "Do not come any closer."

Magnus laughed. The woman pulled her hand back and threw the rock at the unsuspecting man. Magnus flinched and stopped laughing. Everyone held their breath. He touched his forehead, fingers coating in blood. The crimson liquid slid over his right eyebrow, dripping down his lashes onto his cheek. As the first drop landed on his sparkling armor, he narrowed his eyes at Ophelia.

Olivia retreated again and Magnus stalked closer, faster with every step he took towards her. She pondered picking up more rocks, but there were too many men and she couldn't face them all... at all, armed and armored men. Ankle deep in the water, she turned around and plodded deeper, picking up the skirt of her dress, heading for the other side. *Surely their armor will slow them down.*

Magnus chased after her, his men following close behind him.

A roar resounded above.

Fire exploded in front of Magnus. The blast threw him back, away from Olivia, and he skidded on the grass, covering his face with his hands.

The dragon had come.

∞

Fury had boiled in Kaden when he heard Olivia scream for him, her words coated in distress and panic. He had been angry with himself for leaving her on her own in the first place, but when he saw Olivia being chased into water by some knights, rage clouded his vision with red hues. He roared and spouted a ball of fire, missing his target by scant inches. At least he cut off their access to Olivia.

With only Olivia's safety in mind, Kaden descended towards her as she stood in the middle of the stream. Tears ran down her face, then her eyes filled with hope when she saw him.

Conflicting feelings warred inside her: happiness that Kaden had come to her rescue and fear for his safety. These men seemed very dangerous and should not be underestimated. She almost hadn't called out for him, but she knew better. He would be hurt more if she hadn't.

As Kaden approached Olivia, he beat his wings towards the fire, gusting it at the strangers. The blasts of wind forced Olivia to bring her chin down to her chest as she wrapped her hands around her head. Kaden gathered her into his arm, ever so gently, mindful of his keen sharp claws. He shook off the arrows that bounced off his scales as he protected Olivia from them with his body.

When he had her in the safety of his embrace, he beat his wings, once, twice, and they lifted into the air. Olivia unwound her arms from around her head and wrapped them around his scaled arm, clinging tightly.

Magnus scrambled to his feet, pulling out his sword. He roared and stomped, his face filled with ugly red frustration. The dragon was getting away. He wanted the dragon dead and the girl alive. He screamed again when he realized there was nothing he could do to stop their escape. The arrows didn't seem to harm the monster, and he and his men couldn't reach the dragon because of the fire.

Magnus remembered then.

He remembered the weapon the Inventor had given him. He reached for it at his side, cranked it and fired a projectile in the direction of the dragon's head.

The bang hurt his ears, deafening, like a hammer striking hammer, wielded by giants. His aim missed his intended target as the weapon recoiled in his hand.

"Theo! Up!" Magnus ordered, hoping he had at least hit the dragon, slowing him down, thwarting their escape. "Make sure you follow wherever it goes and don't lose sight of it." He planned on chasing after, heading in the same direction. Either they would search for the dragon, or for the girl. She would make excellent bait.

"It's hurt." Theo yelled back down. "They're veering right. They're going down."

Magnus grinned.

CHAPTER 16

Flying away with Olivia in his arms, a loud bang echoed through the air and a piercing pain exploded in the dragon's wing. He faltered in flight but forged on. He had to get Olivia to safety. He beat his wings through the throbbing ache and flew them in the direction opposite from the cave. He planned on misleading the men. He didn't care about the things he was leaving behind, for now or forever, because he had Olivia. She was his real and most valuable possession.

His *true* treasure.

Kaden glanced back over his shoulder. The red-haired man still monitored their flight, perched on the tree.

The dragon cradled Olivia gently to his body. He had been so close to losing her.

Barely managing to clear the treetops, his wing throbbed as he flew, and with each downward beat the pain pulsed through the rest of his body, his muscles spasming. It hadn't started healing yet, and that worried Kaden; something was still inside and he needed to get it out fast.

Veering to the right, down the mountain, he spotted a good place to descend. The alteration of flight made him falter again. His feet tangled in some branches, breaking them.

Olivia squeaked in fright. She clung to the dragon even tighter.

Kaden cursed himself for faltering. He gritted his teeth and clenched his jaw against the pain as they managed to gain some altitude.

"I've got you Liv. You're safe now," he cooed to Olivia, and she shivered in his embrace, cold, frightened and shaken.

Even though she trembled, Olivia smiled, teeth chattering. Her dragon had come when she called for him, when she needed him.

When his legs brushed the treetops again, a frown replaced the smile. Something was wrong. It was as if he were limping in the air, straining to fly.

They descended toward an abandoned field when Kaden deemed they had reached a safe distance from the men. His feet touched down lightly and he let go of Olivia with the last beat of his wings. She took a few steps out of Kaden's embrace and turned to face him. He sat on his haunches, tail twitching from side to side.

Their eyes locked and they just stared at each other for a few suspended moments.

Kaden wished he could just go to her, cup her face in his hands and kiss her as if his life depended on the nectar of her lips. He missed that kind of contact. He needed to reassure himself that she was unharmed as she stood there, heart open to him, soul reaching for its other half, vulnerable. Her eyes brimmed with unshed tears, her fragile body quivered and myriad emotions stormed across her face, spelling out the unspoken words in her heart. The ones that stood out the most were need for comfort. Just a simple hug. Someone to hold her tight and safe.

It awoke primal protective instincts in the dragon. A

different kind of need bloomed inside him, a hunger to destroy and burn anything and everyone that might invoke that turmoil in her again. He had never felt such rage, so foreign, as if not his own. He wanted to roar but he fought and suppressed his anger, calling upon his softer side, the gentle feelings, because that was what Olivia needed now.

"Are you alright?" It was the best he could come up while keeping his temper in check.

Olivia shook her head no as she closed the distance between them. She curled into his chest and cried. Kaden lowered his head behind her and pressed it against her back, pulling her closer, returning the hug in his own way. Sobs wracked her tiny body so he gently rubbed his chin against her back in soothing caresses.

"Shhh… It's alright now. You're safe. I won't let anyone take you away from me." Kaden comforted Olivia, and himself. *Take you away from me*? Kaden winced as soon as the words were out. *Why must you always talk to her as if she's a stolen trinket? Why can't you talk to her like a* — hurt flowered in his chest — *like a man*, he finished, and his anger at the knights who had threatened her was quenched in a sudden, hollow ache. *This is my fault. Because I'm* not *a man. I'm a dragon.* "I won't let anyone hurt you," he promised, flexing his wings. A sharp burst of pain shot along his right side, and he rolled his thick lips back in a grimace that bared all his teeth.

The low timbre of his voice, filled with adoration, enveloped Olivia in an invisible cloak of warmth and love. She shivered. It always had that effect on her, no matter the circumstances.

When her sobs subsided, Olivia pried herself from her dragon's embrace. She dried her face on her sleeve and turned to face Kaden. One hand placed between his horns, she caressed him, while she put the other on his cheek, and pressed her forehead next to it.

"I was so worried about you." She breathed out, rubbing her forehead reassuringly against his scales.

"About me?"

"Yes. They were looking for you," Olivia said as she leaned her cheek against his, arms weaving around his head, embracing tight.

"I don't care about that. I care only for your safety..." Kaden spoke through the ache in his wing as he folded it against his body.

"Oh! I am such a fool... You are hurt, are you not?" Olivia stepped back and looked him over.

"It's... It's just a scratch," he mumbled, sounding unconvincing even to himself as he plopped down, exhausted. Smoke swirled out of his nostrils in a long exhale. He closed his lids for a few moments to gain composure.

"Kaden?!" The alarm and worry in Olivia's voice made him open his eyes again. She was staring at him wide eyed. "Tell me what's wrong... Please. Where are you hurt?"

I wouldn't be less of a dragon if I admit to hurt. Not to her.

"Right wing, I think he hit one of the wing bones," Kaden said and then hissed as he slowly spread his wing out for Olivia's inspection.

She examined it, searching for the wound. "What was that loud boom as we were getting away?" Her fingers whispered over his wing. She bit her lip, the sting grounding her, pushing away the panic and fear.

"I don't know. A new weapon of sorts? I have never seen...or felt...anything like it." Kaden winced when she found the injury. "There."

Oily wetness coated her fingertips. Tears welled up in her eyes as she beheld the crimson liquid. She wouldn't cry again, she needed to focus, to stay coolheaded.

"What should I do?" Olivia withdrew her hand and instinctively wiped the blood on the skirt of her dress.

"There is something stuck inside. The wound is not healing and closing as it should. I need you to look, and if you can't see, try feeling for it." He craned his neck and turned his head so he could see what she was doing.

"Feeling for it? You mean put my fingers in?" Olivia leaned in so she could take a closer look. She was glad for the sun, providing her with light. Not for long though, as darkness threatened to take over the sky, creeping up behind her. She had to hurry because it was her turn to help Kaden, to take care of him.

"Yes, you will need to get out whatever is stuck inside. It will heal once it's out." He offered a reassuring nod.

Olivia took a deep breath, inhaling courage from thin air. "Alright." As she leaned closer, she discerned a circular wound but nothing was sticking out of it. "I do not see anything. Can you lift your wing a bit for me?"

"Anything for you, love." His eyes smiled and he raised his wing above her head.

Olivia walked under, sliding her fingers over his silken membrane as she searched for the wound on the other side.

"No exit," she said after a few moments. "It should be here, judging by the location of the wound on the other side, so there is definitely something still in there."

Finishing her examination, Olivia stepped out from under his wing and he lowered it again with another wince.

"Alright, I can do this," she said more to herself than to him as she rolled up her sleeves. "I do not know anything about surgery or – even butchery. Which might be a help right now. Wish I knew how to do this properly."

"You'll do just fine. I have no doubt about it. Once it's out, we'll rest until late night. The darkness should provide us the cover so we can fly back home, hopefully undetected. I still owe you that tasty lunch of yours." He reassured her, distracting himself from the pain as he braced for what was to come.

Olivia gave back one of her own small smiles. "I would like that very much."

She took a deep breath and closed her eyes for a moment before she began. Inserting her index finger inside, it sank into warm, squishy flesh. Swallowing down the rising bile, Olivia grimaced but never looked away as she prodded deeper, past the soft muscles, until she reached the bone. Kaden tensed, holding his breath, and his muscles cramped around Olivia's finger.

"I am sorry," she mumbled as she clenched her own teeth and felt around for the intruding projectile. A few moments later her finger brushed metal, imbedded into the tissue right next to his bone. It had probably grazed the bone itself, making the damage that much worse. Fortunately, it hadn't broken it.

Kaden hissed through his teeth, holding back the curses that wanted to escape from his lips.

"I found it, just need to get it out now."

Olivia talked Kaden through everything she was doing. It took her a few tries. Kaden sliced the wound wider open with his claw so she could gain better access to it.

Kaden endured it all without so much as a twitch but only a few hisses and painful groans. He held his gaze locked on Olivia. He watched her brow furrow in concentration, while she bit her lower lip as she tried to get the thing out as gently as possible. Beads of nervous sweat rolled down from her temples to her jaw and she wiped them off on her shoulder.

"There!" Olivia held out her hand to display a round iron bullet proudly in her palm. She wondered how such a small object could do so much damage.

Kaden exhaled in relief as his jaw muscles went slack. He had to work out the cramp before speaking. "Finally." He felt like he had flown halfway across this kingdom at full speed while holding his breath.

He was exhausted from it all: the adrenalin and worry that had hit him the moment he heard Olivia's scream, rushing to her, swooping down for her, coming under attack, saving Olivia, getting hurt, flying her to safety with a seriously damaged wing and now enduring the painful process of getting that tiny round thing out. It felt like a week had passed, not a day, the ending of it such a harsh contrast to the soft and tender beginning.

But seeing the relief and a small proud smile on Olivia's face as she stood safe and unharmed in front of him made it all worthwhile.

"Thank you. You really did a great job." Kaden lowered his head to the ground as well, with his hurt wing stretched out and the other tucked in. "I just need to rest a bit and let it heal." He couldn't move any more, and didn't want to.

Olivia's brows furrowed seeing Kaden like that as she cleaned the bullet and then pocketed it. She was past being disgusted by the blood covering her hands, and wiped the last smears on her dress.

"Well, I think that for my excellent skills in dragon care I deserve a new dress," Olivia said in hopes of lightening the mood.

Kaden turned his head so he could look at her better. The sleeves of the dress were rolled up and tied at her upper arm. The fine fabric had blood smeared all over it, but only his blood. He was thankful that none of it was hers.

She couldn't get all the evidence of fishing out the bullet off of her hands. Besides the blood soaking into the fabric, her dress was damp, dirty and dusty so its color was no longer recognizable as light blue.

Kaden's eyes traveled up to her face. Her features, too, were covered in dirt, with a few smears of blood where she had wiped the sweat away with her bloodied hands. Her blue eyes weren't sparkling with life as they usually did. They were clouded with worry and sadness. The exhaustion was evident by the dark circles surrounding them. Some of her hair was plastered against her face with sweat while the rest was a tangled mess around her head, twined with an occasional leaf picked up during their frantic flight.

She looked glorious in Kaden's eyes, his love for her growing. She was no brat, as she had described herself, at least not anymore, but a wonderful woman, although at times quite demanding. The adoration and protectiveness she invoked in him left him baffled.

He also hated seeing her like that - bloody, dirty, worried and exhausted. She deserved better, only the best there was to offer.

"I think I owe you more than just one dress."

"Yes, it seems I could use a clean pair of hands as well." Olivia waved her blood-streaked fingers in front of him.

"Only you could say a thing like that." Kaden shook his head. "Come closer," he commanded gently.

Olivia obliged and stepped closer to him. "Yes?"

"Hold your hands out. I can clean them. It's the least I can do… I'm sorry it's not very – pleasant," Kaden said.

"After what I have just done, hardly anything can be more unpleasant," Olivia responded as she held her hands out. She could only guess what he was about to do.

Her guess was right.

Kaden's forked tongue darted out, and with gentle flicks he licked his blood off her hands. At first, it felt weird, but since his tongue was soft and warm as he cleaned her, Olivia got used to it quite quickly. She didn't mind the wetness of it at all, not after his blood had already painted her hands in red. At times it tickled, so a few giggles escaped past her lips.

It didn't take him long to get the job done as best as he could. His last lick wasn't aimed at her hands but the side of her face where she had a bigger smear of blood across her cheek. It was a playful taste which had Olivia squealing in surprise, and her laugh enveloped him like a soothing remedy.

"Kaden!" she said, another bout of laughter shaking her body when he couldn't resist licking the other side of her face as well. The happy glint was, for the moment, back in his eyes.

"I'm just returning the favor," he defended himself.

"Uh-huh, I bet you are." Olivia winked at him. Her eyes sparkled again, making Kaden's heart feel that much lighter.

"Are you feeling better now?"

Kaden lifted his wing gently before lowering it back down.

"Yes, it already feels less painful. It should heal in a couple of hours."

"I could always kiss it better?" Olivia giggled.

Kaden groaned. "Don't say things like that." He shook his head, but a chuckle escaped him as he lowered his head to the ground, sinking into the overgrown grass, exhaustion taking its toll on him again.

Olivia approached him and planted a smacking kiss between his nostrils. "There, that is my final medicine for full recovery."

"Oh, if it's like that, I should get hurt more often." He winked.

"Kaden!" Olivia glared at him with mock anger. "Actually, you shall only get those if you do not hurt yourself. That should be a good incentive, do you not agree?" She plopped herself next to his head and leaned against his neck.

"Agreed. I don't really enjoy getting hurt, and besides, who could decline an offer like that?"

Olivia sighed and yawned.

"This has turned out to be one… very eventful day. I should have listened to you and your instincts. I am sorry for that." Olivia brought one of her hands up and absentmindedly caressed her dragon. The motion came to her so naturally.

"It's not your fault, love, and you know it." Kaden lowered his lids, enjoying her touch. They faced the sun, catching the last rays on their faces as they watched it set behind the trees.

"But… you would not have gotten hurt."

"And that still isn't your fault. None of it is. I could have argued with you and stayed. I could have been closer, I could have hidden. They could have walked by. They could have ignored you. You didn't invite them. You didn't… Actually… What happened out there?"

Olivia retold the story of what transpired, with no details held back. Kaden deserved to know the truth, no matter how much it bothered him that someone had seen her naked, made advances towards her and said the things that bastard did as well.

His fury was suppressed by her gentle touch. It kept him grounded. He couldn't understand what was going on inside him, his emotions in turmoil, almost out of control, burning a raging storm inside his mind.

"I won't let him take you away. At least not against your wish."

"I know you will not. Hopefully your plan will work and they will follow us out here. Do you think they will figure it out?"

"If they're smart enough to figure out our plan, they will probably think us smart enough not to go back where they first found us. Hiding in plain sight and all that," Kaden said with a shrug. "And if they do come, we will just fly away from there. They'll give up the chase after a while."

"I hope so, because that man... Magnus he called himself, seemed very determined." As the sun set, its warm rays no longer reached Olivia. She pulled her knees to her chest, rolled her sleeves down and hugged herself for the lingering warmth.

"Magnus you said? It sounds familiar." Kaden tried to remember why that name sounded important but couldn't figure it out.

"Yes, Magnus. It really does sound familiar, but I never did memorize the noble families, or the royals... The king is called Magnar, that much I know. Whoever named him Magnus must have wanted a conceited child. I think he really believes he is his own name. He is probably one of the higher nobles." Olivia shrugged and yawned. "Oh! The prince is called Magnus! What if it *is* the prince?"

"What would the prince be doing out in that forest?"

"I thought the same thing... Maybe... Maybe it is just someone named like him. You know, royal names always tend to be popular." Or so she hoped. She winced at the memory of throwing the rock at his head. Although she'd probably still do the same even if she knew for sure he was a prince; maybe she would have been a bit more reluctant, though.

"Maybe; probably not. It doesn't matter now. Come on Liv, snuggle up. We should try and catch some sleep before we fly back. It should be safe to nap. They can't catch up with us that fast," Kaden said as he lifted his other wing for Olivia to crawl under and cuddle closer to him for warmth.

"Good night, my dragon." Olivia smiled against his scales when she settled close. "Thank you for everything." She gave him a soft peck before she rested her head on her hand which was curled under it. She was facing Kaden and her whole body was pressed up against him, her other hand placed against those silky scales. She just couldn't help but keep physical contact with him. It was very reassuring.

"Good night, my love," Kaden murmured as he twisted his head and rested it above hers. His breath made her hair dance around her neck.

It was comforting.

She inhaled his woodsy scent mixed with the aroma of fire dancing on his breath.

It made her feel safe.

And the sound of his breathing mingled with the sound of his heartbeat made her relax.

It lulled her to peaceful sleep.

CHAPTER 17

Theo kept his sharp, light brown eyes trained on the fleeing dragon and the woman it carried in its clawed hands. Jaw hanging open, he could barely believe what he had just witnessed. He wasn't even sure there was a word for how confused he was. *Did the dragon just save the woman from Magnus? Or was she calling out for someone else and it just stole her away?* But that thought didn't seem right to him.

His ma would have said 'befuddled'. He was befuddled by the whole event. He had seen the relief on the woman's face when she had heard the beast roar and he couldn't forget the way she had just stood there, in the middle of the stream, trusting it with her life. He knew the feeling very well, trusting Damien just as much. He pitied them though, because knowing Magnus, the prince was never going to give up on his chase now. The stakes had gotten even higher for the prince. Not only had he failed to kill the dragon, he had just encountered the first woman ever to deny him. Magnus had lost face twice.

As Theo kept his gaze on the retreating forms of the dragon and woman while they veered to the right, his eyes roamed around and he filed in his memory the necessary orientation points. It would help with following the dragon and its maiden as precisely as possible. He didn't want to, but he also didn't think he had much choice at that moment. Nothing was as simple as it seemed. Staying with Magnus, Damien and he might be useful. For whom or what, he didn't know yet.

Down below, Magnus paced, stomping back and forth. He had raw, shiny burns on his arms and chest in the interlacing pattern of his chainmail, heated by the dragon's fire. It had felt like he was trapped in a cauldron being boiled alive. The sleeves of his white shirt were rolled up, his arms an angry red because the heat under the armor had almost reached the blistering point. He was glad he had managed to protect his face, though. A lot depended on his handsome features, but his hair hadn't avoided the damage. It would have to be cut, much to his disappointment. Women loved running their fingers through his golden locks.

When the redheaded scout descended back to the ground, Magnus raised an eyebrow at him. Fury scored his face in a deep scowl, and Theo noticed that there were still streaks of dried blood on his forehead. Magnus tapped his foot, arms crossed over his chest as he waited for an answer to his unspoken question.

Theo nodded. "If we don't stop for rest, we might reach them during the night. The dragon was fast and managed to fly far. But you did manage to hurt it, Your Highness, much to our advantage. They were forced to land. For how long, I don't know."

Magnus's eyes glittered triumphantly, a nasty smile snaking across his lips. "They had it coming! The monster was fortunate this time, but next time it won't be. There will be no stopping tonight, not until we reach them!" Magnus swiveled and stalked away to cool off in the stream once again.

The men checked the horses and supplies, and shared some food, their last meal of the day. An ominous silence settled over their little unit. Now that they had seen the dragon with their own eyes and witnessed what it was capable of, everybody was very wary. Even Reed was quiet, and far more cautious than usual. He checked his armor for weaknesses three or four times, testing the strength of his belt and practicing with his shield, bringing it up to cover his head over and over, keeping his reflexes sharp. Nobody liked the idea of dying by burning to a crisp.

After the gear was packed up, they continued the chase on horseback, going back down the mountain. Magnus still wasn't wearing his armor. His skin had cooled a bit from the dip in the cool water but it was still sensitive, aggravated, making wearing his heavy armor very uncomfortable. He didn't, however, part with his trusty sword.

Theo and Damien took the lead with others following closely behind. Charlie had been quiet since the whole event and her eyes were still wide with wonder, awe and fear. Even Reed throwing hungry glances at her hadn't fazed her. Cassiel, the dark-skinned knight, was the only stoic one among them. He never seemed disturbed by anything, and no one ever quite knew what he was thinking. The rest of the knights were distraught and apprehensive as they followed their prince to their unknown, but possibly deadly fate.

Every once in a while, Theo would get off his horse and climb a tree to check their course. He made adjustments regarding the direction they were heading when necessary and they successfully followed the dragon's flight from below.

As they drew closer, Magnus' fury began to turn inward, channeled into acute concentration, and his scowl froze into an eerie mask of determination. However, the menace never left his eyes. He didn't care about anything or anyone around him, but remained focused solely upon his goal.

With the last rays of the setting sun shining down on them, Theo climbed a tree for the final time and memorized the direction they would need to adhere to.

"This is where they turned right," he said once his feet touched the ground. "We'll need to follow the stars from now on."

"I do *not* care how you do it, just get us there. It is what I am paying you for," Magnus said. His horse stomped beneath him, neighing its consent.

Theo nodded. He swung up onto his horse and neared Damien. They quietly consulted about which stars they would need to follow once the night had fallen, trusting the sky to show them the way.

"Is there a problem?" Magnus approached the pair from behind. He just wanted to move. The closer they got to the dragon, the longer the remaining distance felt.

"No problem at all, Your Highness," Theo spoke up. Damien hadn't ever spoken much in front of the others, except to Theo of course, and Charlie. "I was just consulting with Damien how to proceed further, seeing as the night will fall soon. And not to worry…" he added quickly, "we have it all figured out once the stars are up."

"Good, now get going again," Magnus barked out and cracked his neck to the side as he waited for his guides to take the lead again.

Theo and Damien exchanged a look, reassuring each other and silently agreeing to a future private conversation.

"Yes, Your Highness." They both bowed their heads. Theo rolled his eyes before looking back up. They turned their horses in the right direction.

The other knights, wearing heavier armor than Theo

and Damien, were reaching the point of exhaustion, and their horses as well. Magnus, though, wasn't paying attention to them. He wasn't wearing his armor, so he didn't feel as tired as they did, and saw no point in stopping for a break.

As the night fell, Charlie barely stayed upright. She struggled to keep her eyes open while comfortably settled on the back of her trusty grey mare Raine. Chin dropping to her chest, she jerked upright. Her eyes drifted shut again.

"Lady Charlotte?" A deep voice brought her back from the losing battle against the comfort of slumber. She looked up and focused on Cassiel's concerned face. She could barely make out his features in the darkness, but they were by now used to traveling during the night, lighting up their torches only if necessary.

"I told you not to call me that, Cass. I ain't no lady and you know it." She gave him a small smile that never reached her eyes.

"All women are ladies to me." He bowed his head a tad. "And thus must be treated accordingly."

Cassiel was the only one, besides Theo and Damien, who hadn't used her services. He would come to her, but mostly to talk about nonessential topics or just to enjoy her company quietly. He had always been a gentleman, proper and very kind to her. He kept himself chaste, waiting for the right woman, for his future wife. He was a real knight in every sense of the word. In her opinion, he only had one fault: doing Magnus' bidding. Loyalty, at the same time a virtue and a flaw.

Earlier that day, Charlie had found out that Cassiel was one of the knights not on the prince's own payroll. He was one of the king's guardsmen, just like Reed, Cathal, Galor, Lance and Colin. He had sworn his oaths of allegiance to Magnus' father. The king had assigned him to Magnus as one of the prince's personal bodyguards, same as Reed. Charlie got the impression that the king did not approve of Reed's influence over the prince, but he was too good a fighter to leave out of the prince's party. Perhaps the king had hoped Cassiel would be a balancing force, but Cassiel seemed to believe the prince was responsible for his own destiny, and the king had underestimated Reed. Charlie suspected the king also underestimated the malicious nature of his own son. Or was it inherited?

"Now tell me, my lady, how are you faring?" Cassiel's voice was filled with concern for her, the gentle tone the same one he used when giving alms to beggars or tending the wounded. He saw her as just another poor unfortunate soul, but one worthy of respect.

"I'm alright Cass, just exhausted." Charlie yawned. "Very tired and scared. Did you see its fire? Its size!"

"Yes, my lady. Quite a dangerous beast."

"And we're going after it. Is Magnus crazy?"

Cassiel grimaced and threw a glance in the prince's direction. Glad for not being overheard, he chuckled. "You should mind what you say around him."

"Sorry…" Charlie whispered.

"I was raised not to speak against my prince, but… but if I were not sworn to his duty, if I were just another common man, I would probably have shared your opinion."

Charlie grinned. She reached for her water skin. She tipped it up but nothing came out. She groaned.

"Here." Cassiel pulled out his own from a side saddlebag. "You can have mine." He shifted his horse closer, extending the container to Charlie. "And do not worry," he added as she took it from his hand, "you can have whatever is left in it. I had enough before we departed, and I can always ask someone else to share theirs.”

“Thank you.” Charlie took a few humble sips, enough to moisten her lips and subdue the thirst. She would save the rest for later. “Tell me,” she tucked away the water-skin. “If you don’t mind sharing, how’d you come to be in the service of the royal family?” Pulling out her cloak from a saddlebag, she wrapped it around her shoulders.

“Ah. My family has been in the service of the royals for generations. I inherited the cloak from my father, who was in King Magnar’s service, until I came of age and swore an oath to the King, and then, as I said before, to Magnus himself.” Cassiel spoke in a hushed voice, leaning sideways, closer to Charlie. He didn’t want to be overheard. “It is a family tradition to serve the king or the prince, and I was very proud when my father deemed me ready to take up the duty. He was teaching me and training me since I was barely ten seasons old. And I wish to hold up to our family name.”

“Oh, so you’ve been with Magnus for a long time?” Charlie whispered back.

“Yes.”

“Has he always been so mean?”

Cassiel glanced forward. No one took any interest in their conversation at the moment, but he knew it would only be a matter of time before Magnus noticed, even from where he rode up ahead, right behind Theo and Damien.

“He has always been … difficult. Very…” Cassiel shook his head, “Ah, I should *not* be talking about him, my lady. But I can only tell you that he has gotten worse during this journey.”

Charlie nodded in understanding. Hand covering her mouth, she yawned again.

“Rest on that mare of yours. She is a good horse and I will make sure you do not fall off.”

Charlie graced him with a small smile of gratitude as she let herself fall asleep on her horse. It wasn't the first time she had done so during the long journey. With some practice and the occasional fall on her butt, she had managed to handle it. Having someone keep an eye on her helped her relax and ease into the swaying gait of the horse, lulling her to sleep.

Late into the night, Magnus and his men reached the end of the forest. In front of them spread an abandoned field. They could only discern the overgrown grass, reaching past the horses' knees, stretching as far as they could see under the cover of darkness.

Magnus sat up straighter in his saddle as he looked around. "Is this it?"

"It should be. That is my best guess, though they were far away and barely visible." Theo halted his horse and the others followed his lead. "They might have flown further."

"Torches," Magnus ordered as he got off his weary horse.

Everyone followed suit, grateful for the break in their trek. It had been nine hours since they had last stopped and they had gone over twenty-five miles through the forest. All of them were tired, apart from Magnus who was high on adrenalin and determination.

"Look around for any signs of them." Magnus took a torch of his own and started the search.

They left the horses near the forest and the only person not participating in the search was Charlie. She untacked her horse, used the saddle as a pillow and fell asleep on the ground as soon as she lay down. Damien covered her with his cloak as well, providing extra warmth, before he joined Theo in the search.

The knights spread out and dragged their exhausted forms through the field. All they wanted to do was take their armor off, eat and sleep like they never had to wake up again. Much to their misfortune, Magnus was having none of that. His perseverance was taking a toll on Reed as well, causing the prince's right-hand man to surreptitiously take sips from his waterskin, filled with rum.

An unnatural silence surrounded them. The forest held its breath, waiting to see what they would find and do, watching over them as a godly spectator. The tension was almost palpable, amplifying with each step they took.

After about fifteen minutes of stumbling half-blindly through the field, Galor called out, "I think I found something."

Magnus was the first one to reach him. Holding his torch over his knight's findings, he could see where the overgrown grass was completely flattened, as if a big creature had rested there. "Damien!"

"Yes, Your Highness?" Damien swiftly appeared next to Magnus, who pointed with his torch at the grass.

Damien knelt and studied the flattened area as best as he could under the light of the torch. The other knights joined in, surrounding them with their own torches. Damien circled the disturbed area of the field while Magnus waited, jaw clenched, a fist balled at his side. The prince knew that Damien was the best hunter he could find and that he was an expert at reading tracks.

The disturbance in the field seemed fresh. There were no tracks leading to it, though. Damien could barely make out human footprints, too. It would all be so much easier to figure out in the daylight, but he knew he had no choice about the timing. When he felt around with his palms, the squashed grass underneath still had some lingering heat to it and on the next sweep of his hand something sticky and wet stuck to his skin. Bringing his fingers to his face, he studied the substance, smelled it and even brought a tiny bit to his tongue.

"Someone was here," the hunter said as he stood up and walked over to Magnus, who was now surrounded by the rest of his men. "They obviously rested here. There are no approaching tracks, only in this area. Some big creature was lying over there. A person was with it, too. I noticed a few tracks but it's too dark to be sure. Also, there is some blood." He raised his bloodied fingers to prove his point. "Which would correspond with the dragon being hurt." Damien took a deep breath, bracing himself for Magnus' reaction to his next words. "Obviously, whoever it was, they are not here now. They left, most likely flew away, not long before we arrived." Damien was being objective as usual, not admitting to it being a dragon, but instead just saying it was a big creature, letting Magnus draw his own conclusions.

The prince shut his eyes, gnashing his teeth. *Oh, this dragon is smart… It will make my victory so much sweeter.*

He opened his eyes and stared at the spot where the dragon had lain. He had been so close, twice today. Tomorrow he was going to have its head. Slowly exhaling the held breath, Magnus turned to his men.

"If it is as smart as I have a feeling it might be, the dragon just misled us here. We will go back to the stream and search for tracks there. We might find hers if they walked to the water –" he gave Damien a questioning look and the knight nodded his head in return. "And we can follow her tracks back to wherever they were hiding. We may or may not find them there, but we will stay and camp for a few days if necessary. I do not want to take my chances in case they do return there. If not… well… we just better find them."

Magnus studied his men and only now noticed the exhaustion on their faces. He had really pushed them too far today, but none had complained. He was proud of them, and proud of himself for having that power over them. The adrenalin running through his veins slowed as the events of the day took their toll on his body as well. "We will rest here for the remainder of the night and morning." With nothing else to say, Magnus marched away from his men and back towards their horses.

They set up their camp at the edge of the forest, near to where Charlie had fallen sleep. The men didn't go to sleep yet, since their stomachs were growling for attention.

Magnus ate his meal in solitude. His silence unnerving. His narrowed gaze and flexing fists kept everyone at a distance and silent. It was quite an uncomfortable dinner compared to their usual rowdy ones.

After he finished eating, the prince spent some time whetting his sword while the rest cleaned up. The whet stone stroked up and down the edge of the blade, the sword issuing a soft, rhythmic, metallic scream. Magnus was so engrossed in his ministrations that he didn't notice Theo and Damien sneaking out of the camp together, nor did he notice Reed approaching Charlie's sleeping form with a slightly drunken stumble to his step. Lost in his own world, he imagined hundreds of ways to kill and skin a dragon, chopping off its head. He fantasized about mounting it on the wall, decorating the great hall of his home.

When Reed approached Charlie, he nudged her with his foot. "Wake up, whore," he slurred.

Charlie mumbled and turned to her other side. The nudge was replaced by a slight kick, almost missing her completely when he lost his balance. "C'mon, 'tis time to earn your keep."

Charlie winced at the kick and roused. Rubbing the sleep out of her eyes, she searched for the person who had disturbed her slumber. "What do you want Reed? Go to sleep!" She rolled but Reed's foot stopped her from turning away. He stepped over her, a foot on each side of her body.

"Oh, no you don't. Not tonight." He swayed. "Got some tension I need to get rid of before I can sleep… if you know what I mean." He wagged his eyebrows and licked his lips, smacking them for effect.

Charlie knew better than to argue with him; she had learned her lesson. It would only make him violent and she didn't need that, not after the exhausting day she had. If she handled him smartly, she might get off easy tonight.

"Alright, lover, let's see whatcha got for me tonight," she said as she looked up at him, the light of the fire dancing across her features, the golden glow complementing her fiery red curls.

"You're fucking beautiful." Reed was unbuttoning his pants while he kept his eyes trained on her face.

"Lay down, big guy, and let me take care of you," Charlie said, patting a spot next to her. She threw Damien's cloak out of the way, not wanting to taint it.

Reed took off his own cloak and laid it down next to her before he sprawled his drunken self over it. He reached forward, wanting to grope her breast. Those hands could be quite cruel, she recalled.

"Nuh-uh," Charlie scolded, waving her finger, a seductive tilt to her lips. All the while, she gagged on the inside. But it was a job that had to be done. Her job and she would bear through. "It's my time to play and yours to enjoy." She removed his hands from her body, hoping he wouldn't grab for her again and she rewarded him with an honest smile when she succeeded.

Charlie reached for his drink that she knew he hid from Magnus and offered it to him from her lips. If she could get him even more drunk than he already was, it would all be over sooner, maybe even before she began. Only if he fell asleep. In the morning, he wouldn't remember anything anyway and she would praise him as usual, making him think he got what he wanted the night before.

She took her time unbuttoning his shirt, kissing the trail her fingers made. His hard, athletic body didn't disgust her. She wondered if it were a curse: pretty face, ugly soul. That was her experience so far, with both Magnus and Reed. She shook the thought away; Damien, Theo, and Cassiel proved otherwise. Reed's sloppy, alcohol-laced kisses were the worst to bear, and when he took her roughly, whether she was complicit or not, was the most horrible. She had learned to play along for her own sake.

When she reached his pants, she rubbed his manhood over the fabric in slow, taunting strokes. She hoped he would fall asleep soon, but looking up into his face, she knew he would not leave her alone unless he had some sort of release. After she took his manhood out of its restraints, she rose to her feet, never breaking eye contact as she slowly pulled down her undergarments from under her skirt and threw them at his face with a fake giggle. He wouldn't know the difference anyway.

Reed caught them and brought them to his nose, inhaling her scent deeply before putting them in his pockets, just as she had hoped; it would be his morning reminder of a night he wouldn't remember.

Next, she reached into her saddlebag for her secret weapon: a scented massage oil slightly laced with mint. All the men loved it when she used it. She put a few drops into her palm and knelt next to him.

Her hands rubbed up and down, building up his pleasure. When he tangled his hands in her fiery tresses, a stinging grip of her hair, guiding her head to replace her hands, she leaned over and distracted him by kissing him deeply with a rough bite on his lower lip, just the way he liked it.

The night filled with the sounds of the crackling fire and Reed's grunts of pleasure. The others were used to it and knew not to disturb. Especially when she was with him.

Charlie had learned a few very useful tricks on the streets. They helped her work less than she would in a whorehouse. Using them, she was able to bring Reed a quick release with her skillful hands.

Once done, she cleaned them both and snuggled close. Charlie kissed his chest and settled her head on it as she looked up at him. Sleep already called to him. "You were amazing," she said in a breathless voice and was glad when she saw that a small tired smile appeared on his face. *Good, he will remember that,* she cheered for her small victory as she settled into his tight embrace for sleep. She didn't mind sharing the body heat; it was a chilly night, and it would help her in convincing him the next day that he had had a wild night before falling asleep.

ဆ

About the same time, Theo and Damien snuck into the woods. When they were at a safe distance, Damien reached out and interlaced his fingers with Theo's. The redhead beamed as they continued to walk in silence.

Quietness surrounded them, only the crunch of their footsteps following. Theo inhaled the pine scented air deep through his nostrils and let the peace of the forest settle into his soul. Moments like this, he treasured the most — Damien and him strolling through the forest, undisturbed and free. They walked for a while until Theo pulled on Damien's hand, making him stop. They spent a moment not saying a thing and not moving, just listening to the sounds around them, making sure they weren't followed. It was unusually quiet and Theo was the first one to make a sound by letting out a breath of relief.

Damien turned to face him and brought his hands up, resting his palms on each side of Theo's neck, caressing his jaw. Their eyes locked and Damien pulled Theo close for a soft kiss. As their lips melded, their tongues danced the familiar dance. What started as a soft peck soon turned into a passionate declaration of yearning and love. In the eerie silence of the night only their moans of approval and quickened breaths could be heard.

As they broke apart for some much-needed air, Damien kept his hands on Theo's neck. He didn't want him to pull away so he rested his forehead against Theo's, who in return wrapped his hands around Damien's waist.

"This has probably been the longest day in my life," Damien mumbled.

"I agree…I'm so grateful to have these few moments alone with you at the end of it."

Damien nodded.

"What are we gonna do?" Theo spoke softly as he closed his eyes.

Damien's exhale brushed against Theo's lips. "Honestly? I don't know."

A few moments of silence followed before Damien spoke again. "Stay for now? See what happens next? When a fight breaks out we stay in the back anyway. It is the safest position, and if it gets too dangerous, we get out. Take Charlie with us?"

Theo opened his eyes, stepped away from Damien and led him by the hand towards a tree. He sat down and rested his back against the trunk as Damien settled between his legs, his back to Theo's chest.

"I agree, because I have this feeling we should stay with

Magnus for now," Theo responded as he wrapped his hands around Damien and rested his chin on the other's shoulder. "I have a hunch something big is going to happen and we can't just abandon the others – they'll need us if we're going to face the dragon. I can't just leave now; it wouldn't be – honorable. Reed can die in a ball of flame for all I care, but Lance and Donovan are good men, and Cass, and..." He trailed off, shaking his head. "In time, I think we will do more damage control by staying with him, and when the moment is right, we will know. That's when we will leave."

Damien nodded. He had learned to trust Theo's instincts.

"Alright, back to Charlie then. What do we do about her?"

Theo groaned. "That conversation at the inn… how are we to help her if she doesn't want it? We could easily assist her in getting away. She… no woman should be forced to do that."

"You know she's not forced."

Theo snorted. "Let's not get into that subject. There's a lot she's been forced to do that she otherwise wouldn't have, no matter what she says. I just… It's hard to sit back and let things like that happen."

"I was thinking," Damien said as Theo tightened the embrace, "just because she doesn't want us to help her get away from Magnus, doesn't mean we can't help at all."

"I'm listening."

"We could always intercept others. Mostly Reed."

"Yes. I'd gladly get into a fight with him over her. We can't protect her from Magnus, though."

Damien sighed. "I know. Let's just hope it all ends well, and when we go our separate ways from Magnus, we can take her along, help her find a real job, and a place to live.

Somewhere she'll be safe. Maybe as a maid for someone, or something of that sort."

"Aye. That's a good plan."

They spent some time just snuggled up, basking in each other's presence, sharing the warmth of their bodies. The night wasn't cold, but the breeze of the early spring brought a chill with it.

"I have an idea." Damien said. He twisted around and faced Theo with a mischievous grin on his face while he straddled his lover's legs.

"Oh, no! I'm not sure I want to know. That smile of yours… You are up to no good again." Theo shot a fake glare at Damien and tried to hold back his smile. He loved it when Damien was being playful.

"It has been a very tiring day, both emotionally and physically, and I think we deserve some respite," Damien said while loosening the cord around Theo's pants.

"I'm listening…" Theo didn't bother to suppress the smile stretching across his face as his heart sped up, the flutter in his belly the best remedy for such an exhausting day. He ran his fingers through Damien's short curls.

"I'll let my mouth do the talking… in a different language." With a saucy wink Damien trailed his fingers down Theo's front, unbuttoning the leather armor straps, and then sliding it off those wide shoulders. His hands slipping under the hem of his lover's shirt, Damien raised the dark green fabric, revealing smooth skin that taunted him to taste it. Lips licked, he lowered his head and left a wet trail up Theo's stomach, over his chest, and along the sweet-tasting neck. Once he threw the shirt away, his mouth seared Theo's with a scorching fire, an ardent declaration of love and devotion. He couldn't believe he had been so lucky to find this man, and have his feelings be reciprocated.

"I adore you. I can't wait till all of this is over and we settle down." Damien nipped on Theo's bottom lip and his hand slipped inside the other man's pants.

Theo only moaned his approval, fingers tangling into Damien's black curls as that loving mouth moved lower toward his lap.

ᔆ

"Shite! Do you think Charlie is alright? We've been away for quite a bit," Theo said as they made their way back to the camp, fastening up his leather armor.

"Probably. She was already asleep and everyone was dead tired. Most likely nobody had anything of that sort on their mind," Damien said as he gave a reassuring squeeze to Theo's hand.

Theo raised his eyebrows. "You did."

"Yes. Yes, I did." The proud, smug smile spread across Damien's face made Theo chuckle.

When they reached the campsite, everyone was already asleep. The flames of the fire swirled, washing their surroundings in a soft orange light. Scanning the sleeping forms sprawled out around them, they noticed Charlie huddled up with Reed. Both men's eyes narrowed in a disapproving scowl.

The timber in the hearth cracked and popped.

"He better not ..." Theo said as he stomped towards Charlie's and Reed's sleeping forms.

"Theo!" Damien hissed in a whisper as he hurried to stop the redhead from doing whatever he had in mind. Nothing good would come of it. He knew Theo's feelings for Charlie were growing because he had lost his twin sister when he had been younger, and Damien thought that Charlie reminded Theo of her. His sister had died of lung fever as a child. Their parents had left her in Theo's charge so they could work for the much needed food and medicine. He believed he should have done more to care of her. The guilt still haunted him. Thus, Theo had become very protective of Charlie, and taking into account what she did for a living, this new attitude didn't bode well. They hadn't learned of her history, only that Magnus had found her prostituting on the street. They dared not ask. How did one ask a prostitute, young one as her, why and how she begun that… work. Maybe she would volunteer the answer on her own? He just hoped that Theo would stick to their plan and not make things worse for her.

Damien managed to stop Theo on time, pushed him back and stood in front of him. A frown sat heavily upon his face. "Don't be stupid, Theo," he warned and turned away, not giving Theo the chance to respond.

On quiet feet, Damien approached Charlie and knelt next to her. He brushed away a curl from her face and caressed her cheek with the back of his hand. "Little Red?"

"Hmm?" Charlie mumbled as her eyes fluttered open, fighting off the fog of sleep.

"Is everything alright?" Damien asked as he looked towards Reed.

Still in a daze, Charlie turned her head, almost surprised to see Reed there but then she remembered. "Yes, I'm fine. I handled him well," she said with a small smile as she settled back to sleep. Damien leaned over and planted a soft kiss on the crown of her head. "Sleep well."

He stood up and turned back to Theo, whose face relaxed with relief as he gave a nod of gratitude.

Theo held out a hand to Damien. After making sure everyone was fast asleep, the two embraced and shared a short, lingering kiss.

"I love you," Damien whispered against Theo's lips.

"I love you, too." Theo ran a hand through Damien's curls. "Good night."

"Sleep well," Damien said back, and after stealing one last peck, they parted, heading toward the opposite sides of the fire where they would sleep for the remainder of the night.

CHAPTER 18

Flying back towards the cave, Olivia safe in his arms, Kaden looked over his shoulder towards the field they had left only moments ago. His brows furrowed. Torch lights sprang to life in the field, dancing through the night like flickering fireflies.

They actually managed to find us... well, almost. The knight and his men are more resourceful than I thought. Olivia did warn me.

Kaden gave thanks for the eerie silence which had descended upon them, prompting him to wake instantly. His wing had healed enough, and he had managed to coax Olivia to wakefulness just in time before taking her in his arms again and flying away. He didn't want her riding on his back. They had no rope, and while she was in his gentle embrace, he could keep her warm and safe.

Olivia pressed her face into her dragon, protecting it from the chill air whipping around her head. She trembled, her teeth chattering, muscles cramped against the cold seeping into her bones despite Kaden's warmth. She would never ask him to take her flying during the night again, so high up.

After reaching the clearing from where they usually took off, they walked back to their cave in silence. Olivia was too tired to speak as she dragged her feet along, rubbing her hands together to chase away the biting cold.

Kaden's mind was abuzz with worry as different possible scenarios flitted through his head. He made sure, though, that the result was always the same: Olivia safe.

When they neared the cave, an indistinct noise echoed from inside, which made Kaden groan in annoyance. "Now what?"

"What is it, Kaden?" Olivia took an instinctive step closer to the dragon, coming fully awake instantly.

"Someone's inside," he grumbled, eyes narrowed and ablaze with annoyance.

Can we get some respite? Kaden tilted his head up and looked at the sky. He breathed out a deep sigh and a cloud of smoke enveloped them. Olivia waved a hand in front of her face to clear the air.

"Is it them?" Olivia said as she leaned into Kaden, eyes darting around, expecting an ambush, men jumping at them out of the nighttime shadows.

"I do not think so, unless they left someone behind." Kaden scanned the surrounding trees, his sharp, draconic eyesight penetrating the darkness far better than Olivia's. The forest was awash in greys and blacks but nothing stood out among the trees and bushes, only an occasional hedgehog or a weasel scurrying along.

"I don't see anybody out here." He tilted his head to the side, listening carefully. "And I don't hear anything out of place. You should be safe here while I check what creature invaded our home. Just… just stay close to the cave's mouth. Call for me if anything happens."

Olivia took a deep, brave breath before she answered. "Alright, I will. Be safe." She gave her dragon a quick hug before he went in. She only took one step inside the cave's mouth then pressed herself against the wall, straining her eyes and ears for any signs of trouble or danger. She wasn't concerned for herself, but for Kaden. A few moments later, Kaden's chuckle rumbled, bursting out of the cave, accompanied by growling and then anxious whining. Curiosity got the better of her and she took careful steps deeper into the cave.

"Kaden?" she called out in a hesitant voice. Nothing was visible and she could only hear the dragon's amused laughter and soft whimpers from some unknown source. Her hands followed the rocky wall, leading her deeper inside.

Olivia heard the now familiar intake of Kaden's breath and closed her eyes so she wouldn't be blinded by the sudden light. When the light of the fire danced behind her closed lids, she first opened one eye to peer out at the scene playing out before her. Her other eye snapped open, too, in surprise.

Before her, Kaden was glaring at a tiny creature because it had started growling at Olivia.

A wolf pup, six or seven months old by her guess and black from tip to tail, shivered in the furthest corner of the cave away from Kaden, lying low, now whimpering. It had probably stumbled upon the cave in search of food and shelter.

Still feeling threatened by the day's events, Kaden put himself between the tiny wolf and Olivia. The pup growled at Olivia, warning her back when she tried to step around the dragon. Kaden snarled in return, the sound almost deafening in the echoing cave. Olivia jumped up in fright as she turned to look at Kaden wide-eyed. He even went as far as to bare his fangs and teeth at the little furry creature in front of them.

He really could be a frightening sight.

The pup stopped growling and whimpered again. It

tucked its tail between its hind legs, lowering its head in submission as it pressed itself further away, against the wall of the cave. Kaden continued to snarl, smoke swirling out of his nostrils, and the pup submitted even further. It warily rolled over, exposing its belly to the dragon. It whimpered louder, and its bladder no longer held against the fear coursing through its wolfish little body.

The sound and the sight snapped Olivia out of her trance-like state.

"Kaden!" she snapped towards her dragon. "Stop it! You are scaring him to death!" She stepped forward, placing herself between Kaden and the pup, putting her hands up, fingers splayed.

"He growled at you!" Kaden grumbled once he ceased with the snarling. "He threatened you!"

"Oh, for goodness sake, Kaden, he is just frightened, trying to protect himself. Look at him, he is no threat, even without you around." Olivia pointed her finger at the still whimpering ball of black fur.

"Kaden, please." Olivia pleaded when her demands didn't work. Her voice was gentle and lilting as she tried to coax Kaden to stop glaring at the poor pup with murder in his eyes.

The sound of Olivia's soft voice made Kaden avert his gaze from the pup, towards her. Dark circles around her eyes dulled their sparkle. Her hair was a mess from the wind and she stood there, shivering. He noticed her sway, barely staying awake on her own two feet. Those sky blue orbs of hers were boring into him, begging for some peace, some respite. He couldn't say no to her. Not ever.

Kaden let out a sigh of defeat. The dragon craned his neck around Olivia and lowered his snout down to the frightened pup's belly, nudging him gently. When he got no response except for a terrified whimper, he moved a bit to the side and nudged the pup again, coaxing him to stand up, or at least roll back over. The pup obliged and turned over, still lying obediently on its belly.

"Was that so hard to do?" The sound of Olivia scolding him made Kaden's eyes alight with happiness and amusement; she looked utterly adorable. "And how do you know the pup is a he?"

"I could tell." Kaden retreated after he threw a last warning glare at the now silent and obedient pup. "Are you cold, love?" he asked once he brought his head lower so he could face her. He loved staring into her eyes.

"I am a bit… and tired, too." She yawned. She raised her hand up, instinctively scratching Kaden's snout.

A rumble of contentment escaped from the dragon's throat. "I love it when you touch me."

Olivia's cheeks flushed, a pink tinge spreading over the milky white canvas, and a wide, happy smile crept up her face, the now familiar and constant butterflies taking flight in her belly. "I cannot help it; you are so cuddly." She winked.

"Cuddly? I am cuddly?!" Kaden sputtered, teasing, raising his voice slightly, which made the pup whimper again. The distress in Olivia's eyes when she looked back at the pup made Kaden lower his voice, almost to a whisper. "I am a big, bad dragon. We are not cuddly, we are frightening."

An image of Kaden snarling at the pup, threatening with those deadly fangs, flashed in her mind and she mentally agreed that he could indeed be frightening. At this moment though, with his head lowered, as he fought to keep his eyes open while he enjoyed Olivia's touch and with his words spoken just above a whisper, he seemed quite the opposite of his description.

Olivia had to chuckle at that. "Indeed you are my dear,

scary dragon." She leaned in to nuzzle at his rough-scaled cheek. He would always be cuddly to her.

The pup yipped, disrupting their tender moment. They turned and looked at him. He had been watching the exchange quietly and rather studiously for such a young pup. There was much intelligence hiding behind those pale blue eyes. He yipped again, and looked towards the previous day's fish.

"I think this little boy is trying to tell us something, are you not?" Olivia cooed as she moved away from Kaden and took slow steps towards the pup.

Kaden instantly missed the contact and narrowed his eyes at the little wolf, blaming it for distracting Olivia from their intimate moment.

When the pup made brief eye contact with him, he bared his teeth at Kaden. The action caused Olivia to pause in her step and Kaden to snarl slightly again. The pup understood the warning and looked back at Olivia, laying his head on his paws.

Taking it as a good sign, Olivia continued approaching the pup with measured steps. She outstretched her hand in an unthreatening manner, offering it to the cute little pup for sniffing.

Kaden stood guard behind her.

The pup craned his neck forward and sniffed her hand with reluctance and caution. After he was satisfied that she was not a threat, he licked at her fingers as a gesture of truce.

"Oh, such a sweet puppy. Are you hungry?" Olivia queried in a gentle voice as she kneeled down and slowly brought her hand up so she could pet him. She didn't, though, notice the victorious glance the pup threw at Kaden, making the dragon narrow his eyes at the clever bundle of fur. He would have to keep a close eye on the little wolf.

Kaden snorted. "You do realize he is *not* a puppy." Jealousy laced his words.

Olivia only gave him a look that said, *"Do I look that stupid?"*

Kaden just turned his head away, snout tilted up. "I'll… I'll just go get some food for myself and the little… thing, and you too. We should be safe for the remainder of the night." He spat out another burning blob. "Use that for tonight's fire. If you need anything, check the back cave." His cave was becoming cramped as he carefully turned around.

Olivia noticed the change in his mood and she didn't like it one bit. He was grumpy, and he seemed jealous that she was paying attention to the pup and not to him. She preferred her dragon happy and knew exactly what to do.

"Oh, and Kaden?" Olivia called out to him before he disappeared from her sight.

"Yes, Liv?" He stopped and turned his head so he could see her. His voice was soft and tinged with sadness.

"I will always love *you* the best, Kaden," she said with a bright smile on her face, the light of the fire dancing merrily in her eyes.

Kaden's eyes lit up with immense joy and he even managed to stretch a real grin across his features. Smiling was hard for him; his mouth not built for it. He took a moment to drink in the sight of her, beaming at him, love shining through her bright blue eyes. Kaden bowed his head in respect and gratitude, turned around and left the cave on a much happier note. The butterflies in his belly almost made him fly without the need of his wings. But he did fly, in spirit.

That, in there, was the best moment of his entire life, now and the one from before.

While Kaden was out, he noticed that the craving to take from others had somewhat lessened. The desire to steal came to him since he had been... born as a dragon. Always hard to control or fight off. He wondered why the change now, was it also a part of the curse? Maybe all of it would go away. Maybe it was because of Olivia.

&

Olivia's heart warmed at the happy glint in Kaden's eyes after her proclamation and she turned her attention back to the pup. She scratched him behind his ear gently and said, "You will learn to love him, too."

A few moments later, she rose to her feet, slowly as to not frighten the pup. "Come on, little boy, let us go see what we need from the back cave while we wait for Kaden. You will eat better than that old fish when he returns. We will have to throw it out." She took a couple of steps towards the back cave but the pup didn't follow.

Olivia turned around, crouched down and beckoned the little wolf. "You are safe now. I will not harm you. Come with me," she coaxed in a soft and gentle voice.

The pup studied her, tilting his cute little head to the side. He then looked to where Kaden had stood and then back at her.

"I promise he will not hurt you. You can come with me. I would prefer the company anyway." She continued to talk to the pup as if he were a person, hoping the sincerity and benevolence in her voice would cajole him to follow her.

She smiled when she saw the little wolf make his decision.

The pup rose to its paws and reluctantly made his way over to Olivia, keeping his tail tucked submissively between his legs. He sensed she was important to the big predator.

179

She was the alpha female of this little pack.

"Good boy," Olivia praised him and was rewarded with a small, happy tail wag.

A little while later, Olivia gathered what she thought might be useful and went back, the pup following at her heels. She disposed of the old fish and cleaned as best as she could the spot where the pup had soiled the ground. The stench of it mixing with the stale air was offending her senses. The dry branches of the uprooted tree from the back cave, she put into the fire, and added a short piece of board she had plied off the wagon. Someday, she would make Kaden tell her all the stories about all the things he had taken. Like that chimney... she was most curious about the chimney. And the weird-looking, closed-off wagon with its vials, broken and whole, and drawers and all sorts of equipment strewn about.

Not long after, Kaden returned. He brought some fresh trout for Olivia and a rabbit for the pup. When Olivia started cleaning her fish, Kaden positioned himself between the little wolf and her, so he could protect her from the sight of the hungry pup tearing at the dead rabbit without mercy. The little wolf had retreated with his meal as far away from them as possible, predatory and survival instincts kicking in.

With their stomachs filled, they settled down for sleep. Day once more reigned the sky, and with its victory, the golden globe brought a bit of natural light to the cave. As Olivia ate her meal, the pup spent the time licking the blood off his snout, cleaning himself while Kaden kept an ever vigilant eye on him. The pup had had plenty of opportunity to leave, but he didn't. Obviously, he was not a stupid one. He had a food supply and the safety of a bigger predator, as long as he didn't threaten the alpha female of his new pack.

Olivia and Kaden snuggled up as they did every night. She was on the mattress with Kaden curled around her. This time though, the pup crawled over on his belly, ready to bolt if shooed away. When no one stopped him, he settled at the foot of Olivia's makeshift bed.

"He is so cute, is he not?" Olivia cooed when she noticed the pup curled at her feet.

Kaden sighed, a martyr indeed. "Yes, he is soooo cute," he said, dripping sarcasm, his voice holding no feelings whatsoever.

Olivia jabbed him with her finger. "Be nice, Kaden," she scolded in a whisper.

"Ouch, woman, who knew you had such a violent streak in you?" Kaden exclaimed with dramatic effect, pretending to wince even though he barely felt the jab.

Olivia giggled and kissed the spot where she had poked him, snuggling up closer to her dragon, tracing his scales with her fingertips. This time, he let out a sigh of contentment.

"I feel like I have been here much longer than I have. As if I have lived here with you for seasons, not just a few days. Much has happened, and it is so easy with you," Olivia's voice penetrated the silence, followed by a yawn.

"I know. I share the sentiment." Kaden brought his head around and settled it under his wing, against Olivia's back.

"Do you think they will come back looking for us?"

"I hope not." His voice was muffled against her back and under the wing. The rumble of it caressed her body delightfully.

"If they do?"

"I will protect you," Kaden said, serious and determined. "We will leave. If we can avoid a conflict, I would rather do so. Too many things could go wrong and I do not want you caught in the middle of it. We will just find a new home."

"We would have to make a stop along the way." Olivia kept her hands busy by continuing to run them gently over Kaden's smooth, draconic scales. "I would have to let my parents know I am alive and unharmed. They deserve that. They really are the best parents one could ask for… But I will not stay, no matter how much I love them. I cannot stay there now that I have found you. And I want to explore the world. Experience more adventure! There is so much out there that I still need to discover. Also, I do not care if you are a dragon. No human man could ever replace you." Olivia was a bit surprised by her own thoughts and proclamations, but she knew she loved her dragon and that was enough for her. Her words were true.

If you only knew. A wave of nostalgia washed over Kaden. *Ah, the joys of young infatuation, but who was he to judge, he was obviously the same… and selfish for agreeing with her. Selfishness did him no good so far in life, maybe he could dissuade her after all. But if she insisted… well…*

"It would mean giving up a lot, you know that," the dragon said in a quiet voice. "And the things you would have to leave behind. Being with me would mean just this… Sleeping in caves, or on the forest ground. Being chased, never settling for too long in one place…You couldn't start a family with me." The last part he said with so much sadness and longing in his voice, it broke Olivia's heart.

"I know… But we have our puppy now," Olivia teased, and she smiled against his scales because she knew that mentioning the pup would annoy him. She continued before he huffed or sighed again. "I do not care in any case. We would manage. We can work things out, can we not? Would you mind? Me coming with you?" Olivia pressed her face flush against his soft, silky scales. She closed her eyes tightly, waiting for her dragon's response.

"Never!" Kaden responded without hesitation. He felt Olivia stiffen and he amended his answer immediately. "I mean... I would never mind it. I have been alone for years. And then you came along, and you stayed, un-afraid, and you want to follow me of your own free will. You want to be with me in any way possible... It still amazes me. You amaze me. How could I say no to that?" He let his words sink in and felt her relax against his side again. The sensation of her nuzzling her face against his scales was heaven to him. "As you said, we will work it out either way. We will just be extra vigilant for the next few days."

"Yeah..." Olivia mumbled, sleep taking over.

"Sleep now, my love. You have had a long day."

Olivia didn't respond, and within a minute, her breathing evened out. She was fast asleep.

CHAPTER 19

The sun no longer teased the horizon with its pink blush when Magnus and his men packed up. They had managed about six hours of sleep, enough to pull them through another exhausting day, such as the one ahead of them.

The trek back up the mountain took longer than the journey down, the slopes demanding, leading up, and both people and animals struggled forward. The sun, now shy again, courted the treetops, its rays fighting through the boughs as the fiery globe gave way to the rising moon, and they reached the stream. The scorched grass was the only evidence of their encounter with the dragon.

"Go back. We will camp further in the forest. Theo and Damien, you two scout ahead for any signs of the dragon or the woman's tracks," Magnus said as he stared at the water smoothing over the rocks. Only the day before, this was where he had cooled his burns. Theo and Damien shuffled away and Magnus turned to face the rest of his people. "The rest of you, set up a camp; raise the tents as well. We only have a bit of daylight left."

"Yes, Your Highness," chorused the men.

An eerie silence descended upon them. During their trek, as Magnus' anger and impatience had grown, it seemed the forest only became quieter, afraid to make a sound lest it enrage him further.

While the tents were being set up, Magnus stood in the full glory of his armor, staring toward the path his trackers had taken. The fire had become a part of him, blending with the fury coursing through his being, consuming him. Hands fisted at his sides, his muscles contracted. He had promised himself he would have the dragon's head by now. He didn't like breaking his promises to himself. He had to have it! He had to prove himself. Had to fulfill his promise, and burning desire, to have the monster dead. His people's loyalty would be faultless then, because once he killed the dragon, his might would be immense, and everyone would bow down to him... *Even my father.*

A soft breeze reached him. The air fresh as the scent of spring tickled his nostrils, the peaceful quiet subduing his anger. No animals could be heard, only the sound of the stream murmuring across the smooth rocks, the breeze ruffling the branches, and his men making a ruckus in the camp. He frowned.

Magnus turned to his men. "Could you make any more noise, you bloody idiots?" he snapped. His hand twitched, palm itching. He just wanted to stick his sword into something, preferably meaty. He needed to see blood adorning the sharp blade, and he almost didn't mind whose or why. Red looked so good dripping down the silvery metal of his trusty sword.

The prince unsheathed his weapon and held it tightly in his hands, knuckles turning white. Everyone stopped what they were doing and stared at him in apprehension.

He brought his sword up, tip pointing to the sky as he pressed his forehead against the blunt side of the blade. He cooed to it in a whisper, "You won't ever let me down." He kissed the blade and let the tip turn downwards so it would stick into the ground. Bringing his eyes up, he saw his men staring at him.

"What are you staring at? Did I tell you to stop? NO! I told you to keep it quiet," he snarled, not bothering to hide his impatience. The prince's men hurried to finish setting up without uttering any words amongst each other, keeping the noise down.

Magnus needed to vent, to stop the fury from clouding his mind, or he was going to snap. He didn't want to hurt his men if that happened. He might hate them all at the moment but he was also aware that he needed them. *Except...* his eyes scanned the faces until he found the emerald ones he was looking for, the one person who might help him blow off some steam. *Charlie!*

A shiver of fear snaked down Charlie's spine. She remembered the last time Magnus had been furious, and it hadn't ended well for her. She didn't dare look up and draw his attention to her, although it was too late already. She felt his eyes boring into her. She tried to avoid him by keeping her gaze focused downward while she slyly maneuvered herself out his line of vision, passing between the horses. Maybe she would be able to hide. She knew she didn't usually have that kind of fortune, but she always hoped.

"Charlie." She heard him call out her name, voice cold, as his footsteps drew nearer. The men subtly moved out of the way.

Charlie pretended she didn't hear him as she turned and made to walk away, an excuse that she was going to relieve herself ready at the tip of her tongue.

"Charlie, my little whore." The fury seeped from Magnus' voice unrestrained as he approached the redhead. No one dared to stop him.

The venom in his voice made her quiver with fear as she

turned to face him, but she trained her eyes on the collar of his armor. "I was just about to—"

Magnus' hand wrapped around her throat. Her eyes bulged and she held her breath.

"You listen to me, puppet. You do not walk away from me when I call for you." He pulled her closer by her throat, making Charlie gasp for air, as he spat the words and spittle at her. "You know the deal… Seems I will have to remind you about it tonight, teach you another lesson, eh my dear puppet?"

The word 'puppet' was a bearer of bad news for her, so she nodded her head, frantic with terror.

Magnus tightened his grip for a few moments, preventing Charlie from taking in much precious air. With a wide-eyed stare she begged him to stop as she wordlessly tried to pry his fingers from her throat. As the dread showing on Charlie's face increased, so did Magnus' smirk. Her eyes rolling back, he cast her aside.

Charlie stumbled and fell back onto the ground, bracing herself on her hands and knees. Pain exploded in her wrists and shot up her arms as she landed hard.

"That's where you belong," Magnus spat as Charlie grasped at her throat, trying to suck in much-needed air, coughing around the short breaths she managed to inhale. She looked around in panic, hoping Theo and Damien weren't witnessing this, for they would surely do something stupid and rash. Not finding their faces, she closed her eyes in relief.

When she opened them again, she noticed the others. Most of the men ignored what was going on, turning a blind eye to it because it was easier for them to cope that way. Lance was looking at her with remorse and when their eyes met, he looked away, ashamed. Her gaze shifting to the right, she saw that Reed had his hands pressed against

Cassiel's chest, preventing him from interfering. The dark knight already had a tight grip on his sword's handle. Charlie nodded at him that she was alright, as much as she could be, and his grasp relaxed, his knuckles no longer white.

She saw Cassiel's eyes widen again. Charlie turned back around towards Magnus just in time to see him grab at her hair as he pulled her up, onto her feet. "I am not done with you. *That* was just a warning." The prince shook Charlie by her red tresses. She cringed while her eyes watered in pain. Her heart pounded in her ears. "We are just about to get to the part where I exact the punishment."

In hindsight, Charlie regretted the deal she had made with the prince. She would rather be on the streets, begging and whoring for food and shelter.

"And what a sweet way it will be to get rid of the tension boiling inside me." Magnus brought his other hand up and Charlie closed her eyes.

She waited for his armored fist to connect with her unprotected face.

It didn't, though. Instead, the familiar baritone reached her ears. "Your Highness, my Prince."

Charlie's eyes snapped open and landed on Cassiel standing behind Magnus, his hand on the prince's shoulder, a very daring move. She feared the consequences. Glancing behind Cassiel, she saw Reed wiping the blood from his nose.

Magnus closed his eyes and took a very deep and calming breath.

Cassiel drew his hand away before he was reprimanded for it. He lowered his head as he waited for Magnus to speak. He knew how to deal with the prince when he was like this, but it was still a risk.

"What. Do you. Want?" Magnus hissed through his

clenched teeth. His cold blue eyes narrowed in anger.

"With all due, highly deserved respect, Your Highness, do not let your anger cloud your judgment. We are so close now, you should cherish these moments. Bask in the glory of what is to come. I do realize we have not fulfilled the task for today, but you have waited for so long, what is another day compared to that? Feed on your anger and use it tomorrow against the monster. Channel it then. It will be more useful than taking it out on a weakling like the girl… Your Highness," Cassiel said, looking Magnus straight in the eyes. He knew the prince admired honesty and that he loved peering into people's souls. A few moments of silence after his last words were spoken, Cassiel bowed his head again.

Magnus considered the knight's words carefully. He knew Cassiel was his best tactician and the words he spoke made sense. His dark knight was a wise and cool-tempered warrior. The dragon was, after all, a much better opponent than Charlie. None of them, neither the men nor any woman, were worthy of his time, but the dragon was worthy of his sword.

He breathed in deeply, reining in his anger, putting it back inside the box and locking it up for another day. With reluctance, he released his hold on Charlie's red curls and settled his hand on her cheek. He wiped away the tears with his thumb and leaned in to kiss her, a show of tender affection.

Charlie kept her eyes open as she trembled, his lips touching hers. The swift shift in his mood and behavior carved the dread of him deep into her bones.

Magnus stepped back. He plastered his well-known smirk on his face, gave Charlie a wink and walked off. Cassiel nodded his head in acknowledgment of her grateful look and followed after Magnus.

At that moment Theo and Damien returned. They saw Magnus walking away from Charlie, leaving her frozen on the spot, her eyes dulled with fear and filled with tears, all color drained from her face as if Magnus had just drained her of life. Her hands shook, her whole body quivering.

Theo's mind clouded with a crimson layer of fury. Damien was not far behind him, and both were itching to confront Magnus. Charlie looked at them in distress, shaking her head *no*.

She didn't want them on Magnus' bad side, not now when he was in this sociopathic mood. They didn't deserve his wrath. When Theo continued striding towards Magnus, the tears gathered in her eyes and she threw him a pleading look.

Damien laid a hand on Theo's shoulder. "Go to Charlie. She needs you, and the One God only knows you're in no condition to talk to Magnus now. I'll report to him and then join you." He gave Theo's shoulder a gentle squeeze and watched him walk away.

When he was sure that Charlie was safely in Theo's arms, Damien headed toward Magnus. He had to put on a cold, indifferent expression, ignoring the feelings that Charlie's distress had caused in him, as he went to talk with the prince. He didn't like talking to others, especially Magnus.

"Good. You're back," Magnus said, noticing Damien's approach.

"Is everything alright, Your Highness?" Damien inquired in a cool voice.

"Just perfect." The sadistic grin on Magnus' face made the hunter uneasy. "Hopefully you have good news for me, eh?" he asked with a raised eyebrow.

"Yes, Your Highness." Damien bowed his head as usual, even though he didn't have an ounce of deference for his prince. "We found tracks, human, small and presumably female, and what we think might be the tracks of the dragon. We followed them a bit and they led to a grassy clearing where we found even more tracks and signs of them. It seems they frequent the place so they should be within close walking distance."

"It was a good idea we set up camp here for the night, a little distance away, so they wouldn't stumble upon us. I recommend we stay in the dark, no campfire tonight and keep it quiet," Cassiel said as he helped Magnus take off the breastplate of his armor.

"I agree. Tomorrow we kill him and I will get to sample some new female flesh." Magnus dismissed Damien with a flick of his hand and took the rest of the armor off with the help of his knight.

CHAPTER 20

Magnus and his men crouched low, hiding behind trees and bushes, a safe distance away and downwind from the entrance to the cave. An evil grin stretched across the prince's face as he eyed his Ophelia with lust-filled hunger, watching her play-chasing with a wolf pup.

He wondered where the dragon was lurking while she ran around. Dark curls danced around her innocent face, which was adorned with a wide happy smile. The sun was shining through the trees, worshiping her features as the fresh air painted her cheeks a rosy color.

A black wolf pup was chasing her around, jumping over some boulders, pursuing her around the trees and nipping at the ends of her dress. The pup's efforts paid off when it managed to get a good grip of her dress in its mouth, thus sending Olivia toppling over. The little wolf then jumped on her and started showering her face with wolfish kisses as she tried to push it away, laughing the whole time.

Her laugher echoed throughout the forest. The sound of it reached Magnus' ears and pulled at his lips, a different kind of smile making its appearance. He was enchanted. Her innocent laugher gave him peace, even if just for a moment, before he shook his head to dispel her enchantment as he scowled in her direction. The softness she invoked in him was disturbing, not what a future King, or any man should be. His father was "soft" for his mother, and look where it got him after she had died; ruining his mind.

Soft. Magnus scoffed. The only softness he approved of was that of the female shape.

He saw her lips moving as she spoke to the pup, a squeal escaping her as the little wolf licked her cheek again before she managed to push it off.

Magnus looked back at his men, scanned their faces and gave them a nod of his head, conveying that he was ready. They were going to leave Charlie here. She was already gagged and bound to a tree, leaning against it as she was seated on the forest ground. Her face was tilted up. She stared at the sun and the wind swaying the braches, as she ignored everybody. This was not the first time he had done it. Magnus didn't want to take any chances with Charlie, afraid she would use the opportunity to run away from him.

Again.

Turning back, he put his hand on the hilt of his sword, ready to draw it out when he saw the woman stop and spin around, towards the cave, smiling warmly at someone. She spoke back and her head bounced up and down in excitement.

Then, he saw the beast appear.

The dragon.

It peeked out of the cave and gave something to the woman.

Magnus unsheathed his sword.

80

Olivia had spent the day before resting and catching up on sleep. She had been feeling quite uneasy, and Kaden had kept a close eye on her, hovering with worry.

She did love Kaden but he had been overbearing and overprotective so some time after midday, she had asked him to go out and fetch them some food.

Of course the dragon declined, not wanting to leave her alone for one moment, no matter how much Olivia tried to assure him she would be fine, and that the Pup, as Kaden had named the little wolf, would keep her company and make sure she was not bored and mischievous.

A compromise made, they went to the stream together, avoiding the place of the previous day's encounter. Olivia had never seen anyone catch fish so fast. Kaden didn't want to linger, so they returned to the cave even before the sun reached its midday peak.

"Urgh…" she whined as she scrapped off the fish-scales and pulled out the guts. "More fish. Yay!" she said, sarcasm dripping through her voice, her cheeks gaining a slightly green tinge. "If I have to eat one more fish after today, I would honestly rather starve myself to death," she said, eyeing the fish with disdain.

"Tomorrow, I will take you shopping." Olivia's eyes snapped up at Kaden, filling with hope that she heard him correctly. "We have more than enough goods to trade with," he continued. "I can take you close to a village where you can buy the food you want. Or anything else you might want or need."

Olivia squealed, jumping up and down. She did love the forest and its peacefulness but she missed the quirks of civilization, a warm bath, a soft bed, and a decent meal… oh, and a clean dress. Yes, all those would be marvelous. As she danced around in celebration, Pup joined her with excited leaps and bounds, wagging his short black tail with glee.

"Thank you!" She tackled her dragon around one scaly forearm, and he didn't budge one inch. "That would really be lovely."

"You think of what you need, and I will buy it for you… I mean, provide the resources for the exchange."

Olivia beamed and nodded, the shopping list in her head growing longer and longer… *Soap! And tea!*

"Love?" Kaden chuckled at dazed look on her face. "Olivia?" He nudged her.

"Huh?" She looked up. "Oh… I apologize, I got lost in thinking what I might need."

"Of course you did. I was saying that you might want to consider visiting your parents. Letting them know you are alright."

Olivia bit her lip, her gaze falling to her shuffling feet. "Do you think they will be glad to see me?"

"They will be relieved and happy at first, from what you have told me about them."

"I guess you are right." Olivia shrugged. "I know they will still be disappointed…" She swallowed, and sighed. "Probably angry with me as well."

"Probably."

Olivia's gaze shifted back to Kaden and she tilted her head to the side. "That is not comforting."

"I know, Liv, but in the end, they are your parents, and they love you very much. That love will prevail, so you have nothing to worry about."

"Except that I will be leaving again, with a dragon none the less… Oh goodness!" She ran a hand down her face. "What a mess I have made." She started pacing. "They might not even believe me and then I will have to show you to them and then I—"

Kaden lowered his head in front of her, halting her

frantic walk back and forth. "Olivia," he said as he gazed into her eyes, "We cannot know what will happen. No sense in worrying that pretty head of yours just yet. We will just let things happen, and react when there is something to react to."

Olivia sighed. "You are right."

ໍ

While Magnus spied on Olivia outside the cave, inside it, Kaden rummaged through the piles of his treasure, gathering trading goods for their shopping trip. He wouldn't let Olivia help because this meant braving the unstable mountains of man-made implements, including the sharp and dangerous ones. He had agreed, rather reluctantly, for Olivia to get some fresh air only if she wouldn't wander away from the cave. Pup was just happy to have a playmate.

As he was digging through his hoard of treasure, Kaden kept an ear out for Olivia. Her happy laughter and playful squeals reached his ears, making his soul light. He could live on that sound alone. Olivia had him completely under her spell. And what a wonderful spell it was. *How ironic*, he thought to himself with a shake of his head as he concentrated on his scavenging endeavor.

He pulled out two beautiful cloaks; one lined with velvet and the other with silk, and thought them perfect for Olivia since her last one had been burned to bits when he had saved her from those men. Neither was entirely suitable as an all-weather travelling cloak, but the velvet-lined one would keep her warm, and the other would match her eyes. He heard her laughter echo inside again as she scolded Pup lightheartedly. By the sound of things she was obviously trying to get him off her. Kaden took the cloaks and decided to show them to Olivia.

"Liv?" Kaden called out as he neared the cave's mouth.

"I am just over here!"

He saw her turn around at the sound of his voice, a smile of adoration stretching across her face. When her eyes locked on his, Kaden's breath hitched and his heart sped up. *God, she's beautiful.* The cloaks went clean out of his mind. *Just my luck to meet her* now, *when I'm wise enough to appreciate her and unable to do anything about it...*

"Yes, Kaden?" Olivia prompted him, as Kaden just stood there, not showing any sign he would move or speak any time soon. She bit her lip, holding back her mirth and his eyes snapped down to her mouth.

Kaden cleared his throat and took a deep breath to slow his racing heart. "I found these. I thought you might have use for a new cloak, and these seemed… ummm… pretty? Not all that practical for every day, I know, but -"

"Oh yes!" Olivia nodded her head enthusiastically. "They look wonderful."

Kaden leaned toward Olivia, handing them over to her. As the whisper of silk cut the air, Olivia spinning with the lighter one about her shoulders, he noticed that the birds had stopped singing. Pup had stopped bounding around, and was sniffing at the breeze. Kaden watched the little wolf cub freeze, his hackles rising. His little head pointed in the direction of a dense patch of brambles screening the trees. Then Kaden's keen ears caught the unmistakable sound of metal on leather, a drawn-out rush, part whistle, part hiss. It was a sword being unsheathed, or he was a rock lizard. Then came the same sound, like an echo, one after the other, and he went rigid. He scanned the trees but the whole band were well hidden. One, however, the owner of the first sword, was not bothering to keep himself out of sight. Kaden's eyes narrowed when he spotted him, hidden by the bushes and the branches, the same man that had almost taken Olivia away from him.

Their eyes met.

"Olivia, get in now!" Kaden barked, his gaze never leaving Magnus's face.

Olivia jumped back in fright, the cloaks slipping from her fingers onto the grass. She gathered them up in a hurry, stumbling backwards towards her dragon and the safety of the cave. She hadn't spotted Magnus, but she feared the worst, and the color left her cheeks.

Magnus and his men moved forward. Kaden snarled. The wolf pup bristled, flattening his ears back to his head and crouching low. His snarl betrayed his age, too high-pitched to be really threatening, but the little fangs were sharp enough. He moved closer to Olivia, stepping in front of her, prepared to defend his new pack.

"Kaden, what is wrong? What is happening?" Olivia asked, panic settling in. Her eyes darted around frantically and when the sun glistened off weapons and armors, she saw the men.

Kaden growled, a low, rumbling sound thundering through the forest.

"Liv, get in. Now!" he commanded in a tone that had her scrambling into the cave as fast as she could.

"Pup! In!" Kaden nudged the pup towards the cave with his tail. Pup snapped towards the offensive limb, which caused Kaden to turn on him, snarling. The wolf pup didn't need to be told twice and he hurried inside after Olivia.

Kaden stepped out of the cave, head low, fangs glistening, eyes narrowing. Ten men moved like a harmonious unit, spreading out around the cave mouth, but two men stayed near the leader, flanking him. The dented, well-used armor, weapons handled with ease, bodies poised, wary and ready to spring into action, spoke of experienced warriors. Kaden wasn't sure if he could take them all down. He had never had to fight off that many capable men under circumstances such as these. Sure, pitchfork-wielding mobs had come after him on occasion, but he hated killing so he either scared them away or went away himself. However, killing was sometimes inevitable and he could do it if needed to be done.

With these men, he didn't want to take chances; it would be very challenging for him to fight them, with the cramped conditions in front of the cave not in his favor. He couldn't fly up to attack them from above and there wasn't much maneuvering space for him to slap them all away with his tail or wings; the trees were in his way. He would have to depend on his fire, bite and claws. Those were quite deadly and efficient, but there were ten of them against one of him. If he failed to fight them off, Olivia would be in danger. He couldn't risk that. He couldn't risk anyone slipping by and reaching her.

He didn't know what to do.

Magnus kept his eyes trained on the dragon. Intelligence shone in those fiery orbs, appraising, predicting their actions. Much to the prince's delight, it seemed this beast was going to be an interesting and challenging confrontation.

"Stop!" Kaden called out, anger lacing his voice, and the men froze.

They didn't expect the dragon to speak. Their composure faltered, eyes widened, and they were left speechless and in awe as they looked back and forth between each other.

"What do you want, humans?" Kaden snarled at them again, his voice low and rumbling. He stretched his neck out, making himself bigger, and with his fangs bared, he exhaled slowly, the smoke drifting out of his nostrils, swirling around his snout.

Magnus was the first one to shake off of the shock. He took a step back, bumping into a tree. He leaned against the trunk and rested his sword over his shoulder. Cold blue eyes studied the dragon, its protective stance in front of the cave, the barely suppressed twitch of its tail. *It has something to lose.*

"You speak," Magnus quirked his head to the side, "that is… unexpected, but it will make killing you only sweeter." A malicious smile spread across his face.

"We have no quarrel. Leave us alone and I might let you go unharmed." Kaden spat some fire in their direction and Magnus flinched. He remembered what it could do and he narrowed his eyes at Kaden's satisfied smirk.

"Oh, you see, I want your head to decorate my halls and the woman in my bed." Magnus licked his lips. "She could keep me entertained for many nights. She is a feisty little thing, is she not? Just the way I like them."

"No!" Kaden snapped. "Let her go and I will face you fairly," he offered instead. He would gladly sacrifice himself for Olivia's safety.

"Kaden!" They heard the female voice call out from the cave. "No!"

"Olivia, don't you dare come any closer," the dragon answered back into the cave.

"So her name is Olivia… Seems my sweet Olivia *lied* to me," Magnus taunted, loud enough so his voice would reach her.

"She's mine!" Kaden snarled back, a familiar bout of possessiveness washing over him, rousing the beast inside him. His tail twitched, thumping against a tree.

"Oh my, this keeps getting more and more interesting." Magnus maintained the veneer of amusement, hiding behind it the shock and disgust that a woman like her would willingly stay with a monster like the dragon.

"Olivia, sweetness, come on out, I have so much more to offer than this…this *monster* -"Another ball of fire flew in his direction, almost reaching him, but he continued to taunt. He took a few more steps back and stood behind a tree. "I could make you a real princess… you could have anything you ever wanted… I am after all the Prince of Illirya, and I could give you anything your heart desires." Magnus hoped his wordcs would change her mind.

Kaden snorted. "So you are the prince after all… Tell me… Your father, Magnar, is he still the same bastard he used to be?" Kaden goaded the prince, hoping to taunt him into making a stupid, impulsive move.

"Don't you dare bring my father up, you monster. You're nothing, no one! You are dead!" Magnus snarled back, his face blotched with angry red spots. His eyes drilled into Kaden, wishing he could kill the monster with the look alone. No one was allowed to speak that way of his father… expect Magnus himself. He had had enough of talking and he reached for his new weapon, which he had named The Striker, for the sound it made was that of a hammer striking an anvil.

"Leave us alone!" Olivia yelled back out.

Kaden rolled his eyes as he spoke back to her barely above a whisper. "Olivia, love, please stay back. Let me handle him. I will not let him hurt you or even get close to you." He turned his eyes back towards his adversaries, watching Magnus take something out from a special belt pouch.

Olivia sighed dejectedly. She wrapped her arms around her middle and retreated further into the cave, Pup close to her side. "Just be careful." Her voice wavered. She walked past the hearth, and then stopped. *Hmmmm…* She lit the candle in her lamp and ventured to the back cave, hoping she would find something useful, something she could use to help her dragon. A weapon maybe, though she knew not how to wield any, or maybe something to trade with… *I doubt that would work.* She just needed to try and do something constructive.

Magnus' knights were taken aback by this new development. Theo and Damien wished they were closer so they could talk to each other but unfortunately they had spread out to different sides, their bows ready. They remembered their deal, though; if it got too much, run away: there was no shame in staying alive. Reed stood close to Magnus, on the prince's left, his eyes narrowed, weapon ready for the lunge. Cassiel flanked the prince from his right, standing proud, waiting to act when told. The other knights were spread out to either side, forming a loose half circle around the cave mouth.

"Look, *dragon*!" Magnus spat the word. "We can do this the easy way or the hard way. You know how it goes." The prince cranked some sort of a weapon, drawing Kaden's attention to it, and the dragon realized it was probably the one that had pierced his wing. His eyes narrowed on it. He needed to see what it could do, how much of an advantage it would give them.

"The easy way is that I chop off your head swiftly, hopefully in one try. The hard way, I kill you slowly, letting my men finish you off while I play with my little princess, making you watch and listen to her struggles as she pleads for help. Either way, you end up dead and she ends up mine." By the end of his speech, Magnus raised his hand, aiming the striker toward Kaden's head.

"What will it be?"

"My way." Kaden hissed and the prince fired his weapon. The sound it produced pierced the air as the round projectile flew toward Kaden at an amazing speed, grazing his shoulder when he tried to dodge out of the way.

Kaden flinched and glanced down at his wound, barely registering Olivia's shriek of alarm coming from the cave. He looked back up at Magnus, and watched as he put another projectile in the weapon.

The prince cranked the handle once. Kaden inhaled deeply as he took a heavy step closer, the earth trembling beneath his feet.

Twice.

The dragon inhaled and held his breath, conjuring his fire. He took another step closer.

Magnus raised the weapon and this time, before he his finger squeezed the trigger, Kaden spat out a large ball of fire in a quick, short breath. The prince sought shelter behind his tree just as the blazing projectile hit the trunk and it burst into flames.

Magnus yelled out an array of profanities, as his men sprang into action.

Reed moved first and charged at the dragon with a roar of his own. "Get him!" Lance, Colin and Cassiel heeded his command.

Kaden switched his attention to the men rushing at him from different directions and he used his fire against the closest one. The man retreated, beating at the flames on his sleeve. Arrows flew toward Kaden's head. He dodged one. The other bounced off his scales but the third one penetrated the natural armor of his shoulder just as he retreated into the cave.

He had to come up with a plan; this way at least, if the men tried to enter the cave, he could just fry them halfway in. They would be bottlenecked in the narrow entrance and being caught like that would hopefully provide them with more time for thought.

The agonizing screams of a man burning alive slipped into the cave, bounced off its stone walls and into Kaden's heart as he kept his eyes locked on the cave's entrance.

ॐ

Reed watched as the dragon's fire flew towards Colin, throwing the man back, the flames engulfing him before he hit the ground. His excruciating screams filled the forest. The nearby birds and animals scattered away in haste. Reed still forged on toward the cave, knowing there was nothing he could do for Colin and that Donovan would take care of him. He had a dragon to catch. As he neared the cave's mouth, he caught himself in time and only peeked in, then ducked back when fire flew towards him.

Cassiel and Magnus reached Reed's side. Blinded by rage and long unfulfilled desire, Magnus passed Reed, heading for the cave. Cassiel grabbed the prince's shoulder and pulled him back before he charged head-on toward a certain death.

Donovan ran straight for the burning man, but there was no hope. He took off his cloak and flung it onto Colin in an attempt to choke out the fire. As he pressed his hands against the fabric, trying to wrap up his friend, his palms burned. He flinched, and as the cloak caught fire, he jumped back. A burning substance clung to Colin, kindling the fire until spent. So it wasn't just flame that dragons spouted, but some gelatinous fuel that coated the victim and kept on burning.

The screams turned to gurgles as Donovan helplessly watched Colin turn a crispy black color, causing even the war-worn combat healer to gag at the sight. The smell of burning flesh, and the sight, was too much for the young man to handle; he turned his head to the side and threw up the contents of his stomach. In the end, there was nothing he could do.

The rest of the knights gathered around the cave's mouth with Magnus, trying hard to ignore the dreadful screams of their companion, hoping they wouldn't meet the same fate.

Inside the cave, Kaden waited for the next target to appear, hoping no one else would be foolish enough to charge inside.

"Kaden?" Olivia spoke in a small voice, huddled with Pup in a corner. She had her hands wrapped around the little wolf, preventing him from going out, and holding onto him as if he were her lifeline, burrowing her tearful face in his fur.

When the fight erupted, she ran back, frightened for Kaden's life. She was also angry. Angry for being so helpless. She wished she knew how to wield a weapon, realizing just how useful that skill was, if only to be able to defend herself. She didn't think she had it in herself to take a life. Nonetheless, she vowed she would learn how to fight back, but at this moment, there was nothing she could do. Those were trained men out there. Even though they might not hurt her, or at least she hoped so, her actions could put Kaden in more danger than he was already in.

The dragon turned toward Olivia and his features softened at the sight of her. He approached her slowly, but kept listening to the goings-on outside so he could act in time if needed.

"Liv?" he said in a tender voice, and she looked up at him with fear in her eyes. "I won't hurt you, Liv."

"I know." She took a deep breath as she rose to her feet, the young wolf taking the opportunity to try and charge out. He had recognized the familiar scent of the men who had killed his parents and were now threatening his new pack.

Kaden snarled at the pup, making him withdraw, though the pup growled in return. Olivia stepped back, but the desperate look in Kaden's eyes made her lunge for him.

Olivia threw her arms around Kaden's snout, hugging tightly, nuzzling her face into his cheek, comforting both.

"You know…" They heard a voice echo into the cave, "we find ourselves in a very *exciting* situation."

Olivia didn't let go of her hold on Kaden but she did turn her head toward the sound. Luckily, they were not in the line of sight of the entrance to the cave.

"A situation which, in the end, will not benefit you at all. Quite the contrary, you find yourselves trapped. Now… before you make any stupid assumptions. We will not charge in blindly and let ourselves be fried, but you cannot get out unharmed either. We will be waiting, prepared. You cannot stay in there forever. You will both need food and water. Will you let her starve to death?" Magnus' grave voice carried through the cave. He was hoping they really were trapped with no other way out, otherwise his threats were useless.

"Shit, damnation and … curses!" Kaden hissed in a whisper, making Olivia turn to look back at him. "I am such a fool."

"What? Why?" Olivia furrowed her brow. "Why would you say that?" She stroked his cheek.

"He is right… I got us trapped here. There are no other ways out. I should have told you to run when I saw them. I should have held them back while you ran away… I really am an idiot," Kaden scolded himself as he pulled away from Olivia. He noticed the arrow sticking out of his shoulder like an annoying thorn so he angrily pulled it out with his teeth and cast it aside. The small wound would heal quickly.

"Oh —" Magnus' voice carried inside again, "- and this time, I will not give you a choice about how you will die… you have killed one of my men, it's the hard way for you now."

Olivia whimpered and Kaden closed his eyes. When he opened them again, Olivia noticed a haunted look in his gaze. They both ignored Magnus as Olivia moved to stand in front of Kaden again.

"Kaden, look at me," she pleaded, and was relieved when his eyes instantly sought hers. "You had no choice in killing that man… *We* will have no choice. It will be either them or us."

"I am so sorry, Love." Kaden shook his head, regret and guilt eating at his soul. "I am so sorry you got caught in the middle of all of this."

"I am not, Kaden. If I wasn't here, that would mean never having to have met you. But I did meet you, and I do *not* regret a single moment." Olivia stepped closer to her dragon. "I could never regret meeting you." She brought her hands and ran them over his scales. "We will work it out… we will get out of this…" She leaned her forehead against him. "Will we not?"

Kaden lowered his head and rested it against her back. "Yes, we will." His voice was as uncertain as Olivia's heart.

"Ignoring me won't make me go away." The sound of Magnus' voice made them both groan at the same time, and their simultaneous reaction brought up a chuckle in spite of the dire situation. Their brief moment of mirth faded and died as the seriousness of their situation reasserted itself.

"He really is annoying," Kaden said a bit louder, hoping Magnus would hear him. He lay down.

"I heard that!" Magnus called back. "And I will annoy you out of that cave if need be."

Olivia sat down next to Kaden's head, resting her side against him as she pulled her legs up, wrapping her arms around her knees. "What are we going to do?" she asked, already trying to come up with solutions of her own.

Pup scooted closer to them and settled over Olivia's feet.

"I am thinking."

Those were Kaden's only words for the next hour.

CHAPTER 21

"Charlie? It's us." Theo announced as he and Damien approached the tree Charlie was bound to.

Her eyes snapped up to them, relief washing over her when she saw her friends. She surveyed them, head to toe, and her shoulders slumped in relief when she saw them unharmed. She had heard the shouts, the bangs and clashes, the sounds of battle and the blood-curdling screams. She was only able to imagine what had been going on.

Theo knelt next to her and removed her gag while Damien went behind the tree and cut the ropes that bound her.

"Are you alright?" Theo said in a low, quiet voice.

"Am *I* alright? I should be asking you that. What the bloody poo happened? Those screams…" Charlie shivered involuntarily.

Damien unwound the ropes from around her. "It was Colin. He's dead," he said, his jaw clenched tight.

Charlie rubbed her red, scraped wrists as she looked at her friends, now both crouching in front of her, waiting for them to explain.

Theo sighed. "The dragon spat a ball of fire at him…"

Charlie sucked in a breath. "Shite!" Her eyes widened. "Did ya kill it?" She tried to run her fingers through her mane of red curls only to have them get tangled in it. She frowned at her offending hair.

"No, but… it's so complicated." Damien sighed as he sat back on the forest ground. He crossed his legs and pulled them up, wrapping his hands around his knees.

"What do you mean complicated?" Charlie said and turned around, searching for her dagger which was hidden in the grass near where her hands had been tied. Theo and Damien had given her the dagger as a precaution, and whenever she had been bound, they would hide her dagger close by so she could cut herself free if she found herself in real danger or if they didn't come back.

Theo joined Damien on the ground and leaned on his lover's shoulder, who in return kissed his head.

"He talked," Theo said.

"Who is he?" Charlie asked as she tucked the dagger away in her belt bag and looked down at her dress. It could use a washing, a simple dark green cotton dress with silk trimmings, and four buttons going from her neckline to down between her breasts. She always left the top two unbuttoned. She had a brown leather belt wrapped around her slim waist, accentuating her curves, with one belt bag on each side. She brushed the dirt and leaves away.

Damien handed her his waterskin and said, "The dragon."

Charlie took a sip to soothe her dry throat so when the words registered in her brain, she almost choked on the water. "Wait! What? Talked? *He?*"

Theo then told her everything that had happened, especially that the dragon had talked, was obviously male, that the woman was actually named Olivia and had called the dragon Kaden, and that it seemed he was protecting her. He left out the details about Colin's death. It had been too gruesome a sight.

"Oh wow." Charlie's eyes were wide. "Never knew I'd see a *real* dragon, and definitely never thought he'd talk." She shook her head. "Actually, when I think back now… all the so-called dragon attacks… no one was ever even seriously hurt; that's why I thought the stories were bogus, and I never heard of anyone getting killed, 'til now, that is. Don't you find that odd?"

"I've never thought about it myself but yes. It seems he only stole things, if it's the same dragon. We really don't know how many there are out there. I myself thought them only a myth, stories told to children. And in those stories he mostly scared people away but… hmm… this is all so weird and complicated. I don't know what's right or wrong anymore." Theo ran his hand over his face, suddenly looking older than he really was.

They were all quiet for a few moments, trying to wrap their minds around everything that had happened, Charlie wondered about the young woman. At first, envy suffused her, having that sort of freedom. A freedom to live however she pleased, even if it meant living with a dragon. How had that happened? A dragon! A talking dragon… and now, Magnus was after it, after him… or worse, them. Envy was replaced with worry, than pity, for she knew Magnus, knew he wouldn't give up until he had what he wanted. Charlie had experienced what it meant being Magnus's "property", and the poor woman would be his for the rest of his life. She hoped it would be short. He deserved to die a stupid death!

"We need to go back. We were supposed to have returned by now. Magnus sent us to fetch you and the horses and then we have to go and search around the cave, and the forest, to see if there are any other entrances."

Damien was the one to break the silence as he stood up and pulled Theo with him.

"Yes, right. He's mad enough already, don't need to add oil to that fire." Theo extended his hand towards Charlie to help her to her feet as well.

"What are you going to do?" Charlie smoothed out her dress with her hands.

"We're staying for now, but... I don't think I'll be able to kill that dragon. It's all so fucked up," Theo said, shaking his head as he walked over to their horses.

"It's not like our arrows do much damage, we'll just… miss accidentally if a fight breaks out again." Damien gathered the reins as Theo herded the horses together. He tied the reins in three groups, so each of them could lead one group back to Magnus. "We really don't have much choice; it's not like we can do anything against Magnus, as you've said yourself. It's a bad moment to leave anyways, with him as unstable as he currently is. Maybe we'll leave after this whole deal with the dragon is over. I don't want him to send people after us."

"That would be bad," Charlie confirmed as she took the reins of her horse, two more following behind in a line.

"What's going to happen to the girl? The way you described what happened, she seems oblivious… innocent, even. From what you said, she's obviously been living with him. Maybe they grew up together or something. Why else would she be here living in a cave with a dragon? She might not know any better." Charlie voiced her thoughts as she followed behind Theo and Damien, who each led four horses.

"What did you say?" Theo looked over his shoulder towards Charlie, four horses separating them.

Charlie just shook her head at him letting him know it didn't matter. Magnus would do whatever he wanted to anyway.

℥

Back at the camp, Magnus paced outside the cave, running scenarios in his head, trying to come up with the best strategy to get rid of the monster and "save" its victim. *Yes!* His poor Olivia was the dragon's victim, under the monster's spell and he needed to save her. And protect her. The tales and songs that were going to be sung about how he saved a fair maiden from a vicious dragon would be glorious. Not to mention, women would swoon over the fact that he fell in love with the maiden and took her as his wife. The perfect fairytale story. They were definitely going to love that. His father would have to be proud of him, Magnus would finally earn the respect that went with his title, and his people would fall before him on their knees reverently. He would be the king, also known as the Dragon Slayer.

King Magnus, the Dragon Slayer and a hero to his people.

Magnus smiled as he stopped pacing and sat on a nearby boulder, scanning the faces of his men. He knew some of them were restless.

He kept his eye on Lance, who seemed to fancy their little whore. Maybe he needed a reminder of who his priority was. His scout and hunter were away from the group a lot; he should probably rein them in, too. They also seemed to have developed a connection with Charlie, but otherwise kept quiet and to themselves. He needed to work on that, get to know them better, but it seemed that as long as he paid them, they would do whatever was needed. He didn't really care about developing any sort of rapport with them. He was their prince, after all, and they were bound to do as he demanded.

Donovan and Reed, he had no need to worry about. Neither the twins, or Lance… Cassiel though… even though the man was soft, as long as he held up to his oath, Magnus would heed his good advice.

Oh, and Colin, but he was dead now, so he didn't matter anymore.

None of that mattered at the moment. He needed to figure out how to deal with the dragon. He had already planned for Theo and Damien to scout and find any other entrances to the cave. Hopefully, they would find none. The dragon and the woman would have to come out sooner or later and Magnus and his men would be ready, with Theo and Damien in the back with their arrows. They were quite good, and would at least provide a distraction to the beast. The twins and Lance, he was going to post on the other side of the cave. They would flank the beast when it came out. *But what to do about the fire?* Magnus wished he could have anticipated that. He *should* have anticipated it. Would it have made a difference? The boulders and the trees would have to do for protection. Reed… he trusted Reed and he would be the one to keep an eye on the girl. Yes, it was all coming together. Cassiel, a special task awaited him, an opportunity to prove his loyalty and—

The sound of approaching footsteps and horses neighing brought Magnus out of his plotting. He looked up and saw Damien and Theo return with the horses and Charlie. Lance approached her immediately, helping her, evoking a frown on Magnus' face. The prince *really* needed to put Lance in his place.

Once the horses were settled, Theo and Damien each went their way and Charlie settled a short distance from the cave, sitting behind a low boulder, seeking shelter from any possible fight.

Magnus stood up, sword in hand as he walked up to his men; three of them were just finishing covering Colin's fresh grave with dirt. He was ready to bring his quest to an end, to kill the monster and bring its head back to show it to his father whose words still haunted him.

"If you could kill your own mother without even lifting a sword, a dragon should be an easy challenge for you."

It was then and there he had promised himself that he would have a dragon's head in his palace. If not to spite his father, then to honor his mother, because in the end, his birth caused her death.

"Alright. Cathal, Galor and Lance, you will be positioned on the other side of the cave's entrance. Reed, Cassiel, Donovan and I will be on this side. If they decide to make a run for it, we will ambush them. If Theo and Damien don't find any other exits, we will wait them out, make them come to us. Those two will then stick to ranged weapons; their arrows might create a distraction. The woman is not to be harmed, though. Reed – " the prince's eyes landed on the man he trusted the most, " – you'll be taking care of her. I don't want her running away. She's now a part of my plan. We still have plenty of daylight so stay alert and be ready. Anyone have any questions?"

They all knew better than to doubt his judgment if they didn't have anything better to propose. Only Cassiel had the privilege of questioning Magnus' actions.

"Cass…" Magnus turned to his dark knight.

"Yes, Your Highness?" Cassiel took a step forward and bowed his head in acknowledgment.

"I will need you to take a look into the cave and check if they're still there, maybe see how far back it goes. It's been too quiet. I trust you can handle that." Magnus raised his eyebrows, daring Cassiel to dispute.

"Of course, Your Highness." Cassiel was the only one who always addressed Magnus officially. Right now, hearing his title and being reminded of the dignity that went with it, the burdens of the crown he hoped one day to wear, helped focus Magnus' thoughts and kept his temper in check. This was about the dragon, and his kingdom. *Do not make this personal. Do not fail. Do not make a mistake.*

The girl could wait.

"Good. Take your positions."

Galor quickly stole a look into the cave, and seeing nothing, he dashed to the other side of it, Cathal and Lance following the same way. They settled, not too far from the opening, ready for action whenever needed, talking in hushed voices.

Before Cassiel ventured into the cave, Magnus approached Charlie. When she spotted him coming her way, she quickly got up and bowed her head.

"Do you need to be bound and gagged again?" Magnus inquired of her, tilting her head up with his finger under her chin so he could look into her eyes.

"No, my prince. I'll stay out of the way, keep quiet and won't try to run away," she said meekly, finding it easy to cooperate with him, especially when he was on edge like this. She didn't want to suffer the consequences of being cheeky with him. She was usually feisty and quite a firecracker, but Magnus somehow managed to suck the fire out of her whenever he was near.

"Good girl. You have learned your lesson," Magnus smirked but still didn't release her chin. "You will be off today or for however long it takes us to kill that dragon. I want my men ready and not distracted. Understood?"

Charlie nodded.

"I like you submissive like this." He licked his lips as his eyes landed on her tempting mouth. He bit down on his own lip. He hadn't sampled her flesh in a while now and he decided to make sure he would be her next bedding companion. For now, though, he would have to settle for a kiss.

Magnus leaned closer and placed a soft and gentle kiss on her lips. "I need that for good luck." He smiled, winked and sauntered away, leaving a confused Charlie behind him.

She would never understand him. He had so many moods and personalities that she wasn't sure who the real Magnus was. This soft side of him was so rare that she had witnessed it only a few times, mostly in the beginning of their journey together. When he was in his softer moods, he was a gentle and attentive lover. She had even found herself enjoying his body as well. He could make her forget. But not anymore; she would never be able to relax around him ever again. She would always be waiting for the switch to click off, for him to turn back to the ruthless bastard he usually was.

Charlie sat back on the ground as Magnus approached Cassiel.

"Alright," Magnus said, "You are to go inside. You make enough noise so the dragon won't think you're sneaking in. You may even announce your presence and your wish to talk. If you can handle me, you can surely handle a dragon and try to reason with it... make it come out where it'll be ambushed." Magnus patted Cassiel's shoulder; in return the knight gave a curt nod, his face expressionless despite his soft features.

"Mostly, check that they are still in there," Magnus added. "See how far the passage goes, where the cave starts. Maybe even coax the girl out. Just give me some results."

"Yes, Your Highness."

Cassiel grasped his weapons, a short sword and a war-axe, as he peered in. Nothing moved and no fire flew towards him. He took a step in front of the entrance and waited again, ready to jump back. Still nothing. He took slow and careful steps inside. He knew there was no point in sneaking. Moving in his armor always made sufficient noise that stealth was wasted on him. In the end, it might even be better for him not to sneak up on the dragon on his own. The beast might lash out at him without giving it a moment's thought.

He kept his approach cautious but brave. He had taught himself to always expect the unexpected and not to worry about things he could not influence; the worry would only cloud his judgment. But now, as he moved deeper into the cave his heart pounded hard and fast, the pulse resounding in his ears. His eyes darted around, searching the shadows for any sign of danger. His grip on his weapons was tight, but the sword tip was quivering. His usual coolheadedness didn't make facing a dragon any easier. And what was he to say? How to address the dragon?

"Greetings, dragon," he said in a steady voice as he continued forward. "I wish you no harm."

He held his breath, afraid of being deafened by his own sharp intakes of air as he waited for an answer.

Ahead of him, only darkness loomed; the daylight behind him was his only illumination. Soon enough, the dark would prevail, completely taking over the light and he would be forced to take out his torch.

With his next step, his eyes darted left, and then... he froze.

A warm gust of air brushed against his neck. Ever so slowly, the dark knight turned his head toward the source of the sudden change in the air.

He found himself eye to eye with the dragon himself. Amber and slitted, the dragon's gaze bore into him, unwavering. All the air he had been holding in left his lungs in a gut-punching rush.

The dragon's eyes were narrowed at him, assessing, smoke billowing out of his nostrils, enveloping them in a cocoon of privacy.

Cassiel stood frozen, afraid to provoke the dragon's wrath, his eyes never wavering as he studied the dragon's features. Neither made any aggressive moves towards the other.

For the first time in Cassiel's life, fear held him firmly in place. His father would be proud, though, serving his prince so bravely.

The dragon tilted its head. Waiting. It was hard to understand the dragon's expression. Was it waiting for Cassiel to make the first move so it could burn him? Cassiel didn't want to be burned to death like Colin, such a horrible end. But... he did understand the dragon's actions. If he were protecting the ones he loved, he would have done the same. He would have done anything for his family; even serve a prince like Magnus. And it seemed, the dragon wouldn't attack him unprovoked, so he wouldn't draw blood first... not like this.

Reaching an unspoken understanding, Cassiel bowed his head in respect of the dragon's honor as he took an unthreatening step back, keeping his weapons away.

"Kaden?" They both heard the tentative, quiet female voice.

Cassiel kept his eyes focused on the dragon, knowing how it was very protective of the girl. He didn't want to appear as a threat to her; his own life depended on it.

Kaden showed the dark-skinned knight the same respect as he allowed him to retreat further, never breaking eye contact.

When Cassiel got closer to the cave's mouth, Kaden

gave him a nod of permission to turn around and run away. Cassiel obliged more than willingly as he spun around and picked up his pace, heading for the light.

He heard the dragon's deep intake of breath and in the next moment the heat of the fire rushed up to meet him, without harming him. It was just a cover, a precaution, a sign of power.

The dragon had spared his life, a very humbling experience indeed.

❧

Kaden watched the knight run out into the daylight.

"Kaden? I'm afraid. Are you still there?" The soft, quiet voice of the woman he loved reached him.

"Coming," he said as he walked back to Olivia.

The knight had surprised him; his honorable behavior was refreshing. It was so rare in these times, and he was glad to know that honorable men were still out there, even though he himself hadn't been honorable when he was younger.

"I'm here, Love." He lowered himself next to Olivia. She was now sitting with her back against the cave's stone walls with a blanket underneath her, so Kaden settled his snout on her lap.

Olivia was relieved when she felt his presence once again. He had doused the fire earlier because he didn't want to give the men who were after them any advantage, but the darkness shrouding them brought her a sense of unease.

"What happened?" Olivia lifted her hands from the wolf pup lying at her side and brought them down gently on Kaden's snout.

"They sent someone in to check on us and I sent him

out," Kaden replied simply.

"You killed him?"

"No, I just sent him out. I let him go. He didn't do anything. I would *not* kill anyone unprovoked. That is just not who I am."

"Who are you, then?" Olivia softly stroked the rough features of his face.

"Your dragon?"

She could hear the smirk in his voice. "Now, that is a very good answer."

Kaden summoned from his memories her smile, the one that probably graced her face at that moment. It only made his decision harder, his heart aching even more.

He sighed, the smell of his smoke reaching Olivia's nose. "What's wrong?" she said.

"I know what I have to do."

"And what is that?" She wished she hadn't asked that question, because she knew that as long as she didn't know his plan, they would be here together.

"What I should have done in the first place."

CHAPTER 22

"Absolutely not!" Olivia's voice rang out through the cave, startling the men outside as well.

"Liv, keep your voice down. It is the only way. I cannot think of anything else," Kaden said, exasperated with himself for not having created any emergency exits from the cave, but back when he had taken it as his home, he hadn't had a need for them.

"Are you sure there are absolutely no other ways out?" Olivia asked, a little quieter this time.

"No… and I am beating myself up about it now. There are a few cracks in the stone walls of the cave leading outside, but they are too small even for you to squeeze through. I have never had the need for a back exit. I never had people like that coming after me and I never had anyone to look after. If you weren't here I would have just charged out there, fending them off until I reached a place with enough room to fly away." Kaden paced back and forth.

Olivia stood up, pressed against the wall as Pup retreated a bit further, staying out of the way but still alert. She lowered her head. "I'm sorry," she said; a quiver in her voice didn't escape Kaden's notice.

He stopped his pacing and turned to look at Olivia through the darkness. He couldn't distinguish the color of her dress from the soft tones of her hair, but he could see her tiny form slouched with her head lowered. His heart constricted at the sight. Not long ago she had been laughing happily, running around with the pup, and now… So much had happened.

"What are you sorry for?" The dragon moved closer to her.

"For holding you back… you could have been safe by now." Olivia bit her lip, picking at the hem of her sleeve as she heard him shuffle closer.

"Liv." Kaden reprimanded gently. "Do not even start that trail of thought."

"But—"

"No Liv, nothing is your fault… no what ifs. We cannot influence what has already passed and most of those things we didn't have any power over anyway. We cannot change the past, so what's the point in worrying over it? We need to adapt and move on. Think about what's to come and how we can make it work to our advantage." He was much closer to Olivia now, his warm breath brushing over the top of her head.

Olivia tilted her head up and blindly reached out so she could place her hands on each side of his face. "You should take your own advice, then, and stop beating yourself up about the things you cannot change now."

A chuckle escaped Kaden. "You're right." He pulled back slightly. "But I still think my plan is the only way to go."

Olivia sighed. "But –"

"It's the only way. I would have handled it that way regardless. I will just need to hold them off a bit longer so you can have a chance for a head start. As I said, I will charge out, providing distraction and giving you an opportunity to slip past the fight. You just keep on running. They will be slow thanks to their armor, so you should be able outrun them. Once you are far enough away, I will go to the fly-off place and then I will come and find you once you leave the forest. I will come for you. I will find you. I promise." Kaden hoped his words would come true. He knew it wasn't going to be easy, fighting all of them off, but because it was the only way to get Olivia to safety, he would gladly make the sacrifice.

Olivia stepped up under his head, snuggling into his draconic chest. "I am frightened, Kaden. I do not want to lose you."

Kaden rested his big head gently atop of hers. "You won't." Olivia decided to trust his words; it was easier that way.

"What about Puppy?" Olivia asked, her voice quivering as she held back the tears, trying to stay strong.

"We will tie him up in the back cave," Kaden said as he drew back from her.

Using the sleeve of her dress, Olivia wiped away the stray tears. "What do you mean tie him up?" Her brows furrowed in confusion.

"If I don't, he will charge out after me and get himself killed. This way, if I draw their attention away, he will be safe. And if we don't manage to come back for him, he can easily chew through the rope and run free. We will use a thin rope. It is safer that way for him." The dragon's eyes landed on the wolf pup huddled in the corner.

"Makes sense." Olivia nodded. "Alright, we can do this. Even though I still do not understand how someone can be like this prince and these knights. Why won't they let us be? We have done nothing wrong."

"Greed? Fame? Conceit? I think the list could go on.

And when you take into consideration that he is a prince, then pride as well. I have learned over the years that those things really don't matter in the end, but he has not had the years that I have had to realize that."

"Shouldn't he be taking care of his people, helping his father run the kingdom?" Olivia smoothed out her dress, keeping her hands busy, trying to soothe her nerves.

"He should, but he isn't. What does that tell you about him?" Kaden padded toward the back cave. "Wait here, I will be right back." He left Olivia with the pup and her own scrambled thoughts.

Olivia crouched down and reached her hand out to where she thought the wolf pup was. "Come here, Pup," she called gently and a few moments later he licked her outstretched hand and then rubbed his face into her palm. "There you are." Olivia managed a smile as she huddled next to the little wolf again, finding comfort in the heat that radiated from his little body and the softness of his baby fur.

She heard Kaden coming back, then some shuffling before he came closer to her again.

"Here," he said, and a whoosh of air brushed her, followed by a thud. "It's your mattress with another blanket on it."

Kaden settled around it as he usually did before they went to sleep, though this time shielding Olivia. She crawled over and lay down in between the wall and his warm body. Pup followed her and settled at her feet.

Before Olivia snuggled in closer to Kaden, he placed something in her hand, cold and metallic. "Be careful, don't hurt yourself."

Olivia felt the item in her hands and found that it had a sharp point on one end and a handle on the other. It was longer than a dagger, but shorter than a sword.

"It's a dirk." Kaden answered her unspoken question. "I want you to take it with you, a safety measure of sorts. It is easy to wield if needed. You will take it with you, and if someone tries to take you away, you just stab them with the pointed end."

Olivia simply nodded, knowing that Kaden could see her in the dark. She put the dirk within her reach before snuggling up to him.

"Now what?" She pressed the whole length of her body against him, and gently ran her palms over his silky scales. She loved doing that, and if anything were to happen, one of the things she would miss about him would be the feel of him under her fingers.

"We rest and wait a bit. Give them some time to relax and lull them into a false sense of peace, make them think we are biding our time and then… then we will make our attempt. I don't want to wait until tomorrow; we will both be hungry and tired by then so this will be our best chance." Kaden's eyes drifted shut as the delight of her fingers caressing him spread over his scales. He loved how affectionate she was and that she wasn't afraid to show it through her actions, being honest in her declaration of love.

"Do you think maybe I could try and reason with him?" Her brain couldn't stop thinking of possible ways of getting out of their predicament unharmed. She shivered at the thought of Kaden getting hurt for the sake of her safety, and he most definitely would if he went through with his strategy. Even though she didn't approve of his plan, they had no other choice so she appreciated his sacrifice. She knew he wanted to do this for her and there was no point in arguing about it with him. He would only get upset, they would argue, and Olivia didn't want that; what they had was beyond that. And the main reason, of course: she didn't want him distracted when they made a run for it; she wanted him safe as soon as possible.

She would accept his sacrifice, despite it going against her every instinct and desire.

"It would be in vain, trying to reason with the prince," Kaden said. "I have seen men like him before. When he wants something, he will not stop until he gets it or he is dead. If you try and talk to him, he will just try to entice you, lure you out with false promises and once you are within his grasp, those promises would be long forgotten," Kaden explained as he settled his head above her, the tip of his snout resting on the mattress, his breath brushing over the mess of her wavy dark hair.

Olivia inhaled his breath as if it were the air sustaining her life, the scent of it unique to Kaden. It probably would have bothered others, the smell of burning, but to her, it was comforting because it was all him.

Her dragon.

She had never heard him sound so serious. Sure, in the beginning he was a bit rough and gruff, serious too, but it was a different kind of serious, the wary kind, not as mature as now. All the years of his life finally showing through a bit. He had been more lighthearted and young around her, making her forget that he was probably over a hundred years old.

"I trust your judgment." Olivia said.

Kaden reveled in that part of her, the simplicity and her acceptance of him. It was one of the reasons he loved her, for she took him the way he was. She snuggled even closer, reaching for him tighter as she pressed her lips softly against his scales. He wished those soft pink lips could be pressed against his. Maybe one day it would be possible. If they lived through today.

Her lips were replaced by her soft cheek.

ॐ

"Wake up, love. It is time," Kaden whispered and Olivia stirred. He moved away, taking the warmth with him. She frowned, wanting him back so they would never have to part. With a heavy sigh, she sat up and rubbed her eyes with the heel of her palms.

"So it was not all a dream? With the prince, I mean," Olivia whispered back.

"No." Kaden's clipped answer disturbed her.

"Kaden?"

"I am sorry, it is just—"

"I know." Olivia rose to her feet.

"I will need your help with Pup."

"Alright," Olivia said as she touched the wall and followed it to the opening leading back. "Where is he?"

"Following you, just keep going."

"Good puppy," Olivia praised in the darkness, and she gulped down the nerves fluttering up from her belly.

ॐ

Olivia stepped closer to Kaden, who had his head bowed so his eyes were level with hers. Tentatively, she raised her hands and put her palms on each side of his face. Kaden closed his eyes and soaked up her soft caress. She then slowly touched her forehead against the bridge of his snout and closed her eyes as well. The quiet sounds of the pup's whimpers, whines and protests cracked her aching heart even more. She had a bad feeling about it all but was afraid to voice her thoughts and give them life.

"I love you, Kaden. Please survive and come for me. I need you," Olivia pleaded softly. Her need for him was much stronger than her love. She loved him, yes, but needed him like she needed the air and it scared her. Her feelings for him frightened her; the emotions had blossomed so fast that they hadn't had a chance to settle in her heart. Maybe it was his mysteriousness or her unattainable and forbidden love for him, she couldn't be sure, but she knew her feelings were true, however she tried to rationalize them. She never shied away from her emotions.

Kaden sighed and a soft cloud of smoke surrounded them, enveloping Olivia and him in their little private cocoon, creating an intimate ambience.

"I need you too, Liv." His deep voice sent shivers down her spine and the gentleness in it brought tears to her eyes. "I promise I will come for you. Even death itself could not stop me." The oath rang true in his voice; he meant it with every fiber of his being. "When I tell you to run, you run as fast as you can. Don't turn back to try and help if you think I need it. You know I can handle it. But I need you safe, otherwise the whole purpose of me holding them off would be defeated, not to mention that having you around would keep me distracted so I would worry more about your safety than anything else. So please promise me, Liv. Promise you will run."

Olivia knew there was no point in arguing with him and she didn't want to ruin what could possibly be their last moment together. But she hoped and believed that he would be back for her.

She laid a gentle kiss where her forehead had been pressed and whispered softly, "I promise." And she meant it.

Taking a step back, Olivia opened her eyes and looked up at her dragon. They were closer to the entrance of the cave so some light managed to reach them, providing her with a little bit of illumination, her sight once again getting used to the light.

Kaden was looking her over, trying to commit everything about her to his memory. The soft curls in her unruly hair, the love shining through her bright blue eyes. Her soft skin, the few tiny freckles dancing across her cheeks. His eyes lingered on her lips. He wished he were able to kiss her back just as gently and reassuringly. He just needed to be able to remember her face and he knew that he would be alright, whatever his outcome. As long as she was safe.

Olivia, on the other hand, just watched his eyes roam her face. She would never forget his eyes and the way he looked at her, the way they smiled like she was his whole world. And the way his scales felt under her touch. She would cherish that forever.

Their eyes met. Neither dared say goodbye, only maybe *see you soon*. Kaden inhaled deeply and she knew what that meant. He was ready.

With one last glance at her tear-stained face, Kaden charged out.

The dragon spewed his fiery breath in a long exhale, curving it from his right to his left. The knights were caught off guard; they hadn't expected him. They had heard his approach but there wasn't enough time to react. Galor and Cathal managed to jump back out of range but Lance wasn't that lucky, being burned to crisp on the spot.

As Kaden's fire traveled to the other side, Cassiel managed to push Donovan back to safety while Reed and Magnus ducked behind a boulder, narrowly avoiding getting caught in the blaze of the dragon's fire.

In the distance, Charlie's screams of fear and panic pierced the otherwise peaceful sunset.

The arrows flew by Kaden's head but it didn't escape

his notice that they weren't as precise as the first time. He didn't have the time to ponder that now and search out his friendly foes.

His head snapped back around toward Cathal and Galor when he felt the thrust of their swords into his side. The sight of their burning brother at arms panicked them and their grip on their weapons shook, preventing them from digging their swords in properly. Kaden narrowed his gaze at Cathal. He needed to get rid of one pest at a time. He bit hard on Cathal's shoulder, fangs sinking through skin and flesh, breaking bone, and he lifted him up off the ground then slung him away. That would keep him down and out of the fight.

Seeing his bloodied brother soaring through the air fed Galor's anger and he swung his sword with new fervor.

He had to go next. Kaden needed the opening for Olivia to slip through unharmed.

On his other side, the men recuperated and threw themselves into the fray. Reed jumped, soaring through the air, ready to sink his sword into the dragon's back. Kaden swung his tail out of the cave and sent Reed crashing into Cassiel.

A sword pierced his side, under his armpit where his scales were softer. An angry roar escaped him, adrenalin pumping through his veins, and a primal instinct woke inside him. He had never felt that rush before, as if a caged animal had been set free.

As he turned towards his new offender, another swish of his tail made Galor fly back as well. The man landed on the ground with a thud and all the air left his lungs.

Kaden's eyes clashed with Magnus as he pulled the now bloody sword out with a wicked smile on his face.

"Now, Olivia!" Kaden bellowed, his eyes filled with rage. He achieved the effect he was hoping for, because his attackers paused for a moment to see what would happen. He used their moment of distraction to send Reed stumbling back again with the swipe of his hand, claws scraping the knight's armor.

Olivia ran out of the cave and to the right of Kaden where she had seen him make an opening for her. She ducked under his wing and jumped over a now charred corpse, clutching the dirk tightly in her hands. She looked back for a moment and saw a man stumble back as others continued their attack on her dragon. Out of the corner of her eye she saw the redheaded woman in the background, holding her hands up to her mouth in fear. Their eyes met.

Charlie shook her head no to Olivia, removed her hands from her lips and mouthed, "Run."

Olivia didn't need any other incentive, as she quickly turned around so she could mind her footing, pumping her legs harder, her muscles burning. The sounds of battle faded but the clambering of metal armor followed her.

She glanced over her shoulder again and spotted the man she had seen stumbling backward, now chasing after her. He had a predator's look in his eyes; she shivered and gripped the dirk even tighter.

Behind the man, Kaden followed, trying to reach her pursuer while ignoring the pain piercing through his body as the others continued their onslaught on the dragon. Slowing down from her sprint because she couldn't take her eyes off of Kaden, Olivia narrowly avoided tripping and stumbling.

Since Kaden couldn't reach the man following her fast enough and the others slashing at him were slowing him down, he inhaled and with a quick, sharp exhale spat a ball of fire toward the man.

The inferno hit a nearby tree but not without scorching the back of Reed's head as it flew by, heating up his armor.

His screams rent the air as he stumbled and dropped to his knees. He quickly threw away his gauntlets and snatched off the chainmail hood before it melded with his skin. He then desperately tried to put out the fire burning his head with his bare hands.

Olivia met Kaden's eyes for one last time.

"Kaden!" she yelled, skidding to a halt as Magnus swung his sword down, piercing through the dragon's wing and pinning him to the earth.

Kaden's roar of pain and fury echoed over the mountain, and Olivia saw his eyes turn completely black as he switched his attention back to Magnus and his men.

As hard as it was for her, Olivia turned away and forced her legs to move again. She had promised him. She had now witnessed what a distraction she could be for him and what she might cost him. She dared not turn back around as she picked up speed, because she wouldn't be able to keep from going back to help him.

It was the hardest thing she had ever had done in her life.

She ran as fast as she could, jumping over tree roots and dodging branches as she ignored all the scratches that painted random patterns on her exposed skin. It was like history repeating itself, closing a circle, but this time she was *not* running away of her own volition.

She didn't know how long she ran but her lungs and muscles were on fire when the familiar bang reached her ears. Her heart stopped for a moment… *Did that mean? No, it cannot!* Her eyes welled up with tears and her vision blurred. She let her feet carry her on. No longer watching where she was running, she stumbled down a decline.

The dirk slipped out of her hands as she braced herself with her palms, but the momentum kept her rolling, as she tried to grab onto a wooden limb or a root or just to slow her tumble with her arms. She was glad the dirk had fallen from her grasp. It would be too ironic if she had managed to stab herself. As she rolled to a stop at the bottom, her head made sharp contact with a stone and she didn't fight the darkness that came upon her.

CHAPTER 23

Pain.

It seared Olivia's head when consciousness drifted back to her mind. Her temples throbbed; so did her right hand. Her whole body ached and her ribs were tender. Her eyes were glued together and her throat dry and scratchy, lips chapped.

She tried to raise her hand to rub away the sleep from her eyes, but regretted the action as soon as she did it. The pain shot through her like a lightning bolt. Consequently, her head throbbed even more. She willed the pounding away, hammering to the rhythm of her heartbeat.

A groan, she managed.

"Livvie? My sweet?" A soft, familiar female voice reached her ears, the sound of footsteps following promptly.

"Livvie?" A soft hand touched Olivia's cheek.

"Mother?" Olivia fought through the fog in her brain and managed to flutter her eyes open.

The first thing she saw was her mother's warm but tired smile and her brown eyes filled with tears. "Oh Livvie!" Lady Caroline said as she wrapped her arms around Olivia in a gentle embrace.

Olivia returned the hug with the hand that she could move without any pain and comforted her mother with an awkward pat on the back. She was confused. Her eyes scanned her surroundings blearily and she noticed that she was in her room, lying on her soft bed, in her mother's warm embrace. The light shone softly through the crack in the heavy velvet curtains, which she was grateful for. The brightness hurt her eyes.

Olivia tried to speak again but only managed to croak out something incomprehensible.

"Oh, here… Take slow sips." Her mother unwound her arms from around Olivia so she could press a cup of water to Olivia's parched lips.

When the worried woman put the cup back down, she took Olivia's slightly bruised face gently in her hands and looked at her like she was a miracle. The love shone strong through her tired, red-rimmed eyes. "My dear Olivia, I thought I would never see you again." She kissed her daughter's cheeks, tears starting to flow again.

The last thing Olivia remembered was rolling down the decline, praying to the One God to either make it stop or make her lose consciousness.

Kaden!

Please let him be alright, she chanted in her mind. She needed some answers first.

"Wha…" Olivia cleared her throat before she continued. "What happened?" She looked up at her mother, wincing as she brought her right hand up to rest it against her chest. It was then she discovered that the hand was wrapped up tightly in a splint. A bandage was wound around her head as well.

Lady Caroline saw the physical pain in her daughter's eyes and before she answered her child's questions she offered, "Do you want something for the pain first, my sweet? You must hurt fiercely." She was relieved to have her daughter back, alive. Everything else would be dealt with and would heal in time with a lot of love and care.

When Olivia nodded, which caused her to wince again, Lady Caroline walked over to the desk and prepared the tea of mixed herbs that the young healer had given her for this exact purpose. Returning to Olivia's side, Lady Caroline's eyes welled up again at the sight of her daughter, bruised and battered but safe in her own bed. The days and nights she had spent awake, worrying over Olivia's safety, were all blurred together. It felt like an eternity had passed, but her baby was home now.

"Here." Lady Caroline offered the tea to Olivia's lips. "This should help; do not worry, it is only warm, not hot."

Olivia took the first sip tentatively. When her tongue was not burned and the taste was manageable, she drank it all, quenching her thirst with the tangy liquid.

Putting the now empty cup on the bedside table, Olivia's mother sat on the bed beside her and took Olivia's uninjured hand in her own.

"How much do you remember?" Lady Caroline said cautiously.

"Everything. Until I hit my head; from then on, everything is black." Olivia barely held back her tears. Tears of fear and worry for Kaden. She closed her eyes for a few moments to compose herself before opening them and giving her mother's hand a squeeze and a fake reassuring smile as a sign for her to continue.

"Well, from what we have been told, Prince Magnus and his men had been hunting a dragon for quite a while and when they finally found him, they discovered you as well, being its victim, abused and held captive." Olivia's mother frowned at the thought of her daughter being mistreated and didn't notice the alarm in Olivia's eyes as her throat constricted and no words could pass through.

Her mother continued, "They fought the dragon off to offer you a chance to escape and once the prince killed the dragon, they found you unconscious. Apparently, your foot got caught in a root, so you fell and hit your head on a rock." Olivia's breath halted, trapped in her lungs; the thought of Kaden's death froze all of her brain functions, her heart almost beating its way out of her chest. The shrapnel of her broken heart pierced her lungs, and she drew in a slow, painful breath. Her vision blurred and she could barely make out her mother's words as she continued speaking about how Magnus had taken Olivia and his surviving and wounded men to the first big city they came to. On their way they had passed near her family's estate and happened to encounter a man who knew her family and who had recognized Olivia's unconscious body. Knowing her family had been looking for her, the man quickly led them to her home.

Her mother's words were a mess in her head.

"How long?" Olivia's fingers dug into the sheet at her side, holding together the last cracking pieces of her heart.

"You were asleep for three days."

"Three days?!" The first tear rolled down Olivia's bruised cheek. "Kaden…"

Her voice quivered, "The dragon?" Olivia looked up at her mother, tears now running freely down her cheeks.

"Dead, as I said," her mother repeated, brows furrowed. "They brought its big claw with them. The head was too big to carry without a wagon."

My dragon!

Olivia's eyes widened in panic for a split second before she burst into tears, reaching for her mother, her lifeline.

Lady Caroline mistook her daughter's tears of sorrow and heartbreak for tears of fear and relief that the dragon was dead. "Oh, my dear, sweet child… It is alright now… you are safe." She held Olivia in her arms once more, running a hand up and down her back reassuringly.

Olivia wanted to tell her mother about Kaden, about Magnus, wanted to tell her the truth, but her brain had given precedence to her heart and it did not want to speak but tried to hold itself together, fighting against what she had just heard.

Her mother just held her and offered the comfort of her embrace and soothing words, trying to erase Olivia's worries. Just when Olivia started to gather herself up so she could speak her truth, her father walked in through the door.

"Father?" Olivia whispered reverently. She waited for the chiding and scolding to start. The last time they saw each other, their exchange involved shouting and harsh words. She regretted them all; she loved her father immensely and had never wanted to hurt him.

Lady Caroline stood up so she could give her husband access to their daughter. Lord Connal's tired blue eyes were set on Olivia, the dark circles around them completely out of place on his face. He was a man of great stature and charisma. When he entered a room, he never went unnoticed, and this trait only became more prominent as he got older, his once light brown hair now completely silvery white. But now he looked exhausted, distressed and his actual age. Usually he stood worthy of his title, proud, tall and neat, but now, as he gazed at his only child with nothing but adoration, and with a slight stubble on his face, he looked like an ordinary man.

"I am sor—" Olivia's father cut her off by closing the distance between them and taking her into his arms.

"No. I am the one who should apologize… I am so, so sorry my dear Violet," her father choked out, fighting his own tears.

Only her father called her Violet. Since her parents hadn't been able to agree on a name, they had given her both, Olivia Violet, so hearing her father call her the name that only he used made her cry again, this time breaking into heart-wrenching sobs.

Lord Connal cradled his daughter against his chest. He slowly eased one of his big hands under her knees and lifted her tenderly into his lap while resting his back against the headboard of her bed. His heart wept for her and her pain. Her whole body was shaking, her sobs loud and painful and her breath getting faster and faster.

She was starting to hyperventilate.

When Olivia gasped for air, Lord Connal took her face in his hands and forced her to look into his bright blue, but red-rimmed, eyes.

"Look at me… Good girl. You need to calm down… you need to breathe. Come on, Violet. I am not angry at you. I am just glad to have my girl back, to know that you are alive and safe, and whatever happened out there… you are strong enough to handle it, after all, you are your father's daughter." He offered her a small reassuring smile. Olivia closed her eyes for a moment, grateful to have been blessed which such wonderful parents.

Olivia forced herself to follow the rhythm of her father's deep breaths.

"That is it. My girl," her father praised and planted a soft kiss against her forehead. He tried to wipe away her tears with his thumbs but it was a failed attempt; they just kept on coming strong.

All the crying made Olivia's head hurt worse, even with the herbs she had taken. The headache, her head wound and the stress of crying made her nauseous.

Olivia opened her eyes, searching frantically for her mother. She felt the sickening feeling rising in her stomach so when Olivia spotted her, she quickly put a hand up to her mouth.

Lady Caroline dashed across the room, grabbed the washbowl and brought it to her daughter just in time as Olivia started heaving. Lord Connal held Olivia's hair back and rubbed her back gently.

When Olivia was done, she washed out her mouth and took a couple of sips of water. She snuggled back up to her father, soaking up his strength and feeling of safety. She felt like a little girl again.

It didn't take her long before she fell asleep.

"I am so sorry," Lord Connal whispered against his sleeping daughter's hair as he kissed her head softly. He felt a hand on his shoulder and looked up into the warm eyes of his lovely wife.

"It is not your fault, my dear." Lord Connal's wife leaned over and kissed him on the cheek.

"It is. If I had not forced her… she would not have run away. I should have listened to her and not…not gone off like that on her." His eyes were filled with deep regret. He loved his daughter to pieces and was sorry that his actions had caused all of their late problems.

"It is not only your fault then. If you want to place the blame, then it is on all of us." Lady Caroline wiped a stray tear away. "It was mine and Olivia's just as much as yours. She is as stubborn and impulsive as you are and she acted on impulse instead of taking the time to think things through. She is old enough to know better and I….I just stood by and did nothing. We are all equally to blame."

&

A few hours later, Olivia woke again. She was nestled safely in her bed and felt a weight on her left hand. Opening her eyes, she looked down to see her father's head resting against her unharmed hand. Pulling her hand free, she rested it softly against his hair.

Looking around, relief settled over her as she studied her room. It wasn't anything fancy in her opinion. She had a nice queen-sized, four poster, dark-wooden bed with violet drapes and a sky blue quilt with cloud patterns on it. Her mother had made it for her sixteenth birthday. On each side of the bed were nightstands with drawers, an oil lamp resting on each. They were not burning now as the sunlight poured into the room from the high windows on her right. The violet velvet curtains filtered it, illuminating the room softly. The floor was made from dark wood as was most of her furniture; her dressing table with a mirror that had been in the family for generations, and a wonderfully crafted wardrobe with butterfly and dragonfly patterns carved into it stood next to it. Her study desk and shelves filled with books that she loved rested against the other wall with a pair of velvet-covered armchairs facing it. Her dresser was the simplest piece of furniture. Another mirror was set on the wall above the drawers and a vase with fresh cut roses was set on it, their scent drifting across the room to comfort her. Olivia always loved the scent of her mother's pink roses. On her left side next to the dresser were the doors to her room and straight ahead was the fireplace, a family picture resting over the mantel above it.

Olivia smiled at the sight of it.

Movement to her left caught her attention. Her mother was sitting in a chair next to her father, watching Olivia curiously, a book set face down on her lap. Olivia wondered how she had missed her when she had scanned her room.

She offered her mother a tired smile that never reached her eyes.

"Tea? For the pain?" Lady Caroline inquired and Olivia

only nodded in return.

The movement in the room woke her father as well and he raised his head from his napping position.

"Hello Vee." He smiled softly, relieved that she had settled down somewhat.

"Hello Father." Olivia tried to smile in return.

The door to her room opened and Magnus stepped in, looking worried, offering Olivia and her parents a weak, sheepish smile, showing off his dimples.

Olivia's smile dropped and she sobered up completely. *What is he doing here?!* Her heart started beating fast again. She was just about to tell her parents what had truly happened to her, when he had to come and disrupt her attempts.

"I hope I am not interrupting," Magnus said as he looked at Olivia's father.

"Oh, not at all, Your Highness." Lord Connal beamed at the prince as he rose from the chair.

"No need to stand up on my account, Lord Moore." Magnus was relieved that he was still welcome in the household. He could tell he had arrived just in time before Olivia managed to tell them her side of the story, and he had a feeling her parents would believe Olivia's words over Magnus' any day. He couldn't let that happen. "I was just worried about my princess, so I came to see how she was doing." He looked at Olivia with a full smile on his face as he ran his fingers through his now shorter blonde hair.

"Well, you came just in time. She has managed to calm down now and we were about to tell her about your proposal." Lady Caroline finished mixing the herbs and picked up the cup to bring it to Olivia.

"Proposal?" Olivia couldn't help but to wonder.

Her father squeezed her hand gently before he spoke up. "Yes. I know we had set up a marriage for you with

Lord Mykke, and I am sorry about forcing it on you and we will discuss that later… as I said, I know we already promised your hand to Lord Mykke but that arrangement has been annulled. Lord Mykke has been very cooperative since Prince Magnus asked for your hand in marriage so you could be his queen one day."

Olivia's mouth fell open. All the air seemed to rush out of the room, leaving her gaping in mute, disbelieving horror. She tried to comprehend what her father was saying, for the words to fully settle in her mind, while Magnus grinned over the shoulders of her parents.

"I….I…"

"This time though, we will not force it upon you." Lord Connal looked with a stern face at his prince. "Even if he is the future King himself, it will be up to you to accept, my dear Violet."

Now both her parents and Magnus were looking at her, expecting an answer.

Magnus drew her attention as he raised his hand behind her parents' backs. The cold crept into his gaze, eyebrows furrowed and his lips set into a straight line. He looked pointedly at her mother, then her father and then, very slowly, drew his index finger across his own throat.

Olivia gulped. *Did he just…?* She dared not finish the thought.

"You can take your time to think about it of course. After all, you have been through so much," Olivia's father offered when Olivia didn't respond.

Magnus's eyebrows rose at her.

"I…" Olivia started to say and saw Magnus nod his head at her, letting her know she should say yes before he pointed to her parents again, behind their backs. "I accept." Olivia saw no other choice. She had apparently lost Kaden; she was not about to sacrifice her parents. They didn't deserve it and she already felt like an empty shell. How much worse could it be?

"Are you sure, Livvie?" Lady Caroline asked as she studied her daughter's tired face, still holding the cup in her hands.

With a fake smile, Olivia nodded again. "Yes… I am sure. After all, he is my knight in shining armor," she said as she kept her eyes on Magnus. She couldn't lie and look her parents in the eyes.

An approving smile appeared on Magnus' face.

"I am just tired… and in pain." Olivia's gaze shifted back to her father and her mother, seeking understanding. The haunted look had been in her eyes since she had woken up. It was very hard for them to read her.

"Of course, Princess." Magnus walked closer to Olivia, bypassed her father and leaned over to lay a gentle kiss on her forehead. Olivia barely managed not to gag and vomit at the feel of his lips against her skin. He softly cupped her cheek with his hand. "You rest and heal. As soon as you recover enough we will leave for the palace. I have a future Queen to present to our people."

৪১

Two days later, Olivia was finally allowed to leave her room. Magnus was always around, hovering, threatening her with menacing surreptitious glances, never leaving her alone with either of her parents for long enough to tell them what had happened, under the excuse that he was worried about her wellbeing.

She had learned that he had lost another knight in the fight against Kaden, and that two more were seriously injured, one of them with a severely burned head. A boy named Donovan nursed them. He was also the one who provided her with the mixture of herbs that eased her pain. The redheaded girl that she had seen with them was apparently Magnus' cousin; they were escorting her to the palace along the way. Olivia somehow doubted the whole story.

When she had been left in her room alone, she had cried. She cried for Kaden, and for their bond that had developed so strongly in the few days they had together. She mourned alone, never running out of tears. The grief prolonged her recovery, and an ever-present headache lingered. She mostly kept to herself, her thoughts unsaid. She would rather not talk than be forced to lie to her parents. Talking was hard for her anyways, just another distraction that would bring her walls down, the sorrow threatening to drown her.

In a few days, when Magnus' men had recovered enough, she would be leaving her home and parents behind again, which was going to be another thing to grieve about. At least she could keep *them* safe.

She had heard that Lord Mykke would be visiting today. He had come to visit when she was bedridden, but her parents wouldn't let him see her and now she wanted to apologize to him in person for running away.

She stood at the entrance to the stables, waiting for him to come out.

Her hand was still splinted, nestled safely in a sling against her chest. It would take a month or two for it to heal completely. The few bruises on her face were healing, the colors fading, and her head was much better, the bandages taken off. She had hit the back of her head against a rock and had even needed a couple of stitches. It was healing nicely, but she still had the occasional bout of nausea if she moved her head too quickly.

The door to the stable opened, drawing Olivia's

attention from her mother's flowers to the man coming out through them. He was very tall and a bit on the skinny side. His hair was golden blond, cut short and neat, and a set of slightly crinkled hazel eyes spotted Olivia immediately. Relief washed over his face and his thoughtful expression was replaced by one of joy. A wide smile on his face, showing off his perfectly straight white teeth, drew attention away from his slightly crooked nose.

"Livvie!" the man exclaimed as he closed the distance between them, picking Olivia up off her feet, making her wince in pain. "Oh! I apologize… You are hurt. I am just happy they found you." He gently put her down.

"It is alright, Sebastian. I am glad to see you, too." Olivia managed to reward him with a tiny, honest smile.

"Do you want to go for a walk? Or just sit in the garden? We have some catching up to do and you have some explaining to do as well." Lord Mykke scolded Olivia playfully but when he saw that her face remained serious instead of gracing him with one of her bright smiles, he frowned. "Are you alright, Love?" He cupped her cheek gently.

Olivia closed her eyes and leaned into his palm for a bit of comfort. Him calling her Love with friendly affection brought memories of Kaden calling her that with different emotions behind the words. She held her breath as she fought against the tears.

She drew back, opened her eyes and wiped away the one tear that managed to get past her restraints.

"No, I am not alright. But I will be; I just need some time."

Lord Mykke nodded. "Is there anything I can do for you?" He was always such a good friend, despite the ten-season gap between them.

Olivia shook her head no. "I just need some time alone.

I actually came to see you so I could apologize. For running away when I learned of our betrothal."

"Am I such a bad choice?" Lord Mykke was used to teasing her so it was hard for him not to be playful, and this time he managed to get another smile from Olivia.

"You will be a wonderful husband to your wife someday. You know I love you dearly 'Bastian, you are a wonderful person. But," Olivia shrugged, "you are more like an older brother to me. It would have been awkward at the best. And what would have happened if I had met someone I could actually come to love romantically?"

"I know what you mean, Livvie." Olivia saw something flash in his eyes before he continued. "At the time, when your father asked, mind you it was not my idea, it seemed reasonable enough. Combining our estates, me finally settling down, and I knew you, knew what to expect. It made sense, but after I accepted, I actually thought about it for a few days. When I started spending more time in your company, I came to the conclusion that it was a bad idea after all, for the same reasons as yours. But I could not go back to your father and tell him I had changed my mind. That would have been quite a debacle," Lord Mykke admitted, his voice barely above a whisper.

"I should have talked about it with you. And don't you dare tell your father what I just told you. I am actually relieved that the prince asked for your hand, and may I say that he is a much better match for you." Lord Mykke wrapped his hand around Olivia's shoulder and led her towards the gardens.

Out of the corner of her eye, Olivia saw a man walking by. She recognized him as one of Magnus' men, and the look of resentment he gave her quickly had her agreeing with her friend.

"Yes, he is," Olivia answered as she looked at the

flowers.

"Thank you for your apology; not many would admit to a fault like that. But I always knew you were too nice a person not to feel guilty about it. So I absolve you from all the guilt," Lord Mykke said as he gave her shoulder a gentle squeeze.

Olivia frowned. "Bastian? You seem overly happy about all of this. What is going on? I have never seen you this chirpy."

"Can I not just be happy to see you safe?" It was the slight quiver in his voice that made her think there was something more.

"No… I mean yes, but that is not like you. Usually you are the quieter and more mature one and I am the chipper one, so?" Olivia stopped them and turned to face him, a stern look on her face. "Is there someone else?"

His blush was her answer. "Oh my, there is someone else, is there not, Bastian?"

Lord Mykke let out a deep breath and nodded. "But it is complicated…"

I wish I could have my complicated back, Olivia thought as she locked eyes with him, not letting him look away.

She narrowed her eyes. "Well, complicated be damned!" she blurted. "Do not wait, do not wonder, do *NOT* care what others think. If you really love her and she loves you back, you should be together. Mind, body and soul. Unless you want to spend the rest of your life regretting that you did not take the plunge and wondering what if."

Olivia's outburst caught Lord Mykke by surprise. He had never witnessed such passion in her about anything; it made her passion for horses pale by comparison. "Olivia?"

"Do *not* Olivia me. If you don't marry that woman, I will personally… make sure you never have an heir." She nodded, satisfied with her threat.

"Are you alright?" he couldn't help but ask.

"I told you I am not, but I do not want to talk about it and we are talking about you now."

Raising his arms in surrender, Lord Mykke conceded to Olivia. He had never witnessed her lose her temper like that. She had never been the aggressive type.

"She is one of my servants," he admitted, afraid of more of Olivia's outbursts.

"So? I do not understand the problem." If she could, Olivia would have folded her hands across her chest, but she had to settle by putting her healthy hand on her hip, glaring at him.

"She is one of my servants." He repeated disbelievingly.

"I heard you the first time; I am not deaf. She could be the daughter of a beggar and you will still regret it if you don't do something about it. You are your own man, you have your riches, your estate. You don't have your parents to lecture you or make you worry about their opinion. You can do as you please. Forget about what others think of it. It is your life and they will get over it; if they don't, well, that is just too bad for them; show them the door and kick them on their way out." Olivia took a deep breath to calm herself.

She continued in a much softer voice. "Please Sebastian, do *not* miss out on your opportunity to be happy. If you don't want to be selfish then think of her. Do you want somebody else to marry her… to kiss her and touch her the way you want to? What if she ends up with someone who doesn't love her, maybe even beats her? Do you want that for her or do you want to make her happy with everything you have to offer to her?" By the end of her speech, Olivia was once again in tears.

Lord Mykke wrapped her in his arms gently and held her against his chest. "No, you are right. I don't want anybody else putting their hands on her." He lay his head on top of Olivia's head. "Thank you for the support. For not making me feel guilty if I follow my heart." He kissed the side of her temple.

"But, what is going on with you, Livvie?" He pulled back.

"A lot…" She averted her gaze.

He wiped away her tears and turned her face towards him. "Talk to me. Are you not happy?"

"What is she like?"

"Olivia…" Lord Mykke frowned at her.

She pulled her face away from her dear friend's gentle grasp, pasted on a fake smile and asked again, "What is she like?"

Lord Mykke was well aware of her stubbornness; if she didn't want to talk about it, he knew there was no way for him to make her. He let out a defeated sigh and when he started talking about the woman he loved, his eyes sparkled to life. "She's beautiful… She joined my household a few months ago. Her uncle works for me. She has long blonde hair which is usually braided, soft light brown eyes and her smile is almost as bright as yours, but much more… hmmm… quirky. She's taller than you, perfect for me. She's twenty-eight years old, closer to my age than you are. She's feisty and isn't afraid to talk back. She…" Lord Mykke was interrupted by somebody clearing their throat beside them.

They both turned and saw Magnus standing there. It was probably that man of his who had alerted him to their conversation, Olivia thought.

"Is everything alright here?" Magnus took a step closer towards Olivia, who barely refrained herself from taking a step back. "Have you been crying again, princess?" He turned his eyes to Lord Mykke. "What did you say to her?"

He furrowed his brow.

Lord Mykke was at first taken back by the prince's presence, as he hadn't had a chance to meet him yet.

"I apologize, Your Highness." Lord Mykke bowed. "I am Lord Mykke, Lady Olivia's friend. I just came to see how she was recuperating."

"So *you* are Lord Mykke?" Magnus couldn't help but smirk. "I am sorry to have taken this precious gem away from you." Magnus wrapped a hand around Olivia's waist as he snuggled her against his side.

Olivia forced herself to lean into Magnus. She didn't want Sebastian figuring it out. That would be another set of problems to deal with, and who knew what Magnus might do to him if he doubted something.

"She is very precious, Your Highness, and I know she will be in great care with you." Lord Mykke studied them together. They made quite a couple, so he nodded approvingly when he saw that Olivia didn't pull away, even though the haunted look never left her eyes. He presumed it would take time for it to go away. Who knew what the dragon had done to her.

"She will be. She has been through a lot lately, so I have to apologize for stealing her away from you yet again."

"Yes, of course. I need to speak to Lord Moore, so I will bid you a good day." Lord Mykke bowed again to the prince and gave Olivia one last warm smile. "We can continue some other time."

"Of course, Lord Mykke," Olivia answered and watched her friend walk away.

After Lord Mykke was far enough, Magnus returned his attention to Olivia. "Now my Princess, you will become my dearest puppet. I have to explain to you how all of this will work out."

Magnus led Olivia to one of the garden benches, making

sure no one was around as he made her sit down and took a seat close to her himself.

He put one of his hands on the back of her neck, holding her head firmly in place. Olivia tried to pull away but was still too weak to fight him off and the sudden movement of her head only brought dizziness and nausea. It also didn't help that he tightened his grip on her.

When he noticed her giving up her struggles, he brought his other hand up to caress her face with the back of his hand. He loved the feeling of her bruised skin.

For those who watched from a distance it seemed like a lover's comforting caress and nobody wanted to intrude on their intimate moment.

Looking straight into her eyes, he stated coldly but quietly, "I will have you. You will be mine. You will leave this place with me and accompany me to the capital and the palace. You love your parents, right?"

She nodded apprehensively.

"You want them alive and unharmed?" he asked next.

She didn't like what he was hinting at again so she nodded, tears welling in her eyes. All her smiles had been replaced with tears.

"You will cause no problems regarding our departure. I am more than capable of fulfilling my threats, understand? Accidents happen all the time." His eyes never wavered from hers.

"Yes," she responded firmly and leaned in closer. "Just so we are clear... I hate you."

Her response provoked a menacing yet amused chuckle from him.

"Puppet, I don't care how you feel about me. I will have you —" he paused a bit and licked his lips as he looked her over, "— all of you." Magnus whispered the last words right into her ear, his whiskey-tainted breath fogging her hair.

She managed to pull back a bit so she could turn her head and glare at him but before she could retort, he spoke again. "Of course, I'll let you recover a bit first. So you don't look like a beaten whore. I've had my share of those. And I want you to be able to fight back. I like them feisty. Oh, my dear, dear puppet, the things I'll do to you, we will have so much fun together."

The longing glint in his eyes and the shivers of dread running down her spine left her no doubt that he would not hold back and that he meant every word he said to her so in his venomous soft voice.

"I will – " Before she could finish saying it, Magnus roughly pressed his lips to hers.

Olivia was thankful that wasn't her first kiss.

She tried to draw back but his hold on her was too strong. She had had enough of him; she didn't need to put up with him yet, so she kissed him back, relaxing in his arms, forcing him to soften his lips as she let her own part.

He moaned at her sudden surrender and she used his distraction to bite hard on his lower lip, drawing blood as she clamped down almost hard enough to pierce through his lip with her teeth.

He jerked back, stood up and watched the fire burn in her eyes as he sucked at the blood on his lip. He loved that about her, and if he could not have her love, he would have that fire.

Bringing his fingers to his bleeding lip, he said, "Just as feisty as I imagined you'd be."

He gave her an exaggerated bow. "I will see you at dinner, my lovely puppet." With that, he turned on his heel and sauntered towards the house.

Grim determination burned through her, heating her skin. She would play along for now, for her parents' safety, but she would not make it easy for him. Maybe she would find the solution along the way or maybe the right opportunity would present itself at the castle. Her family would be known by then, and they would be somewhat safe. She could be the worst wife ever, and the best Queen the Kingdom had ever had. She would survive this, it would make her stronger, she could be braver. At least he left her alone for now.

Olivia sighed a breath of relief, but Magnus turned around one last time. He said something that made her shed those tears she had been holding back.

"And remember. Your dragon is dead."

EPILOGUE

"Are you paying attention, Delilah?"

Her mother's voice snapped Delilah out of her daydreaming. "Yes, Mother!" She sat up straighter at her desk and tried to focus her eyes on her mother and away from her doodles and drawings.

No one would have ever guessed that the woman in front of her was her mother. First, she looked young. Very young. She appeared to be twenty-five seasons old but Delilah knew that her mother was much, much older than that. Older than anyone she had ever met. Which wasn't many, really.

When a person compared them at first glance, they looked nothing alike. Her mother had very curly long black hair, stern hazel eyes and a tall willowy figure. She was a beautiful woman. Delilah, on the other hand, had straight. light brown hair and plain brown eyes, her figure smaller and curvy. She was just another pretty girl, at the age of seventeen not yet a woman. But when a person looked closer, their facial similarity was apparent, and when her mother smiled, it was the same smile that graced her own face.

"As I said, two *small* spoons of lizard blood, not big ones… we don't want a repeat of last time." Those stern hazel eyes glared at Delilah. "Write it down!"

"Yes, Mother." Delilah obliged once again as she turned over a page in her notebook, away from her doodles and to an empty white sheet. "Two small spoons of lizard blood," she repeated as she wrote the words down.

Her mother, Lilith, gave her one last glare and turned back to the cauldron bubbling with liquids for her next potion.

They lived in a small wooden cabin in the Witch's Forest, named after Delilah's mother. The forest used to be named differently a long time ago, but since her mother had first settled there, everyone around started calling it the Witch's Forest. The name was more of a warning.

The cabin wasn't big, just enough for the two of them. It had a roomy kitchen, which was mostly used for brewing potions, connected to the living room area. There was also a library downstairs and upstairs were two bedrooms.

The house was surrounded by a garden filled with an assortment of herbs, vegetables, plants and flowers. At the edge of the garden two sheds were leaning against each other, with an outhouse nearby. One shed held the usual gardening tools. Even though it was spelled to be silent, the other was the one that Delilah hated and dreaded. Because once she stepped inside the shrieks, whimpers and cries for release from all the animals would descend upon her as the weight of the world. She loved animals but she feared her mother's wrath more.

Lilith was a mighty witch, probably the most powerful one in the whole Kingdom of Illirya. Even King Magnar himself had sought out her services a few times and never held a grudge when she didn't comply with some of his requests. People, as well as the animals, knew to fear her.

Even though their cabin looked sweet and the garden was beautiful in the spring, the silence surrounding it gave it a very unsettling feeling. No animals dared come near, so when Delilah wanted to enjoy nature's beauty to its fullest, she had to walk for a while to reach the peaceful little pond she usually snuck out to, bringing a book filled with fairytales and brave knights. She would daydream there. Dreaming of a life she would never have. A simple life with her charming knight, a wonderful home filled with children's laughter and…

"Delilah, you're daydreaming again!" Lilith snapped at her daughter as she brought her palm down sharply on the table where Delilah sat, making the younger woman jump up in her seat. "I swear… If I didn't know any better…" Lilith grumbled as she walked back to her cauldron. "You better pay attention now, because I don't plan to waste my time repeating myself." The mighty witch threw one last glare at her offspring, her eyes flashing black.

Delilah gulped; she knew what that look meant so she forced herself to pay attention.

"Good." Lilith nodded her approval as she turned to stir the contents in the cauldron. "As I was saying, since fertility potions seem to be in demand, you need to learn how to make one properly. I already mentioned that you have to use…" She looked over her shoulder at Delilah and raised her eyebrow.

"Two *small* spoons of lizard's blood." Delilah finished her mother's sentence.

"Finally I have your attention. I'll be right back. You make sure you have everything written down correctly; wouldn't want to make someone infertile again." Lilith walked to the kitchen to gather their next ingredients, while Delilah stuck her tongue out at her mother's back.

"I felt that!" her mother yelled from the kitchen; Delilah rolled her eyes.

She started writing down the recipe but to fight boredom she decided to make it more interesting. Instead of writing the word lizard, she decided to draw a lizard, and since the recipe called for two, she added another lizard to keep the first one company. These lizards were known to love basking in the sunlight, so a sun was needed on that page as well. Of course, some greenery was added, too, and she didn't forget pretty flowers. Soon enough, Delilah was once again lost in her doodles and the life of her imaginary lizard family.

She wished she was a lizard; life might be simpler then, instead of being stuck doing all the potion brewing, spell weaving, making up new ones, planting and gardening (the last two of which she actually enjoyed). There would also be no animal slaughtering, no bartering with other people, no threatening those who didn't want to cooperate. She didn't consider her mother to be a good role model, but she was her mother. Nothing she could do about it but forge on.

She would never be able to get away, and she had absolutely no talent or patience for the witchery while her mother thrived on the power and wanted more. For what purpose? Delilah had no idea, but she knew that her mother wanted Delilah to be just as powerful.

Still, despite Delilah's failed attempts, Lilith persisted. Delilah was her only daughter and she could not throw that away. Witches didn't reproduce easily. The stronger the witch, the harder it was for them to be with child. It was all about the magic fluctuating through their bodies… Delilah hadn't really been paying attention that time when her mother had explained the reproductive life of witches, the near-desperate attempts to conceive and the reasons why witches were so few.

Lilith was afraid she would never be able to have a child; she desired one even more after her twin sister's death. This desire drove her to push her daughter, to try to make her fill her aunt's shoes, no matter what the cost. To this end Lilith had decided to find a way to prolong her life, thus giving herself more time, more opportunities to bear a child. Or at least that was the story she told Delilah.

Lilith had managed to find her own fountain of youth, in the form of a curse she had bound to herself as a consequence of her twin sister's death. She probably had to sell her soul to the demon gods along the way. Delilah smirked at her own pun.

A cloying, fetid smell reached her nostrils. She looked up to see her mother glaring at her now doodle-filled page as she held a handful of black cohosh flowers in her hands. The notebook took flight and bounced off the cauldron before falling down into the fire, instantly vaporizing with a little help from her mother.

"Make – the – extract, Delilah." Lilith slammed the flowers down on the table in front of her daughter. "I have been nothing but patient with you, daughter. Raising you on my own, keeping you safe and protected from the outside world and the greedy men who live there. I feed you, clothe you, give you a roof over your head. I teach you the Art so that one day you will be able to at least take care of yourself since it's hopeless, making a powerful witch out of you. I even allow you to sneak out with those books of yours. And how do you repay me?" By the end of her speech, Lilith's eyes had darkened, her voice lowered, hair wisped around her head. "I guess playing nice won't do anymore… I'll just have to—"

A scream burst from Lilith's mouth as she fell to her knees, clutching at her pounding heart. It had stopped for a few beats before continuing at a galloping speed.

"Mother!" Delilah exclaimed in alarm as she jumped off the chair; it fell back with a thud as she hurried to her mother. She might not like the old woman much, but she had no one else. "Mother!" She grasped at her mother's shoulders.

Lilith slowly let go of the tight grip she had on her dress, over her fast beating heart, as she looked up into her daughter's eyes. Delilah had never witnessed before such fear and panic in her mother's eyes.

"He broke the curse!" Lilith said as she tried to get back up on her trembling feet.

"Which curse?" Delilah's question was well placed since her mother had dabbled with more than one.

"The Dragon curse, the most important one!" When Lilith was steady on her feet she swatted her daughter's hands away. "I never thought he'd figure it out. I thought he would either get killed or be cursed forever!"

Delilah knew her mother was now worried with her sudden mortality. She was not used to being vulnerable to aging. "Oh!" was Delilah's clever reply.

" 'Oh'? 'OH'?!?! That's all you have to say?"

"Well… I'm just as shocked as you are, Mother." Delilah started following her mother around like a lost puppy as she went about packing. "What if he's just dead?"

"He's not 'just dead'… I felt the curse break, felt his heart stop beating." A shudder of dread made Lilith pause in her frantic packing.

A confused frown appeared on Delilah's face. "Wait. First you said you thought he'd die before he broke the curse, or be killed… then you felt his heart stop beating, so he *is* dead… so – I don't understand! Now you're saying he's alive? How can you be sure he's alive? Mother, what are you *doing?*"

Lilith glared at her. "I'm *packing*, obviously. We leave first thing in the morning. Now where's my… ah… there it is…" Lilith walked across the room. "The condition of the curse was that to break it, he had to die in a certain way. For a very particular reason. And I know he's alive because the curse had to have one redeeming quality. A prize, if you

will, to balance it out.”
 “Which is?”
 “Life… His prize is his life.”

ABOUT THE AUTHOR

Maya Starling is a writer, a geek, an animal lover and a gamer. She has lived the life of a magus, an oracle, a goth mortician, a star wars rebel. She has led many lives, sitting at a table, and rolling those dice away.

In reality, she lives with her wife and their adorable little boy, and of course two rescue cats, in a small country of Croatia. Reading and writing are her passion, so you will often find her typing away a new story, or eyes glued to the screen of her phone or a page of a book.